Humbug

Merry ∧ Christmas

Once Upon a Jingle Bell

Merry *Humbug* Christmas

Once Upon a Jingle Bell

SANDRA D. BRICKER

B&H
PUBLISHING GROUP
Nashville, Tennessee

*Ronald Reagan said the smartest thing people can do
is to surround themselves with the best people they can find.
I've certainly done that.*

*Deepest thanks to
my steadfast and loyal Marian Miller;*

my delightful collaborator, Julie Gwinn;

and my unstoppable rock, Rachelle Gardner.

*You women GET ME.
I'm so grateful
(and so sorry).*

PROLOGUE

Rich and Betsy Snow, upon receiving their only child into the world on the morning of December 25, showed considerable lack of judgment or forethought when they decided on impulse not to name her after Betsy's favorite aunt Jocelyn as planned. Instead, with beaming pride and perfectly straight faces, they announced their baby's name to the nurse on duty. Betsy spelled it out for her.

"M.E.R.R.Y. Merry."

"Pretty. Middle name?"

"Christmas," Rich had replied.

"Beg your pardon?"

Yep. That's right. On December 25 at 7:17 a.m. in San Bernardino County, California, unto the world a child was born.

Merry Christmas Snow.

Her name had come to seem like a Before & After puzzle from *Wheel of Fortune*.

By the time she reached twenty-five, Merry'd had just about all she could take of her given name. She'd carried the thing around with her like a joke book tucked into the back pocket of her jeans,

1

and frankly, she was sick and tired of the same old punch lines. So on the day after Christmas, the year of her twenty-sixth birthday, Merry Christmas Snow went to court and changed her name to Jocelyn Merry Snow.

She'd wanted to rid herself of the Merry part too. But David Cassidy, grinning down at her from the framed vintage pillowcase on the wall of her home office and urging her to keep some small part of her former life for the sake of sentiment, just wouldn't let her do it. And so she kept the Merry, deciding to hide it behind the simple initial M.

Jocelyn M. Snow.

Very grown-up. And punch line free.

If only the judge would have signed off on a change of birth date too. She didn't particularly like sharing her birthday with someone so famous that people decorated evergreen trees and baked turkeys and pecan pies in His honor. Joss wished for a nice random birth date, like April 3 or May 5.

On the first day of Christmas,
Murphy's Law gave to me . . .

a Partridge with the first name Keith.

1

Joss's best friend Reese giggled at her from across the table at Starbuck's. "You always say that you want a nice normal birthday like May 5. You do realize that's Cinco de Mayo, right?"

"Oh. Right. Maybe not May 5 then."

"You are such a head case."

"What do you know, Dr. Pendergrass?" Joss slumped in her chair, crossed her arms, and slid one leg over the other. "You, with your shampoo commercial hair and all the letters behind your name. Do not negate the influence of my highly dysfunctional life."

Reese thumped her coffee cup down on the table and grinned. "Joss. I was named after a chocolate-covered peanut butter cup. My parents were vegans before anybody ever heard of it, and my brother dances in Peoria in the chorus of *Billy Elliot*. You do not have a corner on the quirky family market."

Joss tossed a good-natured wave at her friend and shrugged. "In fact, I have no family on the market at all."

"Sorry." Reese's tone told Joss that things had turned serious when she wasn't looking.

"Talk to me when you start twitching each and every year as the holiday season arrives and people start wishing you a Merry Reese Pendergrass."

Reese bubbled up with laughter like air blown through a straw.

"Hey," Joss realized. "When I called to ask you to meet me so I could tell you something important, you said you had something important too. What is it?"

"You first."

Joss caught hold of Reese's sky-blue gaze for a moment and grinned from one ear to the other. She yanked the brochure from the pocket of her oversized bag and slapped it down on the tabletop.

"Check it out." She could hardly contain herself. "Go ahead. Check it out."

"What is this?" Reese asked as she examined the brochure.

"It's where we're going this year on our annual Escape Christmas Altogether Girls' Week Out!"

"Oh." Reese's soft features dropped slightly. "About that."

"Come on!" Joss encouraged her. "A little excitement, if you please. Remember I told you I was searching for the ultimate anti-Christmas vacation for us this year?"

"Y-yeah."

"Well, get a load of this!" Joss exclaimed, snatching the brochure from her and holding up the front toward her. "The *Bah Humbug Cruise!*"

Reese chuckled and took the glossy fold-over from Joss's hand. "The what?"

"The Bah Humbug Cruise. It leaves out of Los Angeles for seven days, cruising . . . wait for it . . . the Mexican Riviera!"

"Oh. Wow. Joss."

"Look!" she said, tapping the brochure, and then snatching it away in her enthusiasm. "Cabo. Mazatlan. Puerto Vallarta. A cabin with two beds, a private balcony . . . and that's not even the best part."

"No?"

"No! The cruise leaves L.A. on the afternoon of Christmas Eve and returns to port on New Year's Eve, with not one single mention of Christmas the whole time. And there are still cabins available. Is that too delicious to *believe?*"

Reese popped out a chuckle, but the amusement didn't reach her eyes.

"What's not to love about this, my friend? Not a wreath, ornament, stocking, or reindeer in sight. Who thinks of something like that?"

"I was just wondering that myself."

"I mean, we're not the only ones on the planet who are sick and tired of the whole comfort-and-joy, families-together, ho-ho-ho extravaganza. I know we always vowed we wouldn't go to the same place twice, but this might turn out to be an all-new tradition, Reese. We could do this every single year from this year forward."

"Yeah. About this year."

Joss's jaw snapped shut, her heart began to palpitate, and her mouth went dry. "Oh no. Uh-uh, Pendergrass. You wouldn't dare."

"I'm so sor—"

"No!" she objected, holding up both hands and leaning across the table. "Do not be sorry. Because sorry is always followed up with *I didn't mean to disappoint you, BUT—*"

"But . . . I really *am* sorry to disappoint you." Reese winced and raised one-half of her mouth in a sorry excuse for a smile.

"Then don't," Joss cried in hope. "We've been going away every Christmas for five years now. We said we'd always rescue each other from holiday overload. The only thing that would ever change that was going to be—"

Joss froze, and she dropped her hands and slowly leaned back in her chair and sighed.

"That's your news, isn't it?"

Reese nodded.

"He proposed?"

"He proposed," Reese confirmed, and she held out her left hand and wiggled her fingers until Joss had to shield her eyes from the reflection. She wondered how she hadn't noticed it before.

"Look at the size of that thing. I thought you didn't do flashy."

"I don't," she replied with a grin. "But fortunately . . . *Damian does!* Isn't it fantastic?"

Joss popped from her chair and rounded the table, sweeping Reese into a bouncy embrace as her friend giggled like a schoolgirl.

"It's great. I love Damian."

"Me, too."

She planted a kiss on Reese's cheek and squeezed her arm before taking her chair again.

"The two of you were made for each other."

"Oh, Joss, I'm sorry about Christmas."

Her heart dropped an inch or two at the thought of spending her first Christmas/birthday in five years without the benefit of Reese's fun-filled diversions.

"He wouldn't understand?" Joss asked, squeezing her mouth into a lopsided frown. "You couldn't write it into the vows? You promise to love, honor, and cherish him fifty-one weeks out of every year?"

Reese shook her head and wrinkled her perfect nose.

"He'll understand. Even pediatricians get Christmas off, don't they?"

"We're spending the holiday with his folks in Sugarloaf. Can you believe that? Isn't that the cutest name for a town? Sugarloaf."

"Where is it?"

"In the mountains above Big Bear. They have a place there. It's been in their family for three generations. Oh, and get this. There might actually be *snow*, Joss! Can you believe it? Me and my fiancé and his family and a white Christmas too?"

Joss fell back against her chair, tugging at the invisible arrow through her heart.

"Ooh, but you could come with us!"

Joss glared at her. Then, without a word, she stood up, shoved the brochure into her bag, and drank the last of her coffee. "I have an event to plan."

"Joss."

She paused momentarily and shot Reese a serious expression. "Can I try on the ring?"

Reese grinned. "No."

"Then I'm leaving."

"Joss."

"Congratulations, traitor."

"Joss!"

"Traitor! You're a total traitor!"

JOSS PITCHED HER BAG over the back of the sofa before collapsing with an armful of mail. She opened her electric and water bills first, then the dozen or so Christmas cards.

Joyous sentiments, warm wishes, and envelopes puffed with faith, hope, love, and jingle bells. All very nice, but each of them completely Christmas-centric and particularly stinging right on the tail of discovering Reese would never again be available for their December tradition.

Don't any of you people know me better than this? Joss skimmed over glitter snowmen and embossed hillside scenes, the shiver of it all quickly annulled by a seventy-nine-degree Los Angeles winter on the other side of her bay window.

Caleb, Joss's six-year-old sheepdog mix, lumbered into the living room and peeked at her through a tuft of unruly white fur that blocked all but a fraction of one eye.

"Hey, buddy. You were napping on the comforter in the guest room again, weren't you?"

Caleb yawned in reply and plodded across the living room toward her. First one enormous paw and then the other clawed the sofa cushion, followed by the long, slow crawl to drag his eighty-pound frame up beside her. Joss groaned when he tossed himself into her lap.

"You are one enormous lapdog," she told him, smoothing back the hair from his beautiful brown eyes. "Aren't you, boy?"

He panted at her, and it looked very much like a happy grin. Joss leaned down and kissed him several times on the bridge of his nose. When the telephone rang, it took her two tries to reach it overtop her smiling dog.

"Urgh," she grunted when she finally snatched the handset from its base. "Hello?"

"Are you all right? Did I catch you in the middle of moving heavy furniture?" Ryan Butler, Joss's business partner for the last four years, could never resist an opportunity for a jab.

Joss chuckled. "No. I'm just pinned down by a guy who finds me irresistible."

"How *is* Caleb?"

"Hairy."

"The same then."

"Pretty much, yeah. What's up?"

"Are you coming back to the office today?"

"I don't think so. I've got those releases to write, and I can't think with all the volunteers there stuffing swag bags for the bash this weekend. I think I'll work from the house for a few hours."

"I'm making a run out to the hotel to see how things are coming for the event. Char can keep an eye on the bag stuffers while I'm gone. Then I'll get her started on gathering our stats for the meeting with Jenkins next week."

"Thanks, Ry. I've got the proposal draft almost completely worked up."

Since the day they opened the door at Images Public Relations, Joss and Ryan's working relationship had been like a set of well-oiled gears. The two of them, along with their assistant Charlotte Hunter—the glue that kept it all pulled together—seemed to be separate appendages of the same body.

"Did you get to see the good doctor?"

"Oh yeah," she replied on a stifled groan.

"What did she think about the cruise idea?"

"She can't go. Damian proposed. My December escapes with Reese are officially behind me."

Ryan fell silent for several beats. "So you're not going away? Why don't you come with us to wine country."

"Oh, I'm still going."

"By yourself?"

"Yep."

"Joss, are you joking?"

"No, I'm not joking, Ryan. The only thing that's changed is Reese as my wingman."

"C'mon. We'll ride all-terrains, sip some stuff; it'll be a Top Ten list of fun. Oh, and we have this tradition where the kids—"

"As charming as that all sounds, Ryan, I have to pass."

"Oh, come on. Come with us. You'll have a blast."

"Some other time," she suggested. "But not at Christmas."

"You know, you might be taking this whole thing a little over the—"

"Yeah, so let me know how things are progressing at the Hyatt?"

"Joss."

"Later, Ry."

He paused. "Later, tater."

Joss propped the handset on the back of the couch and combed her fingers through the long fur at the base of Caleb's neck. He sighed and snuggled her knee before closing his eyes again.

"People think I'm a loon, Caleb," she whispered. "But not you, huh?"

No response, but Joss figured that might have been for the better. She'd been running up against people's expectations and judgments about her Christmas aversion for as long as she could remember. It was partially her own fault, she supposed. If she could find the inclination to explain all the gory details to every Christmas lover she encountered, perhaps the opposition wouldn't be so tenacious. After all, what *ho-ho-ho-er* would try to perk her up to enjoy a happy little holiday that fell every year on the same regrettable date that had severed her family ties in one horrible moment?

Joss closed her eyes. While still massaging Caleb's coat with one hand, she massaged her own thumping temple with the other and wondered why those particular memories always had to return so reliable and clear. Her parents had been on their way down from Tahoe on Christmas Eve in the hope of spending the holiday—and their only daughter's birthday—with Joss in L.A.

Pouring rain, heavy winds, and holiday traffic all played a part in the pileup, the highway patrolman had said. But no matter what the cause, all Joss ever really knew was that an inebriated old guy in a Santa hat, with a red bag filled with wrapped gifts on the seat beside him, had deprived her of a lifetime of Christmas spirit in thirty horrible seconds. She occasionally felt sorry that the one who shared her birthday had been the baby Jesus thrown out with the Christmas bathwater, but she was inclined to believe He understood. She'd made a decision long ago not to ask too many questions about the *why* of that turn of events. Instead of turning on God, she'd turned on Christmas, and it had worked fairly well for her until today.

The only living person who knew every private detail of her defective holiday mental health, in fact, was Reese, and she'd been walking in silent loyalty, supporting Joss through Christmases ever since. Before Damian delivered the rock, anyway.

A smile crept across her face at the thought of it, and Joss let out a sigh from deep within her. She hadn't even asked Reese about the proposal. Had he gotten down on one knee? Was it in a restaurant or some other public place? Were there flowers and promises of forever love?

Joss closed her eyes and tilted her head back against the cushion. For some reason a fairy tale popped into her head: a once-upon-a-time romance where the prince descended on one knee and asked the beautiful princess to marry him and live with him happily ever after. Oh, how many times she'd dreamed of finding her own *once upon a time.* As happy as she felt for Reese, the hollow spot at the center of her rib cage rattled slightly with unmistakable regret.

Suddenly she was curled into the arms of her mother again, a five-year-old with unruly auburn hair and wide, hopeful eyes, hanging on every word as Betsy read the fairy tale to her daughter and then closed the book. "There's a handsome prince out there just waiting for you, too, Merry," her mother had promised.

"Do you think so, Mommy?"

"There will be a big wedding with lots of flowers and a shimmering dress, and then you'll have children of your own. And your family will make memories together, and spend your birthday each year gathered around the Christmas tree, and Thanksgivings where three generations of Snows will hold hands around a big oak table with an enormous turkey and cranberries and pumpkin pie."

"Living happily ever after," little Merry finished for her, and Betsy laughed.

"That's right."

Believing used to be so easy.

Her parents had died, taking with them any hope Merry Christmas Snow had left for happy Christmases and family gatherings. In the years that followed, Joss's closest friends had never once hesitated to include her in their holiday celebrations and spectacular, festive meals. But somehow, instead of being part of the jubilation, Joss only felt the sting of standing on the outside looking in while others embraced their children or looked lovingly into the eyes of their spouses. No matter how hard she tried to join in, Joss couldn't manage more than the role of simple observer, never a participant, and the pain of it had finally backed up on her.

She hadn't ever quite figured out why Reese had so readily sacrificed trips home to spend the holidays with her quirky family, choosing instead to forgo all traces of Christmas ornaments, boxes, and bows to create an annual Christmas-free zone with her slightly pathetic orphaned friend. But they'd had a spectacular time doing it.

It had become a bit of a private joke between them, shooting Santas with their fingers and hiding wreaths and poinsettia plants behind shrubs. Joss's December 25 birthday dinner had been the same for the last five years: Chinese food eaten with the required chopsticks, a six-pack of Diet Coke, always preceded by a prayer of thanks from Reese, then a birthday cake and barefoot sing-alongs to their favorite old Motown tunes.

Joss's heart squeezed slightly at the memory, and she picked up the phone and dialed #1 on the speed dial.

"Reese? I'm so sorry. I didn't ask a thing about how it happened or what he said. Please forgive me?"

"Of course."

"How did he do it? Did he get down on one knee?"

"Oh, Joss, it was perfect. We went to dinner at McCormick's, and they led us through to one of those circular tables in the back, the ones with the soft leather booths. And there were red roses everywhere, and about twenty white pillar candles."

"What did you think when you walked in and saw it?" Joss curled her legs under her and closed her eyes as she snuggled into Caleb's thick fur.

"Well, of course, I started to cry like a big dope."

"Of course."

And then Joss started to cry too.

On the second day of Christmas,
Murphy's Law gave to me . . .

two hearty shoves
and a Partridge with the first name Keith.

2

Joss paid the driver and dragged her large metallic pink suitcase out after her, snapping the handle upward and lugging the thing through the World Cruise Center crowd. She pulled her ticket information out of her bag to confirm the berth location again before following the cattle drive toward the check-in booth.

It was half an hour or more before she finally reached the front of the line and handed over her ticket. The attendant immediately scrunched up her pug nose and shook her head while making a clicking sound with her tongue.

"Nah, honey, you need to go check in down at ninety-three."

"No," Joss corrected her, pointing out the berth information stapled to the inside of the pamphlet. "It says here I'm supposed to go to berth ninety-one."

"That was the original information, but this cruise," she said, tapping the glossy fold-over envelope with pointy crimson fingernails, ". . . this one was canceled."

"What do you mean? It can't be canceled. No one contacted me."

"Don't get your stockings in a twist, Red," the woman seemed to sing to her. "You're still cruisin'. You're just doing it on a much bigger ship."

"Oh. Well. Where did you say I should go?"

"Check-in for berth ninety-three."

"Okay. Well. Thank you."

"Merry Christmas, honey. Next?"

Joss took the paperwork back and tucked it into her bag, pulling her suitcase behind her in the direction pointed out by the bright red nail on the attendant's bony index finger.

"Whuh-whoooa," Joss stammered when she saw it.

She was right about a bigger ship. That's the biggest ship I've ever seen.

Joss gazed upward, her jaw propped open at the sight of what looked to be a small floating city.

Her train of thought careened off the tracks as an intense and painful impact threw her shoulder out of the socket before it bounced right back again.

"Owwww!" she screamed, dropping her bags and grabbing her shoulder on instinct.

"Ah, no, I'm sorry," he said. Joss looked up into narrowed hazel eyes. "I didn't even see you there." He picked up her suitcase by the pull handle and offered it to her.

"Th-thank you."

Dirty blond hair grazed the collar of an open denim shirt, under which he wore a navy henley tucked into the waistband of faded Levi jeans. His muscular arms pulled the cotton shirt taut over them, and thin blue suspenders with a crimson pinstripe stretched over broad shoulders.

"Your satchel," he said, and she noticed a faint Irish brogue.

"Oh. Thanks."

When he cracked the steel of his square jaw and smiled at her, she noticed a prominent dimple hiding at the center of his chin beneath the shadowy stubble of a day's worth of beard. He braced her shoulder for a moment with a firm hand, and he cocked an eyebrow.

"You're all right then?"

"Y-yes. Thank you."

He gave her one pronounced nod, then tapped her shoulder and moved away.

"Be careful now," he called to her over his shoulder. "The docks are crawling with clumsy bulls who will roll right over you."

"Good to know," she returned, and he glanced back just long enough to grace her with a wide smile before disappearing into the crowd.

Following the throng of people heading toward ninety-three in lines that were six-deep, Joss struggled not to bump anyone with her oversized suitcase.

"Hey, watch it."

"Sorry. I'm sorry."

It took longer than expected, but she finally found the correct check-in booth, reached the dock, and moved up the ramp along with the pulsing wave of bodies.

"Please move into the first ballroom to check in," someone announced, but she couldn't see who was speaking for all the people.

Feeling like a goldfish swirling with the current of a drain, Joss allowed herself to be swept along, funneled through a large open doorway, and dumped out in a massive hall. Rectangular tables framed the circumference of the room, manned by uniformed attendants with laptops, each of them wearing Santa hats. Joss tugged her pink suitcase behind her and stepped into one of the rows.

The handsome Irish bull crossed Joss's mind, and she scanned the crowd for a glimpse of him. On tiptoes, she looked over a sea of short, silver heads in hopes of a quick glimpse of a six-foot . . . Lumberjack? Sheep farmer? Gladiator?

Joss grinned at the Russell Crowe comparison. But wait. Crowe wasn't Irish.

Welsh? *No. Australian.*

"Are you lost?"

Joss did a double-take, face-to-face with a walking commercial for Christmas at Dollywood.

"Pardon me?"

"You look lost, sweetie. This is your first cruise, iddin' it?"

The platinum blonde's candy cane earrings dangled all the way to her shoulders, blinking with tiny red-and-white lights. Her dark green eye shadow was exactly the same shade as her sweater—a tight Angora number with Rudolph's three-dimensional head plunked right in the middle of her ample chest—and her wrist appeared heavy under the weight of a large chain-linked bracelet clasped with a bundle of small, silver jingle bells and a red velvet bow.

Joss squinted into the woman's blinking earlobes and shook her head. "Uh, yes. It's my first cruise. It's that obvious?"

"Well, you found your way to check-in, at least. You're just a couple of steps away from starting the 12 Days of Christmas Fun Cruise."

"Oh, no. I was sent over here because my original cruise was canceled, and they rebooked me on this ship."

"Oh, goodie," she squealed, and Joss couldn't help but grimace. "This is my third year on the Fun Cruise."

"No. I'm not on the Christmas—"

"You'll have the time of your life, sweetie. I'm Connie Rudolph," she added, taking Joss's free hand and shaking it vigorously. "Like the reindeer?"

"I'm sorry. Like the—"

"The reindeer, sweetie. You know, with the red nose."

"Oh. Right." Joss nodded slowly, hoping to shake her brain back into place. "Rudolph."

"And you?"

"Me?"

"Your name, sweetie. I'm Connie and you are . . . ?"

"Jocelyn. Joss. Joss Snow."

"Snow!" she cried, shaking her head until one of the candy canes became tangled in her big hair. "Well, that's just adorable, sweetie."

"Checking in?"

Joss twirled around to find herself next in line. She fumbled with her bag and suitcase, producing her paperwork as she thumped into the edge of the table and handed the attendant her ticket.

"Jocelyn Snow. You're one of our rebooks," he observed, just about the time Joss noticed the fifty-foot decorated Christmas tree through the glass window behind him.

"Yes. But I think there's some kind of mistake," she said. "I was booked on the Bah Humbug Cruise. You know, their slogan is No-Christmas-None-of-the-Time?"

"Right. That was canceled."

"Yes, so I understand. But why would they rebook me from . . ." —moving both hands to the left—". . . *a Christmas-free cruise to a . . .*"— and then to the right—". . . *12 Days of Christmas Fun Cruise?*"

"Oh, it's not twelve days," Connie interrupted, propping her chin on Joss's shoulder, the bracelet jingling as she patted her arm. "It's the 12 Days of Christmas. You know, like the song? Packing twelve days of fun into a seven-day cruise!"

The last part of it sounded as if she read from a brochure. The attendant pointed his finger at Connie. "You've been with us before."

"Three years now," she acknowledged, her chin digging into Joss's shoulder as she peered around at her.

Joss took a deep breath and held it for a moment before squirming out from underneath Connie Rudolph's grinning face, a grin bearing teeth at least four shades whiter than they should have been. The woman's candy cane earring got caught in Joss's hair as she pulled away from her.

"But it's still a Christmas cruise," Joss told the attendant.

She could have kissed the woman at the front of the next line when she motioned to Connie. "Next! Step over here, please."

"You got something against Christmas?" the young man asked Joss as she watched Connie go. "Oh! Are you Jewish? It's okay because we've got some great Hanukkah activities planned and—"

"No!" she exclaimed. "I am not Jewish. I just signed up for—"

"We gotta wait here all day?" a man bellowed from the line behind her. "Can we move this along?"

"Here you go," the attendant said as he placed a red vinyl envelope of paperwork into her hands. "Here's your sea pass and your ship information, your meal schedule, and a map to your cabin. You've been upgraded to a deluxe suite up on Frosty."

"I'm sorry. What?"

"Frosty the Snowman: that's level eight. They've placed you in a deluxe suite because of the schedule change. You'll go through those doors, across the deck, around the Christmas tree, and to the elevators on the left. Just tell them you're on Frosty, and one of the elves will help you from there."

"Come on, sweetie," Connie cried excitedly, locking her arm through Joss's. "We're both on the Frosty level." Then the woman gasped and pinched Joss's elbow. "Hey! Maybe we can share an elf."

JOSS TALLIED SEVEN ELVES, sixteen wreaths, and countless candy canes between the elevator and her cabin. Well, countless plus two, once she added in Connie Rudolph's blinking earrings. Every cabin door they passed had a striped stocking hanging from it, some of them green stripes and others red, all of them with two white fur pom-poms dangling.

When she finally shook Connie loose around the corner from the elevator, the elf known as Hadji the room steward herded the rest of the group down the long garland-draped corridor. As members of the moving flock reached their individual locations, they scattered like little holiday insects, and Joss was nearly the last to reach her cabin. Hadji continued to natter on for a minute or two with his spiel about daily activities such as a contest aimed at pinpointing the ugliest holiday sweater onboard—for which Joss felt certain Connie should take the prize—and a big-screen, twenty-four-hour marathon of Christmas movies starting at midnight. Joss shuddered at the thought.

"What about cell phone service?" she asked him. "Will I have any trouble connecting? On the cruise I booked, the brochure said there wouldn't be any problem."

"You have a smartphone?" he inquired.

"Of course."

"Then you should be fine, even out at sea. You'll just pay international roaming charges, which can be pricey, but . . ."

"That's fine. Thank you."

Joss broke away and closed her cabin door behind her.

With a deep, throaty groan she clamped her eyes shut, dropped her bag and suitcase, and fell back against the door. Joss's brain buzzed with thoughts of turning tail and running home to spend the next week behind closed doors.

Hey.

Her eyes popped open. Why couldn't she? Everyone would think she'd gone on a cruise. Her phone wouldn't ring; no one would show up at her door. She could cancel the dog sitters and spend the next week of her life in the company of her favorite creature on earth. She and Caleb could curl up on the sofa with her silky chenille blanket, eat a chunk off the roll of sugar cookie dough in the fridge, and make good use of Reese's early birthday gift as they watched the entire first season of *The Dick Van Dyke Show* on DVD.

This is sounding more like a plan by the minute!

Joss picked up her bag from the floor, then snatched the handle of her overturned suitcase. She could be in a taxi, flying down the 101 on her way back to the rolling hills of Los Feliz inside of ten minutes.

Just as her hand hit the door lever, however, the unmistakable blast of a plan going up in smoke pierced her ears.

Joss gasped.

"No."

She jerked her head so hard toward the balcony window that her neck snapped.

"Nooo!"

With her bag and suitcase still in tow, Joss loped across the length of the cabin. Dropping them to the floor, she threw open the glass door and clasped her hand over her mouth.

"Noooo!" she screamed, but the sound of it was completely lost beneath the detonation of the final horn blast. Translation: We're setting sail.

Joss stood there, with no idea for how long, watching the scenery glide by her in slow motion. Crowds of faceless people waved their arms at her, wishing her a bon voyage.

How! How? How did this happen?

She dropped into the chair beside the window, her eyes glazed over with a zombie-like astonishment, holding on to the arms of the chair with white-knuckled strength.

"Why?" she said right out loud. "Why didn't I just grab a cab and turn around and go home as soon as they told me the humbuggers had bailed on me?"

Speaking of bailing . . .

Joss's thoughts darted to Sugarloaf as she wondered how Reese's episode of *Meet the Parents* was going. Maybe she'd give her a call later . . . after the more important one she had to make first.

She grabbed the large Italian leather bag at her feet and produced her cell phone from the side pocket.

"Hey, Char. It's Joss."

"Is something wrong? I thought you were on a cruise."

Joss scanned her surroundings with a grimace. "I am. Sort of." She glanced out the window and wrinkled up her entire face in disappointment. "Oh, man. Yeah. I am."

"That doesn't sound good."

"My first stop is in Puerto Vallarta on the twenty-seventh. See if you can book me a flight out of there to Los Angeles."

"Joss. Are you sure? You don't want to finish the cruise?"

"Oh, I'm sure."

"Well, do you—"

"Text me the itinerary as soon as you have it."

"Okay."

JOSS HAD TOYED WITH the idea of ordering a room-service cheeseburger and eating it outside on the balcony, but as twilight set in, it became a little chilly out on open waters. The information packet she'd been given at check-in had included a flyer titled *What to*

Expect, and amid tips regarding seasickness and a bulleted list of cautions, there was a warning about weather on the cruise. Apparently, warmer temperatures wouldn't kick in until the second or third day.

Just about the time she decided on sharing her burger with Matthew McConaughey, the star of one of the only non-Christmas-related on-demand movies available, her cell phone jingled to let her know a text had arrived.

"Excellent!" She snatched the phone from the dresser and dropped to the bed.

From: Char Hunter
So sorry. No flights avail out of PV to LA for the next 4 days. Ck the next port?

Joss groaned.
"I'm trapped!" she growled as she hit the reply button.

From: Joss Snow
Find me a way home, or I'll swim.

A while later, as she reached for the phone to call room service and order some dinner, a rap on the door interrupted her.

"Hey, sweetie pie!"

Christmas at Dollywood had evolved into *Christmas at the Grand Ole Opry.* Connie Rudolph's full-length dress was red, except for the shape of a green Christmas tree from neck to knee, topped with a silver star, all of it fashioned in sequins. Joss wondered where on earth the designer had found so many of the shiny little things. Or the audacity to design such a dress, for that matter.

"Well, just look at you," she drawled as she moved past Joss into the cabin, her bracelet jingling all the way. "You haven't even started getting dolled up for supper."

Connie's declaration and accompanying crinkled nose and shaking head caused Joss to have a look at her reflection. She'd changed into gray sweats and pulled her straight hair into a ponytail at the top of her head. She'd removed her contacts and perched her rectangular brown glasses on the bridge of her nose.

"You can't go into the dining room like *that*."

"You're right," Joss replied, padding across the length of the room in bare feet that she tucked under her on the chair by the window. "If I planned on going to the dining room, I certainly wouldn't go like this."

"What do you mean?" Connie crooned. "You have to come to supper, sweetie. It's Christmas Eve. There's an orchestra, and there'll be dancing—"

"Perhaps you haven't noticed, but I'm currently without a partner."

"—and a gift exchange—"

"I didn't bring a gift."

"—and a silly sweater contest."

Joss grabbed her sweatshirt with both hands and pulled it away from her body. "I'm afraid this is as silly as I get."

"Oh, come on now. I'm just not going to take no for an answer," Connie insisted. She yanked back the folding closet door and tapped her index finger to the side of her chin as she scanned the contents. "You don't have a single Christmas color in here, Jocelyn."

Joss sank deeper into her chair. "Hmm. What do you know about that."

"Well, we'll either find something here, or you'll march right down the hall to my room and borrow something from my closet."

"No!" Joss exclaimed, propelled to her feet by the sheer horror of what she might encounter in Connie Rudolph's closet. "Really. That's not necessary. I was just going to order something from room service and watch a movie."

"You'll do no such thing, you silly goose. You simply cannot sit here in your cabin alone on Christmas Eve when there's prime rib and praline cheesecake in the dinin' hall."

"Did you say cheesecake?"

On the third day of Christmas,
Murphy's Law gave to me . . .

three French friends,
two hearty shoves,
and a Partridge with the first name Keith.

3

Joss had only packed one "dressy dress," as Connie called it. And since she felt pretty certain this would be the one and only function she'd be attending (even if she couldn't escape the ship and fly home, she could certainly take stronger precautions against this happening again), she hauled it out of the closet in the name of praline cheesecake.

She'd bought this dress at the Beverly Center on a shopping trip with Reese, who had said she looked like a beautiful ballerina when she put it on, and so she bought it on principle.

The dark gray velvet bodice had long sleeves and a round neckline that didn't scoop too low and was trimmed with a thin row of iridescent beads. The skirt—light gray taffeta—flared slightly, with a black sash that tied in a bow at the waist. She wore it with black-beaded ballerina flats.

Simple and elegant, she thought as she examined her reflection.

"Not too festive, is it?" Connie countered when she appeared behind her with her nose scrunched up. "You know, I have a red feather comb with rhinestones on it that we could put in your hair at least—"

"Oh, no. Really. I don't think so," she said as she tucked a few things into a beaded black bag. There was only so much Joss was willing to do for cheesecake, and wearing red feathers and rhinestones . . . not so much.

"All right then. If you're sure."

"I'm sure."

Connie suddenly gasped as an idea seemed to form. "I know! You wanna wear my bracelet, sweetie?" She raised her hand and shook it in front of Joss, the bells jingling like a herd of reindeer landing on the deck. "It's very festive."

"Yes, it is, but . . . oh, no . . . thanks. You need to wear that. How else will I know where you are?"

Connie cackled and then snorted. "I'm not a cat, sugar. I don't need a bell around my neck, do I?"

"It can't hurt," she replied with an arched eyebrow.

In the elevator Connie gave Joss the good news. "I talked to Hadji, and he's changed your dinner seating to my table."

"Hadji?"

"The sweet little Indian elf we met today. Our room steward?"

"Oh. Right. Can he . . . do that?"

"Sure. He can, and he did. You'll be at my table every meal for the whole rest of the cruise! Won't that be fun? We'll just have such a good time, Jocelyn."

Connie slid her arm around Joss's shoulder and grinned at her.

Those are really some white, white teeth you've got there, Connie.

Joss clocked it at half a mile or more from her cabin to the dining room, and she was thankful for wearing flats.

"We're at table sixty-seven," Connie told the penguin suit at the door. "Connie Rudolph and Jocelyn Snow. Isn't that adorable? Rudolph and Snow?"

It sounded to Joss like a crime-fighting duo based at the North Pole, a visual the décor of the dining room only encouraged. Every table in the place was draped in red or green, with candlelit centerpieces that might have been really beautiful if not for the shiny little gift-wrapped packages, reindeer, and candy canes adorning them.

"Isn't it just like heaven?" Connie exclaimed.

But to Joss it mostly seemed like a place where retired Santas went to entertain.

If not for the forced Christmas theme in every direction, she thought the room might actually have been quite beautiful. Large ceramic urns stood on short columns throughout the dining hall, lighting fixtures reaching out of them and extending all the way to the ceiling where rounded sections fanned out into white screens covered by metallic scrollwork patterns of ivy. The border around the sage green carpet paralleled the leaf design, and the camel-colored walls hosted a barely there green floral imprint.

"Oh, honey, wait just a doggone minute," Connie cried. "You have to meet the Auberjonoises."

"I'm sorry. The whats?"

Connie dragged her by the arm toward three oddly similar humans—a male, a female, and a teenager—all of them dressed in black trousers and black turtlenecks with rhinestone wreath pins at the throat, and all three wearing wire-rimmed glasses. They each had varied shades of brown hair, the teen set apart by the crooked black beret atop hers.

"The Auberjonoises," she repeated. "Adrienne and Jean-Pierre, and their daughter Amberly. They're French."

Three deadpan faces met her as Connie pushed her forward.

"Hi," she managed.

"This . . . is . . . Jocelyn," Connie announced to them as if they were hard of hearing.

"Joss."

"Right. Joss." Turning to Joss, Connie added, "They were booked on that same cruise you were booked on, honey. And now here we all are!"

Amberly muttered something in French, and the mother nodded tentatively.

"I was trying to avoid all this Christmas stuff too," Joss told them with a stale, forced smile. Nodding toward Connie, she softly added, "Don't hold her against me, okay? We only just met."

"I'm guessing these are going to be your three new best friends," Connie drawled. "So we'll see you Auberjonoises later, alrightie?"

Joss tossed them a wave over her shoulder, wondering about the actual pronunciation of their last name as Connie tugged her along. They seemed to have reached their destination when she jingled to a stop in front of Joss and greeted the six other people at their table. She did so with such familiarity that it wasn't until she introduced herself and Joss that it became apparent she hadn't already met each and every one of them.

Frank and Doris Henderson, an elderly couple wearing matching sweaters bearing several versions of Santa heads on the front and down one sleeve, were seated next to the other married couple in their late forties. The husband wore an equally hideous Christmas sweater put together like a patchwork quilt, each of the squares displaying an image from "The Twelve Days of Christmas" song.

"Doug and Caroline Denture," he said with a nod, and he stood up and extended a friendly—albeit clammy—handshake. "From Scottsdale."

The Dentures? Joss repeated in her head, biting her lip so she wouldn't laugh out loud. *I know a great attorney who can get you a name change for a reasonable price.*

The elderly woman with the kind eyes beside them introduced herself as Lilibeth Oakes, Caroline's mother.

Caroline Oakes married to become Caroline Denture? That's just sad on so many levels.

Lilibeth dressed like a normal human being, as did the woman next to her who turned out to be Lilibeth's best friend. Kathleen Brenneman had a warm yet aristocratic air about her. Despite her age, which Joss estimated around seventy, she had emerald eyes that sparkled. Her silver-white hair reached neatly back from her face into a pristine bun, and she wore a tailored green dress that contrasted her fair skin. When she smiled at Joss, her eyes reflected a sort of joy that made her whole face shine. Joss immediately gravitated to the chair next to her, and she sat down.

"Are you from Scottsdale too?" she asked as she sat down.

"Yes, we're—"

"Oh, that seat is saved," Lilibeth announced, but Kathleen pressed her hand atop Joss's and shook her head.

"Don't be silly," she declared in a soft Irish brogue. "My son will be perfectly happy to sit anywhere at our table."

Joss's heart began to pound. It was almost too much to hope for. But with that beautiful Irish brogue of hers and the mention of her son—

"Good evening, Mother. I'm sorry I'm late."

It's him!

Kathleen's son turned out to be the gorgeous Irishman Joss had met on the dock that afternoon. But one thing was horribly different, and Joss leaned back to take it in.

The breathtaking man with the dark hazel eyes and dimple at the center of his chin wore . . . a dark crimson crew-neck sweater, every inch of it displaying a colorful, nubby manger scene, complete with fluffy sheep and glitter stars in the red night sky.

He leaned down to kiss his mother's cheek and, upon spotting Joss, he took her hand and kissed it lightly. "We meet again."

"Small world." She couldn't think of anything else to say.

"The two of you have met?" Kathleen asked her son.

"Not officially, no. I'm afraid I mowed her over in my attempt to board the ship today." He rounded Joss's chair and sat down in the empty one on the other side of her, then he took her hand again. "Patrick Brenneman."

"Joss Snow."

"And this is my sweater," he offered without missing a beat. "You may call him Beelzebub."

Joss popped with laughter and returned his handshake demurely. "It's a pleasure to meet you both." Willing her heartbeat to slow down to a safe rhythm, Joss finally peeled her eyes from his and nodded toward Connie. "This is my new acquaintance, Connie Rudolph."

Patrick stood up, and Connie moved right into his personal space and grabbed his hand like a ripe melon she had every intention of devouring. "Pleased, I'm sure. Is that an English accent you've got there?"

Patrick eased his hand out of her grasp and clutched his heart. "Never label an Irishman by any other stamp," he said poetically, narrowing his greenish eyes at Connie with a sly grin, "lest you one day find yourself in need of a dancing partner when there are only Englishmen in the room."

"I don't know what you said exactly," Connie admitted. "But I'm pretty sure you've just promised me a dance."

Patrick kissed her hand and held out her chair before taking the one next to Joss again.

"I see you made it safely aboard," he commented, and Joss smiled. "I did indeed."

What was it, she wondered, about an Irish brogue that made a person want to respond with words like *indeed*?

The waiter appeared and began filling each of the crystal glasses with sparkling cider. "My name is Victor," he told them in a thick Russian accent. "I'll be your *vater* this week. Anything you need, I *vill* be at your service."

"Pleased to meet you, *Vik-ter*," Connie said, and the others echoed their greetings.

"Patrick," Kathleen suggested. "Why don't you make a little toast for our guests before we break bread together."

"Happy to, Mother."

When everyone raised their glasses, Patrick turned toward Joss and met her gaze for a moment.

He has his mother's eyes.

"On behalf of my mother and myself, I bid a very Merry Christmas to all of you," he said, and the former Merry Christmas Snow held back a snicker. "As in the old Irish blessing, may God give you, for every storm, a rainbow; for every tear, a smile. For every care, a promise; a blessing for every trial. For every problem life sends, a faithful friend to share; for every sigh, a sweet song, and an answer for every prayer."

Once again Patrick turned toward her, and this time he winked. Joss was glad she hadn't been standing when her knees grew weak like that. It could have been humiliating when she dropped like an anvil over the side of the ship at the mere wink of a green-eyed guy wearing a Jesus-in-the-manger sweater.

"Joss Snow?"

Joss reeled to find herself face-to-face with—

"Marla? Marla Jenkins!" she exclaimed, hopping up from her chair. "What on earth?"

"Rodney," Marla called, wiggling her index finger at her husband until he followed it toward her. "This is Joss Snow, the young lady I told you about."

"Images Public Relations," he said, shaking her hand. "I thought our meeting was in L.A. in two weeks, Ms. Snow."

"It . . . it is! What are you all doing here?"

"What else?" Marla crackled. "Just like you! Celebrating Christmas!"

Oh. Well, I'm not actually . . .

Rodney Jenkins, CEO of Vandermere Hotels & Spas. This was the target client Images Public Relations had been chasing for the last couple of years. After meeting Marla Jenkins at the annual Women in Business conference in the valley, Joss had wrangled an opportunity to pitch for her husband's account.

But not here, she thought. *Not on the Camp Happy cruise!*

"We like to go somewhere exciting every Christmas, and this sounded like a lot of fun, don't you think so? Is this your husband?"

"Oh," she replied, her eyes darting to Patrick and then back to Marla. "N-no, no. No, he's not. Not my husband."

Patrick extended his hand and gave Marla a warm smile. "Patrick Brenneman. Not the husband."

Joss's heart pounded so hard that it rocked her chest as Rodney shook Patrick's hand and offered an introduction. "Rodney and Marla Jenkins."

"Where are you seated?" Marla asked Joss.

"Right here. Over here. Where are you?"

"Oh, they've set our group up there."

Joss followed Marla's gesture toward a table fringed all the way around with an array of noisy children wearing combinations of colors that hurt the eyes. "It looks like you've been dropped into *The Sound of Music*," she said on a chuckle.

"That's my world," Marla replied with a grin and a shrug. "Just call me Marla von Trapp."

"They're . . . all . . . yours?"

"Yep! All seven of them."

Joss's eyes grew large and round as she surveyed the many members of the Jenkins family flanking the banquet table, each of them wearing sweaters bearing holly wreaths, Santas, and gingerbread men.

"From six to sixteen," Marla declared.

"You've got a hockey team there," Patrick teased Rodney.

He nodded as he laughed. "This group makes hockey seem tame."

"I'm so happy you're here," Marla told Joss, and she poked Joss's rib with her elbow. "I mean, what's more fun than celebrating Christmas, huh?"

Oh, I don't know. Falling overboard?

VICTOR FILLED JOSS'S COFFEE cup again while a server who didn't look like she was more than seventeen slid giant slices of chocolate something in front of everyone at the table.

"What is that?" Joss asked, leaning toward Patrick. When he didn't answer instantaneously, she reached up and touched the girl's sleeve. "Excuse me. What is this? I thought there was going to be cheesecake."

"It is chocolate cheesecake," she replied with a thick unidentifiable accent.

"Oh." She tapped it with her fork and inspected it more closely. "Okay."

"Cheesecake snob, are we?" Patrick asked, and she snickered without looking up at him.

"I was expecting praline cheesecake, but this will have to do."

She poked the dessert with her fork and scooped up a large bite, which she set ceremoniously upon her tongue. When the slight hints of mocha and the velvety cream cheese settled in, Joss's deep and long sigh turned a bit toward a groan in the end.

"Well, that sold me," he remarked, and he took a bite of the dessert from his own plate.

He nodded at Joss, shrugged, and then nodded again. "Yeah. I see it."

"No, no, my friend," she corrected as she sliced off another chunk with her fork. "This is not something to be weighed and considered and then met with ambivalence. Cheesecake is very serious business."

"Is it now?"

"It is."

An announcement through the sound system drew everyone's attention to the front of the dining room. An odd little man stood center stage with a microphone in his hand and a set of antlers on his head.

"It's time," he declared. "It's what you've all been waiting for! It's the Christmas sweater competition!"

Thunderous applause rolled until Joss felt the reverberation against her ribs.

"Our judges have walked the room several times over, and they've narrowed it down to six lucky finalists."

As the table numbers were called, Patrick leaned toward Joss and asked, "Are you a praying woman, Miss Snow?"

"Now and then."

"Join me in prayer, won't you?"

He had a spicy scent about him, subtle and manly. Joss's pulse raced as he pressed his shoulder against hers.

"You have your heart set on winning?" she asked him.

"No!" he objected with a raised hand, and he glared hard into her eyes. "It's important to keep up here. We're praying that I don't win."

When the rest of their table began to hoot and applaud, and Doug Denture rose to his feet and pointed his clapping hands at Patrick, a bit of the color drained from his handsome face.

"No." He swiveled and looked toward the emcee. "Is he *codding* me?"

Joss could only guess what it meant to be *codded* in Ireland, but she felt secure in assuring Patrick that his finalist status was no *cod*.

"Come on up here, finalists," the emcee insisted. "Let's get a look at you all standing next to each other."

Patrick reluctantly stood up. Before heading toward the stage, he paused between Joss and his mother. Pulling his crazy red sweater away from his body with both hands, he leaned down and stated, "Really, Mother. Abuse of an adult child? I'd thought you above such things."

"What would make you think that?" she replied.

Patrick kissed his mother's cheek and gently squeezed Joss's shoulder before he met up with another finalist, and the two of them navigated the jungle of chairs in disarray.

Thinking her new friend was by far the best-looking finalist on the stage, Joss could hardly peel her eyes away from Patrick Brenneman as he grinned and waved for the crowd. When he shook a finger in the direction of his mother, onlookers erupted with laughter.

Good-natured and somewhat playful, he seemed to charm most of the large room, but first prize ultimately went to a welder named Jorgen from somewhere in Minnesota for his three-dimensional Christmas tree on both front *and* back of the sweater—a decision that was met by an unabashed string of surprising obscenities from the sweater wearer next to Patrick in the line.

On the fourth day of Christmas,
Murphy's Law gave to me ...

four dirty words,
three French friends,
two hearty shoves,
and a Partridge with the first name Keith.

4

"I was robbed, I tell ya," Patrick said when he returned to the table.

"Don't be dense, boy," Kathleen teased. "That's a horrible sweater."

"Why'd you give it to me then, woman?"

The two of them shared a chuckle as Joss pushed her chair away from the table.

"And if I ever hear you speak like that gentleman next to you on the stage," Kathleen told Patrick, "I don't care how old you are, I'll wash your mouth out with soap."

"You have to forgive the oaf, Mother," he said. "You saw that sweater of his. He was quite invested in the competition."

Joss giggled as she leaned over toward Kathleen and touched the woman's hand.

"It was so nice to meet you, Mrs. Brenneman."

"Are you leaving us, child?"

"Yes. I really just came for the cheesecake," she confided with a grin. "But I had to stay long enough to see how the great sweater adventure played out." She glanced at Patrick and added, "You really were robbed."

"This is what I'm sayin'," he agreed.

"Patrick, be a gentleman and escort Miss Snow back to her cabin."

"Oh, no. That's all right."

Patrick stood up and nudged his chair toward the table. "You never know when some rogue elf might jump out at you," he told her. "I'll just be along in case one of them needs a good beating."

Joss smiled at Kathleen. "Well, I can hardly turn that down, can I?"

"I'll come back for you, Mother. Don't go anywhere."

Kathleen crossed her heart with one finger and smiled. "I promise."

Connie's cat-that-ate-the-canary grin said it all as Joss passed her with Patrick in tow. "See ya tomorrah," she sang.

A small choir of costumed carolers crooned "Silver Bells" at them, and a random "Ho! Ho! Ho!" followed them down the hall.

"This is what I'd hoped to avoid when I booked the Humbug cruise," she remarked as they boarded the elevator and Patrick's hand hovered over the panel of buttons. "I'm on Frosty. Where are you?"

"Blitzen. What's a Humbug cruise?" he asked.

"Oh, it was canceled, so they rebooked me on this floating extravaganza. It was for all of us Bah! Humbuggers who can't stomach a whole season of this stuff."

"What stuff is that? Christmas?"

"Yeah." She shrugged.

"You don't like Christmas?"

"No."

"Why?"

"Long story."

"It's a big boat," Patrick commented. "By the time we hike it, you'll have gotten the whole long story out of you. Think of it as festive therapy."

Joss looked at him and arched an eyebrow. "I'm sorry. I can't take you seriously in that sweater."

"Imagine how I feel." The elevator doors slipped open, and Patrick backed against the opening, holding the doors for Joss to pass. "Now step out here to my office and tell me why you hate Christmas." He shook his head. "And with a name like Snow."

"Oh, you don't know the half of it."

"Of what? Your name?"

Joss chuckled. "Well," she said with a one-shoulder shrug. "Yes."

She moved past him into the corridor and headed toward her cabin without looking back.

PATRICK LOOKED AROUND AT the garland-draped hallway as they meandered along, Joss explaining how she and her longtime friend always spent the holidays playing the diversion game.

"But Damian—that's her boyfriend . . . well, her fiancé now—proposed, and years of Christmas avoidance came to a screeching halt," she explained, only pausing long enough to poise her index finger and thumb into the shape of a gun to fire off an imaginary shot at a large cardboard Santa hanging on the wall. She made the sound effect of the shooting with her curled-up mouth, barely missing a beat in her monologue. "I mean, I'm happy for her and everything. Damian's a great guy, and they're really suited to one another, but doing this without her is just a little daunting after all these years, you know?"

"I can imagine," he said, nodding. "But you still didn't tell me why you're so opposed to Christmas."

"I'm not opposed to it exactly," she said. "I mean, I like a celebration as much as the next person, and the Lord and Savior of the whole world certainly has every right to celebrate His birthday and to want us to celebrate with Him. But the whole

Santa-elves-evergreens-mistletoe thing, well, what does that really have to do with Jesus anyway?" She stopped in her tracks and turned to face him expectantly. "Can you explain that to me?"

Patrick raised both hands in surrender as he continued down the corridor. Joss hurried to catch up to him.

"So I guess you're one of those Christmas-spirited humans then, huh?" she asked him.

"Well, I wouldn't turn down a glass of eggnog and some wreath-shaped cookies," he replied. "But it's not really what gets my holiday spirit revved up."

"No?"

"No. I prefer a more relaxed Christmas celebration without all of the accoutrements. I like to keep in mind the reason for the season rather than the colorful, conspiratorial assault on our senses."

"This, from the man in the manger sweater, cruising to the Mexican Riviera on a 12 Days of Fun Christmas cruise."

"Hey, I wouldn't be here if not for my mother. She asked me to join her and her friends, and I'm one of those blokes who likes to buy his mother's love by wearing hideous sweaters and escorting her to tree lightings."

Joss snickered. "Hey, far be it from me to criticize a man who loves his mother." After a moment, she added, "And your mom is quite sweet, by the way."

"That she is."

They strolled on in silence until Joss stopped at her door, reached into her bag, and produced her room key. Patrick took it and swiped it for her.

"Thanks," she said, and he handed it back.

"I still don't know why you hate Christmas the way you do, Miss Snow."

"I hear the Irish love a good mystery," she replied, and the pirate smile that slipped across her face made Patrick's pulse start to pound. "Consider me a mystery."

"Wrapped in an enigma," he remarked.

"Inside a conundrum."

"All of it baked inside a nice Christmas fruitcake," he added with a broad smile, and Joss swatted his arm.

"Hey!"

"See you at breakfast tomorrow?"

"More than likely."

"It's Christmas, so I didn't know if you'd come out long enough to see your shadow. But I think I'll step out in faith and save you a chair."

Joss started to close the door, and then she suddenly stopped. "I can't wait to see what you'll wear," she teased him.

"I was thinking of Mother's Christmas bonnet," he volleyed back to her. "Too much?"

"I think you can carry it off."

An instrumental version of "O Holy Night" serenaded his walk down the hall toward the elevators, and Patrick sang softly along with it as he mentally replayed the conversation with Joss.

"She's a corker, that one," he muttered, shaking his head and grinning like an idiot.

He boarded the elevator with several other passengers, all but one of them women.

"Merry Christmas!" one of the ladies sang as she touched him on the arm.

When he looked into her eyes, he noticed a little something more than passing interest there.

"And to you," he replied, returning his attention to the closed metal doors in front of him.

The moment they opened, Patrick gave them all a nod and headed immediately toward the lobby and past the carolers, still crooning at passersby. His mother waited for him near the doorway to the banquet room where they'd had dinner, and she smiled as he approached.

Sliding her arm through his, she commented, "Miss Snow is quite a pretty girl, don't you think so, Patrick?"

"Indeed she is, Mother."

As they slowly walked along, Patrick couldn't help but notice the slight lumbering quality of his once-elegant mother's gait.

"Are you doing all right?" he asked her.

"Fit as a fiddle."

They stopped to join the gathering crowd forming a semicircle around the costumed singers. Patrick had to admit their melodious voices did far more justice to "O Holy Night" than his had done just a few minutes earlier.

He felt his mother's hand trembling against his arm, and he covered it with his own hand and smiled down at her. "Do you need to sit down for a few minutes?"

She nodded tentatively, and Patrick led her toward an open seat on the oak bench surrounding the enormous Christmas tree in the center of the lobby.

"Sit here for moment, and I'll be right back, yes?"

The instant she nodded, Patrick hurried away to catch up with a passing uniformed member of the ship's crew.

"Excuse me," he called out as he touched the boy's shoulder. "Hi. Can you help me? I need to find a wheelchair for my mother. She's feeling a little shaky on her feet."

"Yes, sir. I can get one for you."

"She's seated on this side of the holiday tree. Can you bring it to us?"

"Give me ten minutes."

"Thank you."

Patrick felt a wave of relief push through his chest as he made his way back to his mother's side.

"Shall we head up to our rooms, dear?"

"Let's wait here for a bit," he answered. "So you can ride upstairs in style."

"Oh, Patrick," she said. "What have you done?"

"I've arranged a chariot. It will make Christmas week far more enjoyable for you."

His mother sighed, gracing him with a warm and familiar smile. "You're a very thoughtful son."

"I am, aren't I? I'll bet you thank the Lord above every morning for such a blessing as me."

When the boy arrived with the wheelchair, Patrick thanked him and helped his mother into it. "Tell me, Mother," he said as he began to wheel her toward the elevators, "what's Irish and stays outside all year long?"

"I can't imagine."

"Paddy O'Furniture," he replied. He pushed the call button and leaned down to kiss her cheek before repeating the punch line. "Paddy O'Furniture."

"Yes, dear. It's a sophisticated take on Irishmen, but I do understand the joke."

"BEFORE YOU SAY ANYTHING," Charlotte said by way of answering Joss's early morning call, "I can't find you a flight home within the next four days, Joss. I've tried every airline out there, and I can't get you home. I'm so sorry."

"Actually," she replied, slipping one leg over the other and relaxing into the wingback chair by the window, "I'm calling to wish you a Merry Christmas, Char. Do you have big plans?"

"What?"

"Plans? For Christmas? What are you doing?"

"Oh. Well." She'd obviously caught her executive assistant completely off guard. "I'm waiting for Justin to pick me up, and we're headed to his parents' for the day."

"That sounds like fun."

"Joss? Are you okay?"

"Of course."

In a raspy whisper, she asked, "You're not drinking, are you?"

Joss chuckled. "No, Char, I'm not drinking. You know I don't drink."

"Well, you sound a little . . . out of character for . . . you . . . on Christmas morning."

"Oh. That. Well, that's another reason that I'm calling. You won't believe who turned up on this boat with me."

"Who?"

"Rodney Jenkins!"

"You're joking. The CEO of Vandermere Hotels & Spas?"

"The very same," she exclaimed. "He's here with his family. The guy has . . . like . . . a dozen kids."

"How weird is it that you were rebooked on a completely different cruise than the one you signed up for, and—"

"I know!" Joss interrupted. "I tried to call Ryan, but I just keep getting his voice mail."

"He's traveling. Maybe there's no service."

"Maybe. But be sure and tell him next week, will you?"

"You're staying on the ship then."

"I think I should."

"Are you having any fun at all?"

"Some." Joss swallowed around the sudden lump in her throat. "There's Kathleen, this really lovely woman from Ireland . . ." Her words trailed off, and she smiled as Patrick Brenneman strutted across her mind. "She's traveling with her son and some family friends."

A strange tapping noise—accompanied by jingling bells keeping perfect time—sounded against her door, and the moment she heard Connie singing to her from the other side, she pinpointed the origin of the noise immediately.

"Come on, sugar," she yodeled through the door. "It's Christmas *mooornin'*!"

"Char, I've gotta go. I have three-inch fingernails and a herd of reindeer tapping at my door."

"Pardon? Is it the woman from Ireland?"

"No," she replied with a chuckle. "Connie Rudolph couldn't be any more different from Kathleen Brenneman. I'll call you in a couple of days."

Joss made her way to the door and tugged it open. She couldn't contain the guffaw that flew out of her at the sight of Connie, her platinum blonde beehive surrounded in a halo that doubled as a shimmering Christmas wreath. Large reindeer head earrings stared back at her from both of Connie's earlobes, and Joss felt a sudden urge to shield her eyes from the reflection of her color-blocked Christmas tree blouse.

"Wow. That is quite the festive . . ."—she struggled for the word as she waved her hand from Connie's neck to her waist—". . . ensemble!"

"Oh, thanks, honey." Connie floated past her and bounced down on the corner of the bed. "I brought you a little present."

Joss restrained the groan that threatened to rise into her throat. "That's . . . so . . . well, it's sweet of you." She let Connie push the small package into her hands. "But you really shouldn't have."

"Oh, sure I shoulda, honey." Wrinkling her nose, she gleefully exclaimed, "You're gonna love 'em!"

"No, no," she insisted as she untied the ribbon and lifted the lid from the box to reveal a pair of blinking candy cane earrings like the ones Connie had been wearing when they first met. "You really shouldn't have."

"I thought Christmas just called for something a little more fun than what I see around this place," she said with a wide—and extremely white—grin. "These little darlings will doll up even the blandest outfit in your closet."

Joss lifted one of the earrings from the box and held it up in front of her face to inspect it more fully. "You're sure right about that!"

"So go on. Get dressed. I'll wait for ya, and we'll wiggle on downstairs together."

Joss shook her head and meandered toward the closet.

"And while you're in there, give me the lowdown on what happened with that Irish cutie pie you left with last night."

"Connie, he only walked me to my door. That's all."

"Oh, what a shame," she whimpered. "Don't worry, honey, you have the whole week for him to make his move. And when he does, I want to hear all the yummy details."

"I'll be sure and pass you a note after study hall."

Joss emerged from the closet, planting herself in the doorway with her hands on her hips, waiting for Connie's reaction.

"Oh, honey," she said, looking like she'd just gotten an unexpected whiff of spoiled food. "Is that what you're wearin'?"

"I thought I might," Joss replied, and she resisted the urge to release the chuckle building in her throat. Pulling her hands out of the pockets of her black trousers, she flicked the row of clear beads around the scoop neck of the gray tank shirt. "It's kind of sparkly, right?"

Connie laughed out loud and smoothed her blonde hair with the palm of one hand. "Oh, honey. If you think that's sparkly, you must think I'm a gaudy light show."

"Of course not," she fibbed. "But I'm pretty sure they can see you from space."

Connie pushed her small frame to her feet and shifted atop the four-inch, red-patent leather spike heels. "Not funny," she said, and she picked up the reindeer earrings and handed them to her. "Let's go see what they have on the breakfast buffet, shall we?"

"We shall," Joss replied, stuffing the room key into her pocket as she followed Connie out the door, walking to the beat of her jingling bracelet.

*On the fifth day of Christmas,
Murphy's Law gave to me . . .*

five cold sardiiiines!

*four dirty words,
three French friends,
two hearty shoves,
and a Partridge with the first name Keith.*

5

Patrick tried to peel his eyes away from Joss as she moved through the buffet line, but he couldn't seem to manage it. When her friend—the platinum blonde Christmas tree—said something that amused her, Joss's sparkling laughter lit up the whole room. Jutting out her hip, she bumped the blonde as she plucked a pastry from the table and dropped it to her plate.

Victor stepped into Patrick's line of sight. When he couldn't look around him, he glanced up and met the waiter's waiting smile.

"More coffee?"

"Yes, thank you." On second thought, he turned over the cup from the setting next to him and tapped it. "This one, too, please."

When Joss made her way to the table and began to sit down across from him, Patrick nodded toward the coffee cup beside him and told her, "Over here. Hot coffee with your name on it."

She brightened and rounded the table. "Thank you." She set down her plate and dropped into the chair beside him, adding, "I'm happy to see you decided against your mother's bonnet. Very nice."

"I was going to, but it interrupted the overall look."

She swept him with a lingering glance. "You look . . . really nice, Patrick."

He looked down and grinned. He'd removed the suit jacket and draped it over the back of his chair, and he'd loosened the knot of his black tie and unbuttoned the top button of the starched white shirt.

"Do you have a hot date, or do you have a gig with the rest of the boy band later?"

He wanted to laugh, but instead he arched an eyebrow toward those horrible blinking candy cane earrings tucked into the nest of wavy reddish hair on her shoulder. "And you're meeting up with the other elves after breakfast?"

"Oh, right," she said, lifting her hands to touch one of them. Nodding toward her blonde friend on the other side of the table, she added, "They were a gift from Connie. She thought I could do with some sprucing up."

"I'd say they do the trick."

"We missed you at church this morning, dear," his mother commented to Joss from the chair on the other side of Patrick. "It was a beautiful service."

Joss raised both eyebrows and grinned at Patrick. "You took your mother to church on Christmas morning. How sweet of you. That explains the suit."

He wanted to tell her he'd have gone to church whether his mother had been around or not. He wanted Joss to know his Christian faith played a deep and abiding part of the man he'd become. Out of nowhere and in no time at all, he wanted to share things with this virtual stranger, personal things, things that mattered—

"How did you rest?" Patrick's mother asked Joss, interrupting his private soliloquy.

"Very well," Joss replied. "Once I stuck on one of the patches for seasickness, I drifted right off. What about you, Mrs. Brenneman?"

"Please call me Kathleen."

Joss nodded. "I will. Kathleen."

"I had a very nice night of sleep. Thank you for asking."

"The woman can sleep anywhere," Patrick interjected, and he paused to pop a sardine into his mouth before dropping his fork. "I'm in the adjoining cabin, so I looked in on her. Out like a light."

"Clean conscience," his mother commented, and she squeezed his hand. "It makes for an effortless sleep each night."

"I'll have to try that," he teased.

Patrick suddenly noticed Joss staring at him, her lips parted slightly, and her lovely eyes wide and round as sugarplums.

"What?" he asked her.

"What on earth is that on your plate?"

He looked down at it. "Eggs. Pota—"

"No!" she interrupted. "That!"

He cackled. "You mean this?" he asked, picking up the last sardine and dropping it into his open mouth. "It's a sardine in mustard sauce."

"Ohh!" she groaned. "How can you eat that?"

"I agree with you, dear," his mother chimed in. "My son has questionable tastes when it comes to cuisine."

"I've eaten half a dozen of them with my eggs," he told her, finding ridiculous amusement in her repulsed reaction. "Try one? I'd be happy to go and fetch a few for you."

Leaning forward around him, his mother cut him off at the pass by asking Joss, "So what are your plans today?"

"I don't really know," she managed. One more shudder, and she added, "I hadn't thought that far ahead."

"My friends have invited us to a screening of *It's a Wonderful Life* on the top deck this afternoon. Would you like to join us?"

Patrick noticed the flash of agony that passed over Joss's expression before she masked it with a polite smile. "I appreciate that, Kathleen, but I'm kind of looking forward to being on my own today."

"Translation," Patrick said with a grin. "She's avoiding all things Christmas."

"A little hard to do on a Christmas cruise," his mother pointed out, and she gave Joss a concerned glance.

"I . . . know."

"I have a feeling she's up to the challenge," he said.

"What about Christmas dinner?" his mother added. "You will join us for dinner, won't you?"

"Of course, she will," he cut in. "She has to eat."

Joss tossed him a fleeting glare before she turned away from him and smiled at his mother. "I'll be here."

"Oh, good."

"Now if you'll excuse me, I want to go and say hello to the Jenkins family."

"Of course, dear."

She didn't even look back at Patrick as she navigated her way over to the table of the von Trapps, but that didn't stop him from watching her weave her way through the crowded tables. When the wife invited her to join them, Joss sat down between her and the husband. He envied them a bit for landing in the sunbeam of that toothy white smile of hers, slightly crooked on one side where the corner of her lips dipped ever so slightly.

"She really doesn't like it?"

Patrick snapped back to the moment. "I'm sorry, Mother. What?"

"Miss Snow. You said she's trying to avoid Christmas."

"Oh. Yes. She mentioned it when I escorted her back to her cabin after dinner last night."

"It seems like an odd place to spend your holiday then, doesn't it?"

"It does."

"Very mysterious."

"Wrapped in a conundrum," he added.

When he looked back toward the von Trapp table, Patrick didn't see Joss sitting there anymore, and he scanned the area to find her. When he finally spotted her, she was almost out the door.

"Mother, will you be all right here for a while?"

"Lilibeth said Douglas can push my wheelchair, dear. You go about your business for a bit."

He stood up and pecked her cheek before rushing off. Once he reached the doorway, he sprinted through it and looked around until she strolled across his line of sight.

"Joss!" he called out as he jogged toward her. "Where are you off to?"

She smiled as he reached her. "I was browsing through the guest services catalog in my cabin this morning, and I saw there's a little shopping mall onboard. I thought I'd give it a look."

"Want some company?" His pulse thundered in his ears as he awaited her reply.

"Sure. But I'd like to run up to my cabin first."

He grinned, waving her in front of him to board the elevator as they reached it. The car was a full house this time around, and Patrick stretched to reach around the apparent honeymooners standing so close to one another that air couldn't even pass between them.

"Sorry," he finally said. "We need to stop on Frosty. Could you push the button for us?"

"Oh, sure," the groom replied. "Sorry."

"Frosty," the bride mused. "Isn't that cute, honey?" Looking to Patrick, she told him, "We're on King Wenceslas. We don't even know who that is, do you?"

"He was the Duke of Bohemia," Patrick answered. "Became king at eighteen."

The couple exchanged curious glances before the bride inquired, "What does a Bohemian king have to do with Christmas? I wonder why we didn't get a fun floor name like Frosty the Snowman."

"He was just the subject of the carol because of his generosity toward orphans," he continued, and then he noticed their indifference toward old Wenceslas's history reflecting off Joss's utter amusement. "Well, no matter. Your inquiry was rhetorical, wasn't it?"

The elevator doors slid open, and Patrick reached back and took hold of Joss's wrist.

"Happy Christmas then," he told them, tugging her along after him.

A few yards down the corridor, Joss turned back toward him and began to laugh before pointing at the ceiling. He looked up to find nothing out of the ordinary, and then she began to sing along with the instrumental music piped in from the overhead speakers.

"Good King Wenceslas looked down on the feast of Stephen."

"He looked out. Not down."

"When *Joss Snow* lay round about . . ."

Patrick joined in, fracturing the correct lyrics right along with her. "She was deep and crisp and even."

"Brightly shone, the moon was bright . . ."

He grabbed her arm and gently shook it. "Do you know the right words to any of it?"

She ignored him and ceremoniously continued to sing, ". . . and then Joss was cruuuu-el."

"The frost!" he exclaimed. "The frost was cruel."

As they reached the door to her cabin, Joss continued to laugh. "What are you, the king's personal historian, Patrick?"

He straightened and pasted a mock-serious expression on his face. "I just think you should care a bit about accuracy, that's all."

Their merriment came to a screeching halt as a uniformed crew member approached them with a silver-domed plate in his hand.

"Merry Christmas, Miss Snow."

"Oh. Same to you, Hadji."

"And happy birthday as well," he added, and Patrick watched Joss's expression wilt like a watercolor painting set out into the December rain.

"Oh . . ."

"Is it your birthday?" Patrick asked her.

". . . thank you."

"This is for you," the steward told her, and he handed her the plate. "There's a card fastened underneath."

"Thank you," she said as she took it, but she looked anything but grateful.

Joss swiped her room key and gave Patrick a nod as an invitation to follow her inside. By the time he reached her, Joss had set down the plate and lifted the dome, and she stood there staring down at a small, decorated cake with *Happy Birthday, Joss* flourished across the top of it.

"You were born on Christmas Day," Patrick said as he stood next to her, also looking down at the cake. "Maybe . . . *thirty* years ago?"

She turned to him and smiled. "Nice try. A good combination of an attempt at getting information glazed with unabashed flattery. I like it."

"Ah. *Fifty* years ago then?"

She stuck her tongue out at him. "Thirty-four years ago, nosey."

"Well, you wear it well. And I might bet this has something to do with your aversion to all things Yule related."

"A little something," she replied. After a moment she sighed and looked up at him. "Do you think this cake has to be refrigerated, or can I leave it on the table until later?"

"I think it will do fine on the table."

Joss chuckled. "We could always make a game of it. I could toss it off the balcony, and we could try to guess how many seconds it will take to hit water."

"A sad waste of cake."

"This is a floating smorgasbord," she pointed out. "I don't think they ever run out of cake."

"You might want to read the card first."

"I don't have to."

"Oh, you have a third eye, do you?"

"No, I just know Reese."

Joss sat down on the bed and picked up a discarded square of adhesive. After straightening it, she placed it behind her ear.

"Nausea patch," she told him with a limp shrug. Standing, she added, "Okay. Let's spend some money!"

"COFFEE. BLACK."

"Skinny vanilla latte with a double shot and two sweeteners."

Patrick saw Joss's wheels turning, and he reached out and touched the young waitress on the wrist. Her jingle bell bracelet clinked in reply. When she looked back at him, he nodded toward Joss just an instant before she spoke up . . . as he somehow had anticipated that she would.

"And maybe one of those red velvet cupcakes in the case up front."

The waitress gave him a knowing smile, and Patrick shrugged. "Apple pie?"

"Dutch or plain?"

"Dutch."

"A la mode?"

He shook his head. "No, thanks."

He waited for her to jingle away before he told Joss, "I'll be back straight away."

The gold flecks in her brown eyes glinted with curiosity as he pushed out of the booth and hurried after the waitress.

"Do you have a birthday candle to put in that cupcake?" he asked when he'd caught up to her.

"Ohh," she cooed. "It's her birthday? On Christmas?"

"Let's make a real fuss and really light it up," he suggested. "She'll love that."

He chased away the devilish smile from his face before slipping back into his spot across the table from Joss.

"What was that all about?" she asked him. "Trying to get a date?"

The tiniest hint of jealousy thrilled him to no end, but a date? With the waitress?

"I think I went to school with her granddad," he said. "A little perspective if you please."

Joss chuckled, and it sounded musical, like the bracelet on the kindergarten waitress's wrist.

When the girl reappeared, she carried a tray with two cups and the sweets they'd ordered, Joss's cupcake ablaze with at least half a dozen little candles. Three additional employees of the café followed, all of them singing.

"We wish you a Merry Christmas, we wish you a Merry Christmas, we wish you a Merry Christmas and a Happy Birthday too."

Joss rubbed her face with both hands, and then she glared at him through open fingers. Patrick burst into laughter, mostly drowned out by the singing.

"Blow out your candles," the perky young waitress added as if part of the song. "And be sure to make a wish!"

Joss thought it over for a moment before looking Patrick dead in the eye and grinning. She closed her eyes tight, and said, "I wish . . . I could get Patrick Brenneman really close to the ship's railing."

Before he could react, she blew out the candles and thanked the quartet of singers.

When the festivities commenced and the wait staff retired to their corners, Joss picked candles from the cupcake, licking each one clean before dropping it to the plate.

"Well, that was fun, wasn't it?" he said, and he gulped his coffee.

"Yeah," she said with a broad smile and a nod. "The kind of fun where somebody gets chased with a power tool."

Her sarcasm delighted him, and Patrick grinned. "Does that make me the electric nail gun?"

"If the Black & Decker fits."

"Hey," he said with a chuckle, raising his hands in surrender. "I was just filling in for your candy friend."

"My what?" Her brown eyes became spotlights searching the room, and then golden sparks flickered as realization dawned. "Oh. Reese. Well, no more of this, all right? And no letting on to Connie that it's my birthday. The next thing I know, there will be a neon blinking light over my head, and I'll become an honorary elf held in captivity."

"I see your point," he conceded. "It's our little secret."

"Ours and the café staff," she said dryly.

"Oh, and Hadji, the cabin steward who brought your cake."

"Yeah. I forgot about him," she said. "I think we may have to kill him. The net's getting too wide."

"Maybe after dinner. We'll need our strength."

The amusement in her brown eyes blazed into a sort of terror, and Joss suddenly began scraping the candles from the plate and scooping them into the palm of her hand.

"Here," she said, pressing them into his and yanking her hand back across the table as a small contingent of the von Trapp family appeared tableside.

"Marla!" she cried. "You're . . . here! With . . . your kids! Hi, kids."

"Merry Christmas," the woman said. "I see you had the same idea the girls and I had."

"A latte?"

"Shopping," she corrected. "Our steward mentioned the shops would be open today, and I thought it might be a good time to have some girl time."

"The boys are with our daddy, shooting 'skeeters," the youngest chimed in.

"Shooting . . . mosquitoes?" Joss asked, and she looked to Marla.

"Skeet shooting. Rod's first love."

"Mama, can I have a cupcake like that?"

"I want hot chocolate, Mama. You said I could. With marshmallows."

"Angela," the woman said, and the oldest of the girls looked up from the glass bakery case. "Take your sisters and get a table."

The girl kicked into mother-hen-in-training mode, and she had the flock of them settled in a booth before the young waitress jingled her way toward them.

Patrick had always planned on having a family one day, but a family this size? He couldn't even imagine trying to herd cats in this way.

"So what did you buy?"

"Pardon?" Joss asked, and Marla nodded toward the shopping bags piled beside her. "Oh! Nothing. I mean, nothing much. A dress I can wear to dinner tonight, some earrings. Oh, and a cute little sarong in case I decide to grab some pool time." She reached into one of the bags and revealed a clenched section of the purple floral skirt-thing she'd bought before they ducked into the café.

"Oh, how pretty."

"How about you? Did you get anything?" Joss asked her.

"There's one thing you learn with this many children," she said, and she shot a grin at Patrick before continuing. "It's a slippery slope when it comes to purchasing *en masse*."

"So, what?" Joss teased. "You never actually buy anything?"

"It's very complicated business, Joss," Marla said in a hushed voice, leaning on the table with a smile. "I keep track of those things that really speak to me—for me and for each of the girls—and then I sneak away later to zip through and pick them up. So we've had a nice time together, everyone gets a little something in the end, assuming there are no battles during the process. Everybody wins."

"Except the boys," Patrick said with a laugh.

"Oh, there's a whole other system for the boys."

Joss chuckled. "So what you're telling me is that, to be a mother, you also have to be a sort of evil genius."

Marla grinned at Patrick. "Hold on to this one. She catches on fast."

On the sixth day of Christmas,
Murphy's Law gave to me . . .

six teeth a-breaking

five cold sardiiiines!

four dirty words,
three French friends,
two hearty shoves,
and a Partridge with the first name Keith.

6

For a dress she hadn't tried on before she bought it, this one looked pretty good.

Joss turned slightly and examined her reflection in the mirror. Not over-the-top like some of the getups she'd already seen onboard but dressy enough she'd fit in with the Christmas dinner crowd. And if it turned Patrick Brenneman's head a little in the process, so be it. She poked the new sterling earrings into her lobes, and they skimmed her shoulders. She grabbed her purse on the way out the door.

The main dining room shimmered under low lights and what looked like a thousand flickering candles. Upon closer inspection on her way across the room, Joss realized the flames were simply battery-operated facsimiles. With several yards to go before she reached her assigned table, her breath caught in her throat when her eyes met Patrick's and he smiled at her.

Black silk tie on black shirt beneath black suit jacket: he looked positively James Bond—in a scruffy, slightly incorrigible sort of way.

Her poor heart had hardly been able to take it when he'd worn a casual Friday version of a suit to breakfast that morning; she'd continually forced herself to look away from him during their shopping escapade to avoid staring too long.

"I thought I might have to come and find you," he said as he stood up and held out her chair. Once she'd been seated, he leaned over and whispered, "Happy Birthday." She inhaled sharply, but he placed his hand on her shoulder and added, "Simmer down there. It's my final offense."

"Wait until you see the menu, darlin'," Connie sang from across the table. "We have one gorgeous thing after another to choose from."

Patrick handed her a menu, and he looked over her shoulder as she reviewed it.

"You should have brought your cake with you," he said softly. "We could have all shared it and maybe sung a rousing chorus of 'Happy Birthday.'"

"You're a laugh riot," she remarked without looking up at him. "Besides, I ate most of it."

"Seriously? How?"

"Me and a fork and a cake. That's really all I needed."

"Hollow leg, right?"

Joss chuckled as their waiter approached. "Good evening, Miss."

"Good evening, Victor."

"Have you decided?"

"I'll start with the pear and pomegranate salad. Then the prime rib with cheesy mashed potatoes and asparagus."

"How would you like your prime rib?"

"Medium rare."

"Very good."

Joss glanced at Patrick. "You've already ordered? What are you having?"

"Turkey and trimmings. I was on the road for Thanksgiving and didn't get to have the usual suspects."

"Patrick loves cranberry sauce," Kathleen piped up. "I often wonder if that's not why he remained in America after college. Why, when he saw pumpkin pie on the dessert menu tonight, I thought he'd have to be revived."

"Your American Thanksgiving is inspired," he added with a shrug. "I admire genius."

"You said you were traveling over Thanksgiving," she said. "What exactly do you do? I've never asked."

"Patrick is a brilliant architect," Kathleen said.

"Historian, Mother." He smiled at Joss and clarified. "I'm an architectural historian."

"I don't . . ."—she hesitated to admit it—". . . know what that means."

He grinned. "Short version, I research specific buildings and compile reports on them."

"Like . . . for what purpose?"

"National registries, preservationists, sustainability evaluations."

Joss mulled it over, shaking her head. "I'm sorry to tell you I never even knew that was a profession."

"What about you?" Kathleen asked her. "What do you do, Miss Snow?"

"Joss. I'm in public relations."

"And how do the von Trapps fit in?" Patrick asked, and Joss laughed at the reference.

She glanced over at the Jenkins's table, noting only about half of the usual family members were seated there.

"Rodney Jenkins is the CEO of Vandermere Hotels & Spas. My partner and I have been trying to get their account for several years."

"Partner." He'd repeated it somewhat casually, but Joss read between the lines.

"Business partner. Ryan Butler. We've been in business together for nearly four years."

"Four years. That's a long time."

Joss grinned and leaned toward him. "Relax, historian. The only history between Ry and me is of the professional variety."

Patrick suppressed a smile as he nodded. "Good to know."

"And you? Any partnering I should know about in your line of work?"

"Nope. Lone wolf out there, all on my own."

She mirrored his nod. "I see."

Patrick angled toward her and whispered, "No attachments whatsoever."

She looked up at him. "And you think this matters to me, why, exactly?"

"No reason. I just appreciate full disclosure myself."

Joss chuckled. "Subtle. No attachments back on land for me either."

He nodded slowly. "I see. Good to know."

Victor and a sidekick began delivering salads and bowls of soup to the occupants of their table, cutting off the conversation at the knees. Joss had to work hard to squelch the squeal of delight that lingered in her chest at the wonderful news that Patrick Brenneman's dating passport could be cleanly stamped: Available.

"Is there anyone at the table who would be offended by a prayer over our meal?" Kathleen asked them, and the others looked at each other for verification.

"I think that's a delicious idea," Connie sang.

"Wonderful," Kathleen said, reaching for Joss's hand. "Patrick, why don't you do the honors with an Irish blessing."

Joss slipped her hand into Patrick's, and he squeezed it lightly. A surge of excitement shot through her. She struggled to follow the others' example, and she bowed her head and closed her eyes.

"The light of the Christmas star to you," Patrick said confidently. "The warmth of home and hearth to you; the cheer and good will of friends to you; the hope of a childlike heart to you; the joy of a thousand angels to you; the love of Jesus the Son, and God's peace unto every one of you."

He squeezed Joss's hand one more time before adding in his sweet Irish brogue, "*Nollaig Shona Dhuit.* Happy Christmas to everyone."

Kathleen let go of her hand, and Joss's eyes fluttered open. She glanced at Patrick. He hadn't released her hand; instead, he stroked it gently with his thumb for several seconds before he clasped it tightly one last time.

Joss felt her heart quiver when he finally let go, and she wondered if he'd noticed that her palm had gone clammy.

Never mind that, she thought as she unfolded the linen napkin and placed it on her lap. *Why am I trembling like this?*

Joss jumped as a hand grasped her shoulder, and Rodney Jenkins leaned down toward her.

"I'm sorry. I didn't mean to startle you," he said. "I just wanted to stop over and wish you a happy holiday. I've got to get back up to the cabin before Marla jumps overboard. A couple of the kids had an incident today, and we're taking our turns staying with them."

"I hope everyone's all right," she exclaimed. "Is there anything I can do?"

"Do you have children, Joss?"

"No, I don't. Just a sheepdog," she said with a laugh.

"Well, never let your dog have a jawbreaker."

"Oh . . . dear . . ."

"They're six-for-six with two of the children in the Jenkins suite. Six jawbreakers, six broken teeth."

"Oh, you're joking," Patrick commiserated. "That's horrible."

"We'll survive," he said with a shrug. "Just another day in paradise."

"Let me know if there's anything you need." Joss offered.

"Enjoy your holiday," he said with a smile. "Once I get a doggie bag of soft food up to the cabin, I think all will be well in the world again. For at least thirty minutes. After that, who knows?" He smacked Patrick's shoulder gently and gave Joss a nod. "Merry Christmas, you two."

"Same to you," he returned.

"Send my love to Marla."

Once he'd retreated, Kathleen turned toward Joss. "How many children does that man have?"

"Seven," Patrick answered.

"Oh, my. Can you imagine?"

Joss leaned back against her chair and sighed. "No. I really can't."

"No, I can't either," Patrick concurred. "I'd still like to have children one day, but as much as I'd like my own small hockey team, I'm fairly certain I'll have the good sense to stop after three or four."

"What if you fall for someone who wants an even dozen?" Joss asked him with a straight face. "You'll just nix her whole dream?"

He froze for a moment. "A dozen?"

"You like hockey," she said dryly. "I'm a fan of soccer myself."

Kathleen snickered from the other side of her before whispering to Joss, "I like your spirit, child."

THE DECK GLISTENED BENEATH the twinkling strands of lights hanging over their heads, and the section of railing where they'd chosen to stroll after dinner shimmered with red foil garland looped around it in a candy cane pattern. Joss slipped her arm through Patrick's, and his pulse began to race.

"Isn't the water beautiful?" she asked him softly. "It seems to go on forever."

"The reflection of a full moon doesn't hurt," he added.

"It's a perfect night."

Patrick cleared his throat and ran his tongue along his front teeth in the hope that no turkey dinner remnants had stuck around. Screwing up the bravery to do something he'd wanted to do almost since he first met her, he came to a stop and looked at Joss. The ocean breeze caught her hair and nudged all but one lone strand away from her pretty face, and Patrick picked up the dark auburn lock with the tip of his finger and combed it away.

"A schoolmate of mine owns a winery in the Napa Valley," he told her as he traced the curve of her jaw with his finger. "I spent the New Year with his family last year, and at midnight he opened a very special bottle of their wine . . . a sparkling variety of white. I don't normally enjoy the sweeter wines, but this one was spectacular, largely because of the gold flakes meandering about in it."

Joss grimaced. "Gold."

He nodded once. "Twenty-two karat gold flakes. Floating right inside it."

"I think I had a piece of wedding cake once with edible gold leaf on it," she told him. "So I guess your friend's wine won't kill anyone."

"I'm still standing," he replied as he rubbed her temple delicately with his thumb and gazed into her eyes.

"Were you making a point?" she asked. "Or did you just find yourself thinking about wine?"

"Oh." He dropped his hand from her face and snapped back to the moment. "Your eyes. They have gold flecks in them."

She connected the dots. "Like your friend's wine."

"Exactly."

She paused for a few beats before she looked as if she might make a move to continue their stroll around the deck. Patrick couldn't let the moment pass, and he slipped his arms around Joss's waist and pulled her closer.

"Can I?" he asked.

He could feel her warm breath on his face in the silence that followed. Finally, "Can you what?"

"Kiss you," he clarified.

The corner of her mouth twitched. "You want to?"

He sighed and replied, "Very much."

"Why?"

Patrick could hear his own heart pounding in his ears, and he wasn't entirely sure he hadn't misheard. "Why?" he repeated.

"Yes. Why do you want to kiss me?"

He snickered. "The usual reasons, I suspect. I'm attracted. . . . I find you quite charming and unexpectedly beautiful. . . . Oh, and if I don't, I'm not sure I'll be able to stand it."

Joss's smile spread across her entire face like warm butter on a hot roll.

"Then I guess you really should," she said.

He moved closer. "I think you're right." Patrick took her face into both of his hands.

"What does that mean, *unexpectedly beautiful?*" she asked him with a grin.

"I'll explain later," he replied, and he pressed his lips against hers.

He'd wondered if the moment would ever arrive. Feeling like he'd known her several years already—and been deprived of her kiss for all of them—Patrick indulged at last. And Joss slid her arms around his neck and surrendered.

"DON'T MAKE ME PUT you over my shoulder and carry you up there."

The way Joss twisted up her beautiful face at him made Patrick laugh right out loud.

"Come on. Do you want me to carry you up there?" he asked her, and the tangled knot of her expression transformed into a full-on glare. "Because I'll do it."

"I'll tell you what," she told him, nearly shouting over the karaoke rendition of "Wind Beneath My Wings" screeching from the stage. "You go first."

"Can I get you folks anything else?" the waiter bellowed at them.

"Another Diet Coke for my friend," Patrick yelled. "She needs to lubricate her voice. She's planning to sing."

"No!" she broke in, smacking his arm. "I'm not!"

"Would you like to see the catalog?" the waiter asked.

"The what?" she called.

"The catalog of song choices," he answered, pulling what looked like a menu from his back pocket and setting it between them on the table. "You can make your choice, and I'll deliver it to the DJ. Then he'll call your name when it's your turn."

"No, no," she insisted. "I'm really not—"

"Just leave it with us," Patrick asserted. "We'll talk it over."

The waiter nodded, and the moment he headed toward the bar to retrieve Joss's cola, she clamped the fingers of one hand around Patrick's forearm and squeezed until he folded into the pain.

"Hey! Stop it! What are you doing?"

"I'll tell you what I'm *not* doing—"

"Come on, where's your sense of adventure? Just have a look," he said, pushing the catalog toward her. "Maybe you'll see something that appeals to you and change your mind."

She pouted at him for a moment before opening the booklet and glancing over a random page.

"I don't karaoke," she told him, but the catalog clearly had her attention. "Although, if I was actually going to do it—which I am not!—you would be doing it with me, I assure you."

Patrick chuckled as he gulped the last of his coffee, and she scanned the song listings. He watched as something grabbed her attention. She squinted and looked closer, the corner of her mouth twitching with amusement.

"Let's pretend then," he suggested. "If you were going to, what song would you sing?"

"Well, this would be it," she declared, slapping the catalog to the tabletop. "Hands down!"

He looked at the listing beneath her tapping index finger.

"C'mon Get Happy"—the Partridge Family

"You're joking."

"I never joke about David Cassidy."

The waiter returned and set another large glass of soda on the table. As he removed Joss's empty one, he asked her, "Have you decided?"

"This one," Patrick snapped. "The Partridge Family."

The waiter cackled. "Good choice. No one's done that one in forever."

"No, really, I—"

"Her name is Joss," Patrick informed him.

"Joss. Got it. There are three others in front of you, but Lonnie will call your name when you're up."

"Wait! Really . . ."

"Oh, come on," Patrick teased. "You've made your choice, and it's David Cassidy."

Joss began gathering her things, an expression of sheer terror commandeering her demeanor, and she stood up from her chair in such a rush that her purse emptied on the tabletop.

"Simmer down there, Sparky," Patrick said on a laugh as he helped her pick up her belongings and stuff them into her purse. "It's all in fun. You wanted to put thoughts of Christmas behind you, didn't you? How far can you get from carols than Partridge Family karaoke, huh?"

"Really, Patrick, you're maddening. I said I don't want to."

"Why don't you tell me about your fascination with David Cassidy," he proposed. "Come on. Sit down."

She plopped back into the chair and glared at him, clutching her purse to her chest and twisting her hair around her finger.

"Keith Partridge," she muttered, and he hardly heard her over the transition onstage to a middle-aged couple's off-key rendition of the old Peaches & Herb song, "Love Is Strange."

"Keith Partridge," he repeated, and she nudged her purse back to the table. "Aren't you a little young for Partridge Family references? Wasn't that show over in the seventies?"

She glared at him and shrugged. "1970 through '74."

"You were like . . . what? . . . a decade shy of even being born?"

"Not that much."

"So where did your love for him originate?"

"Where else? Nickelodeon. It was in syndication in the nineties. And I fell hard."

"For David."

"No. For Keith."

"Keith Partridge," he clarified.

"Yes. I had pictures of him all over my closet door, and my mom got me a vintage pillowcase with Keith on it. I slept with that thing every night until I went away to college."

Patrick chuckled, and Joss slipped with an accidental smile in response.

"It's framed and hanging on the wall in my office right now."

"Oh, you're joking! That's brilliant!" he cried, wondering how much more adorable this girl could get.

A couple of twenty-something girls stepped up onstage and kicked into a rather silly rendition of Carly Rae Jepsen's "Call Me Maybe."

"The brain worm song," Patrick interjected. "No matter how you try not to, you'll be hearing this one in your sleep next week."

Joss giggled and fell back into her chair with a groan. A moment later she leaned forward and told him, "Three years ago, for our annual escape from Christmas, Reese and I went to Las Vegas and saw David Cassidy in concert." She blushed as she added, "I stood there and waited for him after the show like some sort of stage-door groupie."

"Did you get to meet him?"

She narrowed her eyes at him, as if she might be wondering if she could trust him with state secrets of some kind. After a long few moments, she produced a cell phone from her purse and navigated to a photo that she held up before him: Joss Snow, beaming so brightly that Patrick's sweet tooth ached, and a surprisingly fit-looking— albeit advanced in age from his Keith Partridge days—David Cassidy.

Patrick guffawed, snatching the phone from her hand to get a closer look.

"Be careful," she said, tugging on his wrist until she could get the phone back from him. "And don't mock."

"Oh, I'm not going to mock," he said with a chuckle. "I just can't wait to see you singing his song!"

"Us."

"Us, what?"

"*Us*, singing his song."

Patrick turned stoic as he considered her words. "Well," he finally said, "I don't even know that song. I can't sing it. But you can. Just lean into it. You'll enjoy it."

"You know, that's the great part about karaoke," she told him, pointing toward the stage. "They put the words up for you. All you have to do is read it and sing along."

Patrick slowly turned his head toward the stage as a probably intoxicated balding gentleman took the microphone and proceeded to serenade his uncomfortable date. His version of "Merry Christmas, Darling" became an epic fail in the first two lines.

"I think we're up next, genius," Joss called to him.

"Not me. You."

"We."

"You're the one with the Partridge in your pear tree," he quipped.

"Yep. And you're the one who shook him loose from the tree. So you're singing with me, my friend."

"I don't think so."

"Ohh," she growled. "You're singing with me."

On the seventh day of Christmas,
Murphy's Law gave to me . . .

seven songs a-shrieking,
six teeth a-breaking,

five cold sardiiiines!

four dirty words,
three French friends,
two hearty shoves,
and a Partridge with the first name Keith.

7

Joss couldn't deny it. Patrick had been right.

She'd leaned into it, as he suggested, and she ended up having the time of her life. She'd dragged him onstage with her, and "C'mon Get Happy" had just been the appetizer as it turned out. When the next karaoke crooner announced their intention to belt out a Christmas carol or two, Patrick had offered them twenty dollars to leave the mic in their hands for a second Partridge Family tribute, "I Think I Love You." Most of the audience had jumped to their feet and joined in.

And for dessert: Patrick's choice. "When Irish Eyes Are Smiling."

"You're so predictable," she muttered to him before the music began.

"Hey," he mugged for the audience. "I'm Irish. What did you expect?"

She'd just stood back and let him croon most of the song on his own before joining him—and the rest of the onlookers—in the final verse.

It had turned out to be a really fun non-Christmasy Christmas evening. Just the way she liked it. Afterward, they decided to "take the long way home," as Patrick called it, and they strolled around the outside deck. Balmy Pacific breezes caressed Joss's face, and she turned into them, closing her eyes as they meandered along.

"What a great night," she said on a sigh. "Better than I ever expected when I ended up on this boat alone."

"Alone?" Patrick challenged. "There are about four thousand people on this barge. You couldn't be alone if you tried."

"Well, not alone," she said. "Without Reese."

"You miss her?"

Joss chuckled. "So much. It's strange spending a holiday without her."

Patrick offered her his elbow, and she looped it with hers.

"I was thinking. When we dock in Puerto Vallarta . . . do you have any interest in going ashore together?"

Joss nodded. "Yes!"

"Have you ever been zip-lining?"

Her heart thumped. "Like hanging from a thin wire, flying through the trees?"

"That's the simplified version, yes."

"No. I never have," she admitted. "You?"

"Several times in my travels. It's exhilarating. Want to give it a try?"

She didn't want to admit her trepidation, so she nodded tentatively. "I think so."

"There's a pamphlet in your cabin. Give it a read and let me know if you're—"

When he stopped mid-word, Joss looked up to find his attention had been diverted. Following his line of sight, she noticed Connie Rudolph up ahead of them, alone and leaning on the railing, staring out at the moonlit water.

"Is she crying?" Patrick asked softly.

Upon closer look, Joss was inclined to agree. "I think she is."

The two of them stepped it up and came to a stop next to Connie.

"Connie?" Joss said.

She jumped, and once she'd seen them, she turned away, quickly dabbing her eyes. Joss couldn't help grinning at the jingle bell music of the action.

"Well, hi there, you two!" she exclaimed, and she pasted on a brave happy face as she reeled back toward them. "Where have you been off to?"

"You would never believe it," Joss replied.

Patrick moved next to Connie and placed an arm around her shoulder. "Everything all right, love?"

"Oh, I'm fine," she insisted in that Southern drawl of hers. "I just got to thinkin' too much, you know?"

"Do you want to talk about it?" Joss asked, stroking her hand.

"You two don't want to spend Christmas night coddling an old fool like me," she told them. "You just go off and have yourselves a good time. I'm just dandy."

"Connie. Come on," Joss encouraged her, and Connie sighed.

"It's my first Christmas alone without Rayburn. I'm just a little blue, that's all."

"Rayburn?"

"My husband. He died in August from a massive coronary." Joss's heart fell to her knees and bounced around for a moment. "I haven't spent Christmas without him since I was nineteen."

"I'm so sorry."

Patrick drew her closer and squeezed her shoulders.

"Rayburn loved him some Christmas celebratin' too," she said with a sniffle. "You could always count on him to keep the party goin' straight into the New Year."

Joss realized she'd never actually noticed Connie had spent the entire cruise without companions—other than the ones who had no choice, of course.

"You came on this cruise completely alone?" she asked.

Connie nodded. "Just like you, honey."

Her heart dropped again. No wonder Connie had insinuated herself into Joss's personal space the way she had. *She was lonely!*

"Why don't you walk with us for a bit," Patrick suggested.

"Oh, no, honey! You two go ahead and be alone. Anybody with eyes in their head can see there's a budding romance gettin' started here. I don't want to jam up the works. Besides, I hear they have a scrumptious dessert bar set up in the lobby by the Christmas tree, and they're going to be carolin' and all. I'm gonna make my way over there in a few minutes anyway."

"A dessert bar?" Joss perked up and feigned interest, despite the threat of Christmas caroling. "Patrick, let's go with her! That sounds like fun."

"Yeah! I'm game," he said, catching on immediately. "Do you mind if we tag along, Connie?"

"Mind?" she exclaimed. "No! Of course not! You really want to?"

Joss nodded. "Apparently, you haven't known me long enough to know you had me at *dessert bar*."

Connie giggled and dabbed under her eyes with the side of her index finger. Patrick stepped between them, offering an arm to each of the ladies in his company.

"I'm so happy I met y'all, I tell ya! Hey, what are y'all doing when we get to Puerto Vallarta? Do you think you'll go shoppin'?"

"Oh, get this," Joss cried. "This nut case wants to go zip-lining!"

"Zip—! You've got to be joshin' me," she said to Patrick. "Boy, it's a good thing you're pretty because you sure aren't too smart."

Patrick and Joss exchanged smiles over Connie's shoulder.

"You wouldn't catch me with my feet that far off the ground for all the tea in Chinatown! Joss, you're not actually going, are you?"

"I don't know. I thought I might give it a try."

"Well, I'll just hit the shops in town while you do then. You can tell me all about it when I come to visit you in your hospital room."

"Do you know what he had me doing tonight?" Joss exclaimed. "Karaoke."

"Karaoke!" she cried, and then she began to laugh. "Patrick, can she sing?"

"Weeeeell . . ."

"Hey!"

AFTER DOCKING, YOU WILL drive approximately forty minutes to a zip-line circuit consisting of eight different lines. Enjoy breathtaking views from the interim platforms, and then soar like a bird over canopies of trees, rock formations, and moving water.

The description sounded friendly and peaceful, almost relaxing; however, once Joss took on all of the gear and stood on that first platform, her pumping heart seemed anything but relaxed.

"You two will go in tandem," the instructor told them. "Just like we showed you."

Joss locked on to Patrick's eyes in the hope of something reassuring. Instead, she found herself engulfed in flames of utter excitement for whatever the adventure held for them.

"Joss, you go first. And Patrick, we'll latch you in behind her. The first one is easy, just a warm-up."

Easy.

"Easy?!" she cried as they barreled across the canyon below, a hundred feet away from solid ground of any kind.

"Don't look down," Patrick called out from behind her. "Keep your eyes forward for the first few runs."

Few runs. Joss had hoped that, after one unnatural, out-of-control flight through the air, they might call it a day.

"Wasn't it fantastic?" he bellowed once they reached the platform and the guide steered them to a full stop. "Admit it. You loved it!"

"You did great," the muscular guide reassured her as she tried to find her land legs again. "The next one is just a little longer and steeper. About eight hundred feet, about a hundred feet high."

"Oh. Dear."

"C'mon," Patrick encouraged her with a beaming smile. "It's exhilarating."

Joss had to admit Patrick's assessment had been correct; the runs became more fun and less terrifying as they progressed. With harness, belay gloves, and protective helmet in place, she became a more willing participant with each glide, clutching the steel handle with less desperation each time they soared. By the final glide of twenty-seven hundred feet—three hundred feet off the ground— she hooted and howled right along with Patrick.

Afterward, the two of them trekked to the top of the canyon and rewarded themselves with a Mexican feast at the restaurant there. When the shuttle got them back to the pier, they had to run in order to board the ship on time.

"You two look like you had a good time!" Marla Jenkins called out to them as they passed, and Joss noticed she and the four children with her had taken quite a bit of sun.

"You guys, too! I hope you packed some aloe."

"We swam with dolphins!" one of the youngest spoke up, and Joss immediately identified him as one of the jawbreaker victims.

"Did you? I've always wanted to do that."

"You shoulda come," the boy said as he fell into step beside Joss and Patrick. "We had fun! Did you go someplace fun, too?"

"We did!" she exclaimed. "Do you know what zip-lining means?"

"Uh-uh," he said, shaking his little blond head.

"It's where you strap on a harness and wear a helmet," Patrick told him, "and they hook you to a cable and send you barreling through the air over the tops of the trees."

The boy gasped, wide-eyed, and Patrick grabbed him at the waist and hurled him into the air over his shoulder. The child descended into a fit of laughing hysterics as Patrick demonstrated to him how it felt to fly.

"That sounds like fun," he said when Patrick put him onto his feet again. "Can we do that, Mama?"

"Yes, you may," Marla said from behind them. "When you're thirty."

The boy's sister stepped up between them and tugged on Patrick's hand. "Mister, can I fly now?"

"Becky!" Marla reprimanded. "Don't bother them."

Patrick stopped in his tracks and looked down at the girl. "Are you brave enough to fly, Rebecca?"

She nodded emphatically.

"Are you sure?"

"I'm sure."

Without a moment's hesitation, Patrick whipped the girl over his shoulder and mimicked the sound of the zip-line as they flew ahead of the pack. Marla seized the opportunity and nudged Joss.

"He's adorable, isn't he?"

"I'm afraid so," she replied.

"Do you have plans with him tonight?" Marla asked. "We're all going to the stocking-making class on the mezzanine. Would you like to join us?"

Even less than I'd like to intern for Santa himself.

"If you can stand that many Jenkins family members in one place, that is."

"You're all going then?"

"From Rod to Ashley, and everyone in between."

Joss's pulse quickened. She'd been looking for an opportunity to socialize a bit with Rodney Jenkins. This might be just the chance she'd need to butter him up before their meeting back in L.A.

"What time?"

"Seven-thirty."

"What's at seven-thirty?" Patrick asked as he and Becky made their way back toward them.

"A stocking-making class," Joss informed him. "You in?"

He looked down at Becky and asked, "Are you going?"

She nodded and grinned. "We're all making new stockings for Santa to fill next year. It's gonna be a new tarnation."

"Tradition," Marla corrected.

"That sounds like a good one," he told her. Looking to Joss, Patrick grinned. "I'm in."

"Goody!" Becky bellowed.

Marla counted down her children and nodded. "Good, we're all here. Let's get back to the cabin and tell your brothers and sisters all about the dolphins."

"They picked the horses," Becky told Patrick, reluctant to let go of his hand. "They rode horses, I mean."

"Well, that would be fun too," he said. "You can fill me in over making our stockings."

"'Kay!"

And with that, four children scurried off with Marla across the ship's lobby.

"Sorry to rope you into that," Joss told him when they'd gone. "I'm hoping to lay some groundwork with Rodney Jenkins before we get back."

"No problem. I don't have my own stocking anyway. I think it's high time, don't you?"

THE ROOM HAD BEEN arranged with a dozen or more large rectangular tables for twelve, and between the entire Jenkins family, Connie Rudolph, and he and Joss, they filled their table to capacity.

"So there you have it," the proper English instructor told them in a rather shrill voice. "It's a beautiful Christmas stocking to hang on the mantel for Santa each and every year. Let's get started, shall we? And if you have any questions, I'll be walking around the room to answer them."

Becky Jenkins led Patrick by the hand toward the front of the room to choose the trinkets and trims to decorate their stockings. She picked several glittery felt hearts, some red-and-white gingham bows, and a handful of shiny buttons.

"I think you should use some buttons too," she suggested. "The bows aren't right for a boy."

Patrick furrowed his brow. "No? Why not?" he asked, and he held one of the tiny bows up to his temple. "It doesn't look good on me?"

Becky giggled. "Nooo. You're a boy."

"Well, I suppose you're right," he conceded. "Perhaps I'll use one of these glittery paints instead."

He glanced around the room until his eyes landed on Joss surrounded by several more of the Jenkins clan, including their mother. Rodney Jenkins had already returned to the table with his youngest sons, one of whom had quite the jagged jawbreaker-induced smile.

"Are you growing something on your chin?" Becky asked, drawing Patrick's attention back to her.

"What do you mean?"

"You're stubbly."

"Oh," he replied with a laugh. "Don't you like it?"

"I like clean chins, like my Daddy's."

"Do you?" he asked, rubbing his shadowy beard with the side of his hand.

"Doesn't it itch you?"

Patrick laughed. "Not too much. Do you want to feel it?"

Becky's eyes lit up. "Could I?"

He nodded and leaned down toward her. "Go on then. Give it a rub."

The little girl timidly touched his cheek, giggling. "I think that would be itchy."

"Do you now?" he said, and he darted toward her, rubbing her face gently with his. "You think I'm itchy, do you?"

Becky's laughter warmed his heart, and he watched after her as she rushed back to the table with her trimmings clumped into both hands.

"I'm afraid my daughter has a bit of a crush," Marla said, and he turned to find her standing beside him.

"Does she? I guess I hadn't noticed because of the one I have on her."

Marla chuckled. "Well, don't let her break your heart now. She can be quite fickle. Until she met you, our cabin steward was the object of her affections."

"The story of my life, fickle women."

The two of them headed back to the table just as Joss stood up, her cell phone in hand.

"Where are you off to?" he asked her.

"I noticed I have a connection, so I want to make a quick call before I lose it again. I'll be right back."

Patrick sat down between Becky and her smile-challenged brother, paying far more attention to their creations than to working on one of his own.

"I knew it!" Marla exclaimed, shaking her head. "I knew if Rod saw someone making a call, he'd be on his before you could say, 'Ho-ho-ho.'"

Patrick caught sight of the back of Marla's husband just as he pushed through the door and left the Christmas stockings behind.

"I KNOW! FOR SUCH a colossal disaster, it really couldn't have worked out any better," Joss told Ryan. "I don't know how much business talk I can squeeze in between Christmas stockings and noisy kids, but I think I'm forging a relationship anyway. Maybe laying a little groundwork for our meeting in two weeks."

"Joss, are you having any fun at all?"

"Actually, yes. Get this! I went zip-lining in Puerto Vallarta!"

"By yourself?"

"Well, no. I've sort of . . . met someone."

"You've met someone? You sure know how to bury the lead, my friend. Tell me about him."

"That can wait until I get back. It's just a ship thing. You know, something to take my mind off all the merriment."

"Careful, Ebenezer. I happen to be enjoying the merriment."

"You do that, Ry. Get your fill of sugarplums and eggnog and jingle bell rocking while I represent our company here with Santa Jenkins and his band of merry little elves."

"And the someone you've met."

"Believe me, there isn't an Irish brogue *brogue-y* enough . . ."

"Oh. He's Irish?"

". . . to make up for what I'm taking for the team. So if you'll excuse me, I need to get back to my stocking-making class."

"You're joking."

"I wish. Give my love to the fam, and I'll see you soon."

Joss disconnected the call and dropped her phone into the pocket of her jeans. But as she turned back toward the door, she screeched to a stop to keep from running straight into Rodney Jenkins where he stood behind her.

Everything she'd just said to Ryan squealed at fast-forward in her ears, and she could hardly catch her breath as she wondered how much of it Jenkins had heard.

"Oh. Mr. Jenkins, I . . . uh . . ."

"Better get back to the torture chamber, Miss Snow. Your friend with the Irish brogue is saving you a seat."

"Oh. No. I—"

"Now excuse me while I make a call."

And with that, Rodney Jenkins stalked away—taking his six-million-dollar account with him, no doubt.

Joss clutched her chest as she inched toward the door, her breath caught somewhere beneath her throat. She felt as if she might hyperventilate, but she walked into the room anyway. Somehow.

Her eyesight descended into a sort of tunnel vision between herself and Patrick. As if on instinct, he glanced up at her almost immediately. She nodded over her shoulder one time, and then she turned and walked out the door again. She hadn't even made it to the end of the corridor before he reached her.

"Hey. What's going on? Is something wrong?"

"Yes."

"What is it?"

"Me."

"You. Are you sick?"

"Yes."

"It might be time to change that seasickness patch then. Why don't you—"

"No."

"No?"

"No, that's not it," she managed.

"Then what is it? Can I walk you back to your cabin?"

"No need. I'm just going to . . . to . . ." She didn't know what she was going to do, truth be told. But then the inspiration came to her in a flash. ". . . throw myself overboard."

On the eighth day of Christmas,
Murphy's Law gave to me . . .

eight careers crashing,
seven songs a-shrieking,
six teeth a-breaking,

five cold sardiiiines!

four dirty words,
three French friends,
two hearty shoves,
and a Partridge with the first name Keith.

8

"You'll just wait until tomorrow, and you'll talk to him. Rod seems like a very reasonable bloke, Joss. Tell him what you've just told me. . . . Well, maybe not *everything* you just said, . . . but I'm sure he'll understand."

"Yeah, I'm sure you're right, Patrick," she said, still clutching her heart. "I'll just say, 'Look, Mr. Jenkins, I'm a Christmas hater from way, way back. It's nothing personal, but I only pretended to have the kind of holiday spirit of someone who, say, brings their twenty-seven children on a Christmas cruise and spends their time singing carols and decorating stockings, all so I could get closer to you and snag your business.'"

Tossing herself hard against the leather booth, she clamped her eyes shut and groaned.

"Perhaps if he knows why you're inclined to avoid Christmas—"

"Stop!" she growled without opening her eyes. "Please just stop."

A clamor drew her attention as a server set down two cups of coffee and an enormous slice of cheesecake she didn't remember ordering. Joss inspected the cheesecake for a moment, and it morphed into the shape of a life preserver—drizzled with caramel. She scraped the plate toward her, seized a fork, and stabbed it. As it hit her tongue, she sighed loudly.

"Should I get her a fork, after all?" the server asked Patrick. "Or can I bring you a second piece?"

"No. We're fine."

In a flash, she remembered. Joss had told the waitress all she wanted was coffee. Patrick was the one who'd asked for the cheesecake.

"I'm sorry," she told him as she sliced off another hunk. "I have no self-control."

"It's fine," he said with a grin. "Enjoy."

Joss didn't speak again until the last morsel of cheesecake had been devoured. Before setting down her fork again, she mimed stabbing herself in the neck with it.

"Ah, Patrick, what have I done? I just keep going over it in my head, imagining what Jenkins must have thought when he overheard that conversation." She sighed and sank into the booth, looking across the table at Patrick. "I'm defective. You should really know that about me. I'm unfit for human interaction, I really am."

"All evidence to the contrary," he replied softly. "Look, I need to check in on my mother. Can I walk you back to your cabin?"

"Go ahead. I'm just going to hang here with the memory of the six thousand calories I've just consumed."

"I'll see you tomorrow?"

She nodded and tried to smile at him, but her lips refused to curve upward. "I may stay clear of the main dining room though."

"I'll sneak you some food."

"And a life raft so I can head for home?"

"You've got it."

He slipped out of the booth and stopped to press a kiss on the top of her head before departing.

"Sweet dreams."

Joss wondered if she'd be sleeping long enough to conjure up any of those.

PATRICK ARRIVED AT HIS mother's cabin to find her sitting safely on the edge of her bed with Lilibeth.

"Oh, Patrick, there you are, dear. How was your evening?"

"It was fine, Mother. How about the two of you?"

"Caroline, Lilibeth, and I went to the salon and played a rousing game of Reindeer Bingo," she said, beaming. "Look what I won."

A large red basket wrapped in clear cellophane and tied with curled ribbons filled most of the table angled into the corner on the other side of the bed. He walked over to inspect it more carefully.

"There are Christmas ornaments and beautiful little hand towels," she told him. "Oh, and some lovely chocolates I'm thinking of sampling."

"Kathleen was the belle of the ball," Lilibeth said with a smile. "She had a line of gentlemen vying for the honor of pushing her wheelchair."

"I missed you though, dear," she added. "Tell us. Did you enjoy your time with Miss Snow?"

"Very much."

"I'm so glad. She's a lovely young woman."

"Yes, she is."

After an hour or so of hearing about all of the ins and outs of Reindeer Bingo, Patrick left his mother in Lilibeth's capable hands to help her get ready for bed. With the memory of that just-missed slice of cheesecake to spur him, he decided to pass his cabin door and head downstairs to see if anything similar could be had.

The enormous geared clock in the atrium read 10:14, and he'd just begun to wonder if it might be too late for such things. However, a familiar steward directed him to one of the smaller salons where snacks and sweets could be found at just about any time of the day or night.

A stunning, middle-aged African-American woman in a red sequin dress with white fur trim stood at a microphone in front of the piano in the corner of the room, crooning a pretty fair imitation of Etta James. After lingering in the doorway for a moment, Patrick navigated the occupied tables and headed for the buffet. He poured a cup of decaf and gave himself a self-congratulatory smile when he spotted the cheesecake, and he placed a slice on a small plate, along with several gargantuan strawberries.

As he scanned the room for an ideal spot to enjoy the music, he spotted Rodney and Marla Jenkins sitting alone at a small table. He made his way to the empty one beside them and sat down.

"Evening," he said with a nod when Marla noticed him.

"Patrick. Join us?"

Her husband stiffened before courtesy got the better of him. "Please do."

"Don't mind if I do."

He scraped a chair toward them and sat down next to Rodney. "I had a near-miss earlier tonight with dessert," Patrick told him softly. "I couldn't sleep until we reconnected."

Jenkins snickered and nodded. "We're trying out one of the cruise line's sitters to see how the children do."

"I don't imagine you two get much alone time away from the brood," he said. "I don't mind moving to another table if you'd like to make the most of your escape."

"As long as you don't tug on my coat or whine at me to get you something, I think we're ahead of the game here."

Patrick took a swig of coffee and returned the cup to the tabletop before speaking. "Actually, I would like to tug on your coat sleeve for just a quick second."

Jenkins kept his eyes on the singer as he responded. "I had a feeling."

"Joss is pretty torn up about your encounter earlier."

He waited for a reply, but none came.

"She's a pistol, that one," he continued. "Talks a pretty tough game."

"Does she?" It came as more of a statement than a question.

"You and I," Patrick said, "we have the ties to make Christmas a family affair. Joss doesn't have that. So she's developed a fairly robust defense against it all that can come off as pretty . . ."

"False?" he asked, still without turning toward Patrick.

"Harsh," he corrected. "But that's all it is . . . a defense. And what you overheard was a bit of bravado for the sake of her business partner who, I might add, was speaking to her from some idyllic location with his own family gathered around him."

Marla leaned forward and looked at Patrick across the forward stare of her husband. "Are you two talking about Joss? She doesn't have any family?"

Patrick shook his head and casually sliced off a chunk of cheesecake and poked it into his mouth. "Family non grata."

"That's so sad."

"Yes," Rodney remarked. "But it does make her the logical choice then to . . . how did she put it? . . . *take one for the team*."

"As I said," Patrick reiterated, "just a hard outer shell. I've found Joss's inner workings to be surprisingly quite tender." He took a moment to wonder which side of Joss might face off with him over the interference. "I think she and her business partner have spent a good bit of time preparing to meet with you after the holidays. It would be a shame to miss out on what they can offer your company simply because you overheard a misstep about something so personal to her as spending Christmas alone."

"What's she doing on a Christmas-centric cruise then?" Jenkins asked him coolly, and then he turned toward Patrick to await his reply.

"That's a funny story, really," he said, leaning in to include Marla. "She normally spends Christmas with a friend, and they make it a point to avoid the holiday altogether. She'd actually signed them up for a sort of anti-Christmas cruise called a Bah Humbug journey."

"I've heard of that," Marla told him, and she squeezed her husband's arm.

"They apparently didn't get enough interest, and Murphy's Law came into play. She was booked on this ship instead."

"And where's her friend?" he asked.

"Turns out the girl recently became engaged to be married. She's spending the holidays with her future in-laws."

"Oh. Poor Joss," Marla cringed.

"Anyway, it's none of my affair. I just thought you should know that she feels awful about the way things went."

"What things?" Marla asked, and she angled toward her husband. "Rod? Did something happen between you and Joss?"

"I think I'll let you two have your date night," Patrick said, and he drained the last of his coffee. Placing a hand on Rodney's shoulder, he added, "Thanks for the company. G'night then."

"Good night."

DESPITE THE FACT THAT their guide had been meticulous in instructing them how to use torso rotation and upper body stance for purposes of navigation, Joss's shoulders burned when she and Patrick finally stopped for a rest. The blue-green Pacific waters seemed far less choppy as they steered their bright yellow kayak toward the exquisite coastline rock formations.

"Mazatlan was founded in 1531," their nearby guide called out, and the seven other two-person kayaks in their tour paddled into a semicircle around him. "Settlers were Spaniards and Indians, and the seaport mostly dealt in equipment for mining silver and gold."

Joss loosened the strap of her life vest and stretched out the muscles of her neck as several ospreys squawked overhead. Despite the gorgeous scenery and the great company on the tour, she struggled to stay focused on the experience. Instead, the butterflies swarming in her stomach continually called her attention back to the look on Rodney Jenkins's face when she'd turned around to find him standing there.

"C'mon," Patrick had persuaded. "Let's just go with the tour into Mazatlan as planned, and I'm willing to bet you feel like a new person."

But she didn't feel new. She felt weighted down with guilt . . . and regret. If she thought she could pull it off, she'd strap that life vest a little tighter and swim her way home. Anything to avoid getting back on that ship and risk running into Rodney Jenkins and his family.

"Hey, you two!" Brett Wiley called out. He and Corinne, the thirty-something newlyweds they'd sat with on the skiff, paddled toward them, and their kayaks nearly collided. "What are you up to when we get back?"

"What'd you have in mind?" Patrick asked.

"We were thinking about sticking around after lunch," Corinne told them, "and maybe going horseback riding on the beach, or taking one of the tours around the area. Are you interested in joining us?"

Joss wasn't particularly intrigued by the idea, but it would be an effective way to stay away from the ship a little while longer. She leaned back and craned her neck, gazing into Patrick's eyes.

"What do you think?" he asked her.

"Sounds good."

He smiled, nodding at Brett. "I was reading about the older section of the city, and I'd be interested in checking out some of the architecture."

"There's a two-hour tour that starts at the town square," Corinne told them. "It's called Plaza Revolución."

"Let's talk about it over lunch," Brett suggested.

The large group dined on warm empanadas, chips and salsa, and an array of fresh fruit. While Corinne and Joss changed out of their swimsuits and into clothes they'd brought along in tote bags, Patrick and Brett worked with their kayaking instructor to set up half a dozen members of their group with a Latina friend of his who arranged to shuttle them into town for a couple of hours before taking them back to the ship in plenty of time.

An hour later Joss and Patrick climbed off the bus in an old section of the city.

"These structures date back to the nineteenth century," Patrick told her as they strolled through the main square, surrounded by palm trees and colonial-style buildings.

In the center of Plaza Revolución sat a strange sort of gazebo with a wrought-iron bandstand on the top. Joss reached for the small digital camera zipped into the pocket of her tote bag and snapped photographs of a large Moorish church with twin blue and gold spires.

Corinne stepped up next to her, a guidebook in her hands. "It's called the Basilica de la Immaculada Concepción," she told them. "It took fifteen years to build in the 1800s."

"Corinne," Brett called to his wife, and she smiled at Joss.

"We'll meet you back here in a while?"

"See you then," she replied as her new friend jogged toward her husband.

Patrick reached for her hand and led Joss toward the Gothic cathedral. Inside, polished wooden pews faced an ornate gilded altar, and a massive Parisian organ inspired Joss to start snapping photos again.

When she rejoined Patrick, he sat in the back with his arms draped over the pew as he took in the beauty surrounding them. She sat down next to him, and he tugged her close to him and smiled.

"It's just unbelievable, isn't it?" she whispered.

"This is the kind of Christmas holiday I enjoy," he replied. "Sitting quietly in front of such beauty, where millions before us have paid homage to the Savior."

Joss turned and looked at him for a moment, taken completely off guard by his words.

"Do you mind if I just sit here and pray for a few minutes?"

She tossed her hair over one shoulder and cleared her throat. "N-no. Of course not. I'll just leave you to—"

"You don't have to go," he said, and he cupped her hand between both of his and raised it to his lips. "I'd like it if you stayed." And he kissed her knuckles lightly.

A moment later Patrick bowed his head, closed his eyes, and began to pray silently . . . leaving Joss to sit staunchly beside him. She wasn't sure she'd ever known a man who openly *prayed*, and she wondered what it must be like to have such a cemented foundation of faith and reverence for something so clearly . . . unclear.

"Did I make you uncomfortable?" Patrick asked, breaking the silence just above a whisper, yet shattering it to shards in Joss's ears.

"What? No. Of course not," she lied.

"Sure," he said with a smile. "Of course not. Because you're not the least bit tense. I can tell by the way you're sitting there, erect and shell-shocked."

Joss chuckled. "Okay. I was a little taken by surprise."

"By prayer in general?" he asked. "Or by me praying here and now?"

She sighed. "I don't know. Maybe both. I guess I thought that, if you were so eager to help me avoid all things Christmas, maybe it didn't mean so much to you either. But what you said just then . . . it . . . surprised me, I guess."

Patrick leaned forward, angling toward Joss as he took her hand between both of his. "You know, Joss," he said in that appealing Irish brogue of his, "the thing about Christmas—for me—is this whole commercialization that we've done to it. That's the part I don't take seriously. But my faith is a different matter entirely. There were no wreaths on the stable door and no elves waiting to greet the visitors there. And I feel pretty certain not one of the three wise men was wearing a sweater bearing a reindeer whose nose blinked at five-second intervals. It's not that there's anything inherently wrong with all the rest of it, but forgetting why we celebrate Christmas in the first place is a terrible fate this one holiday doesn't deserve."

Joss swallowed around the lump in her throat and rubbed the goose bumps that had risen on her arm.

"Too much information," Patrick observed as he rubbed the stubble on his jaw. "Sorry."

"Don't be sorry," she softly replied. "It's encouraging somehow to see someone like you with beliefs he can really stand on."

"It's not limited to someone like me, Joss. It's a universal possibility."

She looked into his dark hazel eyes, and when he smiled at her, that ridiculously adorable dimple in his chin deepened.

"Ready to make our way back?"

Joss nodded. "More than."

On the ninth day of Christmas,
Murphy's Law gave to me . . .

nine Scrooges hiding,
eight careers crashing,
seven songs a-shrieking,
six teeth a-breaking,

five cold sardiiiines!

four dirty words,
three French friends,
two hearty shoves,
and a Partridge with the first name Keith.

9

"Are you sure you won't come to the dining room?"

"No," Joss insisted. "No, really. I . . . can't."

"You can."

"Okay, I can. I just don't want to."

Patrick leaned against the doorway and sighed. "Then how about this," he suggested. "Let me arrange dinner for us up on the top deck."

"Will they do that?" she asked.

"I read about it in the guest services book in the drawer. You choose your menu and phone it in, and they serve it to you right out there at a private table."

"I don't know. I was sort of thinking about hiding out alone in my jams, watching something on the television."

"Your jams?" he repeated. "What are jams?"

"PJs. Pajamas."

He chuckled as Joss tilted her head slightly and stared him down for one intense moment. "Well," she said, pausing to shake her head. "What do they serve? Anything good?"

"What strikes your fancy?" he asked her, and her heart fluttered slightly. "Steak and lobster? Pasta and shrimp? What sounds good?"

"Something cheesy and Italian," she declared. "Will they do pizza, or lasagna, or something?"

"I'll find out. What do you like on your pizza?"

"Everything except anchovies," she said, and then the memory of those sardines on Patrick's breakfast plate inspired a gasp. "Do I need to say this? No sardines!"

"Got it. No anchovies, no sardines. I'll make all the arrangements, and I'll be back to get you at seven-thirty."

"Perfect. Is this party casual or black tie?"

"Casual," he replied with a wide grin. "Feel free to wear your jams."

"Funny."

"And bring a jacket or a sweater. It may get breezy up there."

Joss let Patrick leave before she leaned against the doorjamb and watched him make his way down the garland-draped corridor, her heart pounding, and a sort of ridiculous grin forcing its way across her face. She never could have imagined meeting someone like Patrick when she booked that Bah Humbug cruise for her and Reese. The absolute best hope had been a little distraction from the real-life season that rolled around each and every year, ready or not.

Once inside she glanced at the clock next to the bed. With two hours before dinner, she decided to make the most of it. After a long bath and moisturizing mask, she dug out her nail kit and settled into one of the balcony chairs for a sunset do-it-yourself mani-pedi. She curled up on the bed to meticulously apply her makeup, and then she took a crimper to her hair. By the time she pulled on her favorite jeans and charcoal shell sweater, the pre-date jitters had kicked into high gear.

Joss sat down on the corner of the bed and watched the clock tick away the minutes. When 7:30 quickly became 7:39, she started to fidget again. But the 7:40 knock at the door shot through her, and she jumped to her feet.

"YOU'LL START WITH A Caesar salad and warm garlic knots," the server explained as he set the first course in front of them. "The entree will be baked ziti and spears of grilled zucchini with fresh Parmesan."

Patrick grinned when Joss let out a soft moan. "You said you wanted Italian. And they didn't offer pizza up here."

"It's perfection!"

The small table sat at an angle in a private corner behind a large column, and a plexiglass and steel railing allowed a perfect view beyond them: dark water stretching out to the horizon under a perfect silver moon and a million bright-white stars.

"Can I pour you some wine or get you a cocktail?" the waiter offered.

"Do you have iced tea?" Joss asked him.

"Certainly. And you, sir?"

"The same."

Resisting the urge to reach across the table and touch the wavy lock of reddish hair caught on the sea breeze, Patrick unfolded his napkin, placed it on his lap, and picked up his fork. "I'm a little disappointed in your attire," he said seriously.

She gasped. "Are you? I'm sorry. I thought you said casual."

"And I thought you said pajamas." She cocked her head and shot him an I-am-not-amused fake smile. "But admit it," he added. "Even though you had to dress, this is much better than what you had planned."

"We'll see," she teased. "You'll have to do pretty well to top my bunny jams and matching pink socks. Let's just see if you burp your ziti before I pass judgment."

"There's an Italian place about a mile from my house," he told her. "They make an amazing baked ziti that comes with freshly ground sausage. I have high hopes for this meal, but I'll be hard pressed to like it as much."

"I have a place with a dish like that near my place too. Carmine's," she hummed. "They deliver to me at least one night a week."

"Carmine's," he repeated, and a surge of adrenaline shot through his chest. "On Glenoaks?"

"Yes!" she exclaimed. When it settled in on her, Joss asked him, "Patrick, *where do you live?*"

"In Glendale."

"Glendale? I thought you lived in Arizona."

"No. My mother and her friends live there. I'm in Glendale."

"Are you joking? I'm in Los Feliz, in the hills above Griffith Park!"

Patrick couldn't stop the flames of the smile that completely engulfed his face. "We live . . . what? . . . ten minutes apart?"

"If that!" she cried. "How bizarre is kismet like this?"

"Not bizarre kismet, Joss," he assured her. "Destiny."

A stain of color washed over her face and neck, and she looked suddenly—and surprisingly—shy. She twisted a lock of hair around her finger and stared out at the stretch of ocean.

"It's beautiful," she said on a sigh.

"I can't believe you know Carmine's," he said in hopes of putting her at ease again.

It worked, too, because she slipped to the edge of her chair and exclaimed, "I know!"

Dinner conversation took on a whole new dynamic as they compared notes about their neighboring communities, and Patrick could almost picture Joss in one of those beautiful old Spanish houses perched in the hills or stretched out on a blanket and reading a book on the main lawn at Griffith Park. He passed her neighborhood every Sunday morning on the way to church, and he couldn't help wondering how many times they'd shared a waiting line at Trader Joe's or pulled up next to one another at the stoplight near Atwater Village.

Over tiramisu and coffee they exchanged tales of concerts at The Greek, the Fourth of July fireworks at the Hollywood Bowl, and countless movies at the Burbank AMC. Joss told him about Mavis, the crazy groomer in Glendale who had mistaken her instructions for Caleb, her sheepdog, and shaved the poor thing completely bald a year prior.

"Mavis *Weatherly?*" he clarified.

And once he explained how he knew that, Joss squealed like a grade-schooler. "What are the odds that you would live across the street from her, Patrick? This is just absurd! We could have known each other for years already!"

He decided not to reveal he already felt like that had been the case in the spirit of keeping her from leaping overboard. Instead, as a small trio began to play an almost haunting version of "I'll Be Home for Christmas," Patrick stood up and offered his hand to Joss. "Come here."

She smiled curiously and took it, following him around the table. Careful not to intrude upon other diners at intimate tables dotting the deck, he stayed close to the railing as he took Joss into his arms and they swayed softly to the melody.

"This is the best Christmas holiday I've had in . . ."

When her words trailed off, Patrick chuckled. "Ever?" he suggested.

With a soft giggle, she conceded. "Could be."

"Very unexpected."

"Very."

"Filled with promise." When she didn't comment, he pulled back slightly and looked into her gold-flecked eyes. "No promise?"

"I suppose," she replied. "Now that you haven't burped the marinara, I'll say yes. Very promising. Speaking of which, if you're going to kiss me, keep in mind I had three of the garlic knots. Approach at your own risk."

"Kiss you?" he teased, drawing her back into his embrace. "I hadn't even considered it."

Joss took her turn at pulling back, and she stared him down, the gold flecks in her brown eyes flickering like flames. "Ah, that's too bad. I was all geared up for it too. But you know what? The rest of my tiramisu will do me one better."

"You think so, do you?"

"Oh yeah," she said, and she turned in the direction of their table.

With a chuckle, Patrick gently tugged a small bouquet of holly and mistletoe out of the glass vase on an empty table near them.

Pulling her back again, he grinned and lifted the sprigs above their heads.

"Well, now we have no choice," she said, stepping beneath it.

Patrick brushed her forehead with the mistletoe before he pressed his lips softly to hers.

"WHERE DID YOU TWO come from?" Kathleen asked as Joss and Patrick sauntered up to the row where she was seated inside the small theater.

"Patrick told me you all were here to see *The Bishop's Wife*," Joss said. "I haven't seen it since I was a little girl."

"You do remember it's a Christmas movie, don't you, dear?" Kathleen gently asked her.

Joss chuckled. "Yes. But Cary Grant was a special favorite of my mom's, and this was her favorite movie. I thought it might be fun. Besides," she said, nodding toward the paper tub inside the circle of Patrick's arm, "there's free popcorn."

Patrick led her to the row behind Kathleen, Lilibeth, and the Dentures to the two empty seats on the aisle. The minute they settled and she opened one of the two bottles of water and handed it to Patrick, the lights dimmed, and a huge blue velvet curtain lifted from in front of the screen.

Almost two hours later the popcorn tub sat empty on Joss's knee, and Patrick held their two empty water bottles. Hand to heart, Joss sniffed and blinked back the moisture from her eyes. It had been years since she'd watched a Christmas-themed movie or television show of any kind, aside from the ten minutes of *How the Grinch Stole Christmas* she'd sneaked in like a ten-year-old in an R-rated movie when she'd happened upon it by accident a couple of years back. And now, like the Grinch himself, Joss thought that Cary Grant and Loretta Young—and all of those fresh memories of her mother—had caused her heart to grow two sizes in the movie theater that day.

She glanced over at Patrick to find him watching her closely.

"What?"

"I'm just wondering," he said. "You look very pensive. Regret that we came?"

She scratched her sweater where her heart pushed toward it and shook her head. "Not at all. I'm just remembering my mom and how much she loved the movie. She was a real sap when it came to some things."

"Take after your father, did you?"

Joss poked out her tongue at him, and Patrick laughed.

"Feel like a walk?"

Joss nodded and pushed up from the soft chair. She stood in the aisle waiting as Patrick leaned over his mother's shoulder and kissed her cheek.

"Do you need help getting back to your cabin?" he asked her softly.

"Oh, no indeed. You two enjoy yourselves."

"Can I arrange a special date for us tomorrow?" he whispered, and Joss watched the two of them with envy. "How about we have breakfast in your cabin, just the two of us."

Kathleen nodded. "That sounds just lovely."

Clutching her hand, he kissed her cheek again, and then the top of her hand. Instead of leaving, Patrick stepped over toward the Dentures. "My mother says you all have everything in hand?"

"Absolutely," Caroline replied. "We'll see her safely home."

He thanked them before squeezing his mother's shoulder one last time, reaching for Joss's hand. "Ready?"

She wished Kathleen a good night as she took it, and the two of them strolled toward the theater entrance.

Patrick deposited the bottles and popcorn tub into the trash can as they passed.

"You are so sweet with your mother," Joss told him as they followed the throng of people out of the theater.

"She's easy to be sweet with," he answered.

"I'm envious," she admitted.

"You and your mother were close?"

"As close as a woman-child can be with her mother," she said with a smile. "She died when I'd just reached that pivotal age of working up a good resentment, blaming her for everything wrong in the world."

"Ah," he replied, nodding. "I never really had that with my mother."

"Boys and their mothers have a very different dynamic. Did you at least resent your father?"

"Nope. Sorry to disappoint you. I had a nice rebellion without hating them."

"Figures."

He chuckled. "What does that mean?"

"Your perfection annoys me."

"No worries," he reassured her. "You just need to get to know me better. You'll be thrilled with all of my issues."

"Promise?"

"I do indeed."

Patrick pushed open the glass door that led to the deck, and a whoosh of cool air blew Joss's hair back from her face. He placed his arm around her shoulder as they headed toward the railing, and they seemed to wander on instinct to just the right spot to peer out into the night sky.

"It's kind of sad how close I live to the ocean," Joss said, "and how seldom I take the time to enjoy it."

"I know what you mean. I went surfing in Santa Monica with some buddies back in August," he told her, "and that was only about the third time I'd been on the water all year."

"You surf too?"

"I just learned a couple of years back."

"Do you ever just lounge around on the couch and eat potato chips?" she asked in hope.

"I don't like potato chips."

"Of course you don't."

"But I've been known to polish off a large pizza and a bag of Chips Ahoy in one afternoon."

She turned toward him and folded her arms across her chest, shaking her head. "I don't think I believe you."

"It's true."

"Nope. I think you're just feigning imperfections now to make me feel better. Vegging out with pizza and cookies? I don't think so. You'll have to prove that one."

"I think you'll be quite stunned when you discover how dormant I can be when I really want to."

"I live in hope."

He moved closer, their faces separated by no more than a few inches. "Do you now?"

Joss's heart thudded against her chest, and she wondered if Patrick might actually have heard it when he hovered there staring into her eyes that way.

"Kissing you now," he whispered, and he waited just long enough to make her question whether he was a man of his word.

And then he delivered. Thankfully.

When they parted, Joss struggled against actually swooning.

"You're very good at that," she told him softly. "A lot of practice, I presume."

"In our case, I think it's more about chemistry than skill."

"Well, there is that," she admitted with a chuckle. "In fact, I'm not sure I've ever had this much chemistry with a man in my life. But I don't really think you should underestimate your talent . . . you know . . . where your lips are concerned."

Patrick laughed. "Then we are a mutual admiration society."

"Bon jour, mademoiselle."

The two of them turned to find the Auberjonoises approaching. For some reason Joss could only remember the first name of their daughter Amberly, who wasn't with them, of course.

"Hello!" she exclaimed, a little too eagerly. "How are you? . . . Patrick, these are the Auberjonoises. . . . Did I pronounce that correctly? . . . Connie introduced them to me when I first boarded."

"Jean-Pierre," the husband said.

Of course! Jean-Pierre.

"And zees is my wife, Adrienne."

"Good to meet you. Patrick Brenneman."

"Irish," Jean-Pierre observed as they shook hands.

"Yes. And you're French," he returned with a smile.

"*Oui.*"

"Have you and your daughter been enjoying yourselves?" Joss asked.

"I suppose," he answered, and Joss thought at first that he might be joking. But without a hint of amusement showing on his straight, deadpan face, she reconsidered.

"My husband has had enough of the cruising experience," Adrienne told them. "He's even considering disembarking in Cabo San Lucas and flying back to Los Angeles."

"Oh," Joss replied. "That's too bad."

"It's just a bit contained for my taste," he added.

"We're going on a scooter tour in Cabo," Adrienne said. "He'll feel better once he gets out in the world again. Oh, perhaps you would like to join us? We'll see the migratory water birds and various varieties of local plants, and end up at the botanical gardens."

"Oh, that sounds lovely," Joss remarked, hoping Patrick would get them out of the invitation somehow.

"It does," he said, and she looked up at him. "But Joss and I are going parasailing."

"We are?"

"We are. I was going to wait to tell you until we docked so you didn't have time to mull on a good excuse to get out of it."

"A good plan," she replied.

"Too bad," Adrienne said. "Perhaps we'll see you again before we get back to port in Los Angeles."

"I hope so."

"Enjoy yourselves," Jean-Pierre added as they walked away. "*Bonsoir.*"

"Good night."

Once they disappeared from earshot, Joss turned toward Patrick and planted a hand on her hip.

"Parasailing. Really, Patrick?"

On the tenth day of Christmas,
Murphy's Law gave to me . . .

ten sharks a-snapping,
nine Scrooges hiding,
eight careers crashing,
seven songs a-shrieking,
six teeth a-breaking,

five cold sardiiiines!

four dirty words,
three French friends,
two hearty shoves,
and a Partridge with the first name Keith.

10

As the parasail caught the air and sent them floating high above the water, Joss's legs pumped as if she could run back down to the ground. Arms flailing, she screamed at the top of her lungs until she ran out of breath, then she gasped for more air and took up the screeching right where she left off.

"Calm down," Patrick shouted to her from the parasail tandem beside her, but she didn't seem to hear him. "Joss! Calm down, love."

"We're going to fall," she insisted. "Patrick, we're going t-t-t—"

"No, we're not. Look! Look at me."

"You said it would be smooth and easy," she squealed. "You said it would be *majestic*, and smooth and easy!" Seething, she added, "This is not majestic, Patrick!"

Patrick laughed and reached toward her. "Joss. Calm down and enjoy the ride. Just hang on to the straps and enjoy it."

"I . . . I can't," she screamed. "I can't!"

"Yes, you can."

"Why? Why couldn't we rent scooters like normal people?" she called to him. "What is wrong with you?"

"You thought the French couple was normal?"

She seemed to think it over for a moment before shouting, "No."

"Did you really want to spend a whole day with them?"

She deflated a bit. "No."

"Okay then. Just take a few deep breaths and——"

"What's that? Patrick, look! What is that down there?"

Patrick followed the invisible line between Joss's outstretched arm and the blue-green water beneath them. It only took an instant to make the connection, and he began to debate whether or not to lie to her in the name of comfort.

"Do you see them?" she screamed, and Patrick debated on how to respond. Just as he started to suggest they might be friendly, non-human devouring dolphins, Joss screeched. "It's SHARKS!!"

Joss had figured it out for herself. There, swimming in the waters below them, he couldn't deny it: the clear shadows of several lurking sharks.

"Those are sharks down there! It's time for their lunch . . . and we're lunch!"

After that Joss's screams dwarfed the verbiage. But then it didn't matter that he couldn't make out exactly what she howled toward him; the spirit of her hysteria translated.

"We're going to be *shark lunch*!"

"No, we're not," he reassured her. "We're two hundred feet above them."

"You know what?" she wailed. "If someone dangled a cheesecake two-hundred feet above me, I'm pretty sure *I'd follow it*!"

"They're not going to follow us."

"No? Then why are they FOLLOWING US?"

Patrick had to admit, if only to himself, that it did look strangely like those sharks were keeping right up with them.

"It's okay, Joss. By the time we come down, they'll be far behind——"

"Faith!" she shouted suddenly, interrupting him.

"What?"

"Faith!" she repeated. "One of us has it. So make use of it, Patrick."

He knew better, but he couldn't help himself, . . . and he laughed.

"Funny? You're laughing? You better thank your lucky stars I can't reach you right now because I would choke the life right out—"

"I get the picture," he shouted. "I'm sorry."

"Good! Now why don't you make yourself USEFUL?! You like to pray, Patrick. Right? So pray we don't get eaten. Okay? Will you please?" She waited no longer than two split seconds before pleading, "Please, Patrick. Pray your fanny off, *right now!*"

He wanted to laugh out loud, but he thought better of it this time. His chest ached from working so hard to hold it back.

"Are you doing it? Are you praying?"

"Yes," he called out.

Father, I ask in Jesus' holy name that You would bring some peace to this woman—

"Are you doing it?"

"Yes, Joss, I'm praying."

"Pray harder."

And forgive me for such a lousy idea as parasailing.

"REMEMBER AT COUSIN BRIAN'S wedding when Aunt Agnes was attacked by that bee? That's what Joss looked like, hopping around up there in the air, waving her arms and screaming her head off."

Embarrassment cascaded over Joss in a heated wave, and the backs of her eyes stung as Patrick gleefully told everyone at the dinner table, especially Kathleen, about their parasailing adventure that morning.

"That's a perfect example," Kathleen said, patting Joss's hand, "why weddings should be held indoors and humans should remain on the ground whenever possible."

"That is my thinking as well," Joss concurred. "But your son has an inexplicable desire to hurtle through the air at every opportunity. Really, I'm surprised he's not an astronaut . . . or a paratrooper."

"The best part," Patrick continued, and Joss elbowed him, "was when she wailed at me to begin praying."

Joss looked around at the others, and their amusement fueled her irritation at Patrick. "She screeches at me, 'If you don't pray right now, I'm going to choke you to death!' and, 'There are sharks in the water underneath us! We're lunch!'"

Connie's laughter sputtered away with one serious gasp. "Oh, now sharks are no laughing matter, y'all," she told them. "Rayburn loved to watch that *Shark Week* on the Discovery Channel, and it's just terrifyin' how many people are killed or maimed every year by those things."

Patrick launched into singing the menacing theme to Jaws as he leaned closer and closer to Joss.

"Doot-doot. Doot-doot-doot-doot."

"Honestly, Patrick," Kathleen reprimanded him.

"Thank you," Joss said to her before glaring at Patrick.

She happened to look up at just that moment when Rodney and Marla Jenkins stood up at their table. While Marla rounded up the children, her husband's glance crossed Joss's, and a surge of hope swelled. But he lingered for just one moment before purposefully diverting his eyes and joining the attempt to wrangle his family. Joss felt the disappointed thud of her heart as it dropped.

"Go on over and talk to him," Patrick softly prodded, but Joss shook her head.

"No. I messed up, and now I need to call it a day. There's no coming back from it."

"Joss—"

"Patrick," she cut him off. "I know you don't like to let anything go, but you need to do it on this subject. Let it go."

He raised his hands in surrender. "Okay."

The attraction to Patrick Brenneman had crested to levels Joss had never known before, and finding out he lived so close had fueled fantasies of an actual future between the two of them. But frankly the man was a bit of a bully. Just because it suited him, he pushed the people around him into whatever struck his fancy, from zip-lining to parasailing, karaoke to Christmas movies, even sacrificing solid, appealing plans for pajamas and TV. Joss wasn't entirely sure she could endure him on a daily basis. He exhausted her.

But then she turned toward him and became momentarily entangled in those dark hazel eyes; she stumbled over that ridiculous dimple set beneath his perfect lips; and she found herself frozen still as he lifted his hand and sweetly brushed back a lock of her hair.

"Would you like to walk off our dinner on deck?" he asked her, and Joss felt as if the world around them had come to a standstill. No one was left in the huge dining room—just the two of them, connected there in the deep green waters of Patrick's eyes.

"I don't think so," she said as she waded free. "I'm tired. I think I'd like to go back to my cabin and turn in early."

He stroked her forearm. "You're sure?"

"Yes."

"I'll walk you."

"No. Thank you, but I'm fine on my own." Joss stood up and leaned over toward Kathleen. "Good night."

"Oh, are you leaving us, dear?"

"I'm exhausted."

"All right then. Sweet dreams."

"I'll see you tomorrow?" Patrick asked her, but Joss gave him a gentle, noncommittal nod before she rounded the table.

"Good night, everyone."

HE TRIED NOT TO, but Patrick craned his neck to get a look at every person who passed through the door or moved through the line for the breakfast buffet. He'd felt quite disoriented by Joss's speedy departure from dinner the night before, but when he'd stopped by her cabin on his way to breakfast that morning, she'd either been hiding out behind the closed door or had already left the room. Now that she didn't appear anywhere in sight, a surge of anxiety churned in his chest.

"Settle back and enjoy your breakfast, boy," his mother told him. "She'll be along eventually. She said she was tuckered out last night. Perhaps she decided to sleep in."

"You're probably right."

But Patrick didn't believe it for an instant.

Maybe he'd gone too far in teasing her about her behavior on their parasailing excursion. She'd changed when she'd seen Rodney Jenkins at his dinner table the previous night. Maybe Marla had told her that Patrick had intervened on Joss's behalf with her husband. He should have told her himself.

Half a dozen other scenarios wound their way around the curves of his mind, but Patrick couldn't land comfortably on a single one. And he despised the way it made him feel to think Joss might be irritated with him or that she might not want to see him again once they sailed into port in a couple of days. He hadn't known Joss Snow long enough—or well enough—for her to matter so much.

But she did.

And worse yet, Patrick couldn't do a thing about it.

He'd begun to imagine a future relationship with her even before they'd discovered they lived so close to one another. But knowing she occupied one of those little Spanish houses he'd often admired in the hills of Los Feliz solidified the reverie and morphed into Saturday morning coffee at The Village Café, afternoons strolling around Griffith Park, and even Sunday services together at the little chapel where he'd attended church each and every week for the last three years. In that one instant Joss had taken her place as a promising—albeit apparitional—fixture in his real daily life, whether she liked it or not. And from all indications, she had possibly decided she did not.

After breakfast, on his way up to Joss's cabin, Patrick made a vow to himself. He'd never been the type of man to chase a woman who clearly didn't want to be caught, and he wasn't going to change now. He would knock on her door and give her one last opportunity to fess up and explain what had changed between them and how they might work it through. If she rejected the chance, then he would move on, no turning back. There would be no chasing, no convincing, no hopeful nudges. She could either accept a heartfelt invitation to invest a little something in their relationship, or she could reject it.

What was the worst that could happen? He'd leave the ship alone just as he'd boarded. Not such a tragedy, really. Patrick had a full life, after all, and he hadn't come on a Christmas cruise in search of anything besides a holiday trip with his mother.

So why are my palms sweating?

He wiped both hands on the back pockets of his jeans and rapped on the door to Joss's cabin. His pulse pounded out the seconds that passed.

He knocked again. Still nothing.

One last time. And then I walk away.

He gave the door two final whacks and leaned toward it. "Joss? It's me, Patrick."

After waiting several beats beyond a perfectly respectable amount of time, he let out a deep and laborious sigh.

"Okay, Joss. Ball's in your court then."

And with that he meandered away without looking back. Except for that one brief moment, of course, when the couple across the corridor from Joss's cabin opened their door.

Patrick stamped out the ember of hope they'd ignited and headed along his way. He rode the elevator to his floor and went straight to his mother's cabin and knocked.

Caroline Denture opened the door and greeted him with a smile. "Hi, Patrick. Come on in."

Lilibeth sat on the corner of the bed next to his mother.

"Your mother was just telling us you ordered breakfast for the two of you out on the balcony the other morning," Caroline told him. "She said the food was heavenly."

He smiled and sat down next to his mother and pecked her cheek. "But it was far too much for me to have eaten before flying hundreds of feet in the air."

Kathleen chuckled. "I don't know why we didn't think of that. Did you find Joss, dear?"

"No. I didn't quite catch up to her."

"A choral group is giving a concert on the mezzanine level," Lilibeth told him. "Why don't you join us? They're doing one of your mother's favorites."

"Handel's *Messiah*," he replied knowingly.

"Oh, do join us, Patrick," his mother implored.

He smiled. "Why not?"

"Excellent. This will be a lovely afternoon. Do you want to call and invite Joss?"

"I don't think so. Not this time. What time does it start?"

"We were just preparing to head up now."

"Then I arrived just in time," he said, offering his hand to his mother.

"OH, COME ON, JOSS. I can tell you like him. Is he cute?"

"He's delicious."

"Then what's the problem? He's yummy, and you like him."

Joss twisted a lock of hair around her index finger and gazed out at the blue-green water as she held her cell phone in her other hand. Adjusting one of the wired earbuds, she replied, "I like him just fine, Reese. That doesn't mean I see us starting a whole . . . thing."

"A whole thing. You mean a *relationship*? You can say it. Come on. Say it with me."

"Oh, hush. You don't know this guy. He's one of those macho types, thinks he knows what's best for everybody, including me. You wouldn't believe what he made me do on Christmas night."

"Do tell."

Reese's giggle infuriated Joss, and she groaned before revealing, "Karaoke." The giggle turned into full-on laughter, and Joss growled at her. "And then there was zip-lining."

"You . . . zip-lined? Was it amazing?"

"Well, it *was* kind of fun. Eventually. But then there was forced parasailing."

"This is me you're talking to. No one forces you to do anything. But . . . you parasailed? Joss, I'm so proud of you! How was it?"

"Before or after the sharks gathered beneath us?"

"You're such a head case."

"You know what? I just realized why he irritates me so much. He's a male version of you! He's *you* on steroids."

"Then I love him, . . . and I have a feeling you do too. What did you sing at the karaoke party?"

"Partridge Family."

"Oh, you're joking. And he wants to keep seeing you?"

"I guess."

"Joss. Who knows you better than me?" Reese asked her.

"Why? . . . Nobody. . . . Why?"

"Because I'm in the unique position of seeing that you're finding fault with this guy because you're scared."

"I am not."

"You are. You don't like change, and he represents change. He makes you uncomfortable. He pushed you into doing things you might not have done otherwise, and I'm guessing a little piece of you enjoyed it against all of your best efforts not to. He's making you feel things you haven't felt since who knows when, and so you're scared. He's upset your orderly little apple cart of a life. So here's what I think you should do—"

"Hush! Tell me what you've been doing, traitor. Have you and Damian had a Very Brady Bunch Family Christmas?"

"There's too much to tell to get into it now. When do you get back?"

"We dock on New Year's Eve morning."

"Then you're coming New Year's Day, right?"

"Of course. Just like always."

"Wonderful!" Reese exclaimed. "Football, food, and friends. And by then, we'll have left another Christmas flat in the dust."

"Thankfully. I can hardly wait to get home."

"Me, too," her friend admitted.

"What? You mean it's not snowflakes and evergreens up there in God's country?"

"I'll see you soon," Reese diverted. "And Joss? Feel free to invite him. The more, the merrier."

"Hanging up now."

"Give the guy a break, Joss. See how it plays out."

"Good-bye, traitor."

"You might be surprised how—"

"Say good-bye, traitor."

"Good-bye, traitor."

On the eleventh day of Christmas,
Murphy's Law gave to me . . .

eleven schemes a-forming,
ten sharks a-snapping,
nine Scrooges hiding,
eight careers crashing,
seven songs a-shrieking,
six teeth a-breaking,

five cold sardiiiines!

four dirty words,
three French friends,
two hearty shoves,
and a Partridge with the first name Keith.

11

Joss glanced at the time display at the bottom corner of her laptop and wondered how it could possibly be nearly midnight. She'd had a quick conversation with Ryan around 4:30 p.m.—at least until the ship's connection dropped their call—and told him about what had happened with Jenkins. After the initial panic had passed, Ryan had convinced her that, unless Jenkins outright canceled their meeting scheduled for early January, they were going to march in there prepared to knock the guy's argyles right off his feet.

"Do or die," Ryan had declared. "We'll bring him something so good he won't be able to let his personal issues come into play. I'll have Char block out all next week so we can brainstorm and work on improving what we have. We'll overcome every objection he doesn't even know he has."

"You're a crazy person, you know," she'd said to him.

"And that's why this works, Jocelyn. We're two nut cases with one mission."

After the call, inspiration had struck. Now that Joss knew Jenkins better, she realized the angle they'd taken in their initial marketing plan was all wrong.

"He's a family man," she'd said aloud as she paced the cabin alone. "He responds to family values. He won't react to improving the wheel when he can have something completely new that appeals to families."

With the lightning bolt still fresh in her mind, Joss ordered up room service and set about deconstructing her entire proposal for Vandermere Hotels & Spas. She tossed the slick corporate vibe and rebuilt it with family vacation packages and points incentives, a kid-friendly advertising campaign, and a solid list of slogan possibilities branding the hotel chain as a high-end destination for parents and children alike.

She pushed the laptop aside and nestled into the mound of pillows behind her with a stretch that wriggled down the entire length of her stiff body, from neck to toes. Yawning, she closed her eyes and pulled the terry cloth band from the messy ponytail she'd pulled together at the top of her head. She tried to convince her eyes to open, her body to carry her to the bathroom to get changed for bed, but cooperation eluded her.

Just about the time she began to really embrace the idea of sleeping right where she was, fully dressed, a rap at the door drew her attention and her eyes snapped open. She listened carefully, wondering if she'd imagined it, but a second knock provided confirmation.

"Joss. It's me."

Patrick.

She sighed. She hadn't wanted to have this conversation until she felt more in touch with her own feelings; however, the time she might have spent working that out had been conveniently diverted by work. And hadn't that become her usual *modus operandi*? Anything she didn't want to think about, that made her uncomfortable or insecure, anything about which she felt unsure, none of it could stand up next to her full-on confidence in her professional life. There wasn't a problem in the world that couldn't be avoided by a sweet treat by her side and a straight nosedive into work.

Joss glanced at the remnants of her earlier room service dinner. More than half of the meal remained untouched; the dessert plate, however, was a different story entirely. Not a crumb or speck of chocolate cake remained as a telltale sign of its existence. That plate, in fact, looked a little like it had never been used.

Patrick knocked again. "Joss? C'mon. We need to talk."

He was right, of course. They did need to talk. Joss just wished she knew what she needed to say.

When she tugged open the door, fully expecting to find Patrick on his way back down the hall, he stood there facing her instead. Leaning against the doorjamb, he gave her a smile that didn't quite reach his weary eyes.

"Thank you," he said. "Can we talk?"

She nodded him inside, and by the time she closed the door behind him and followed, Patrick stood there inspecting the cart of dishes next to the bed.

"That's why you didn't come to dinner."

"I was working," she replied, consciously acknowledging the half-truth.

"Look," he said, and he ran both hands through his shaggy hair with a sigh. "I told myself to walk away and just let it be, but I just couldn't manage it. I had to try one more time to get you to talk to me. What's going on here, Joss? What happened?"

She breathed in sharply, expelling it through twisted, puckered lips. "I'm sorry, Patrick."

"For what exactly?" He scraped the desk chair over toward her, turned it around backward, and sat down on it, draping his arms over the back of it. "Look, if you haven't been feeling what I've been feeling, and you just want to call this a shipboard type of thing, I can live with that. I just need you to make me believe it. I mean, you changed pretty dramatically in a matter of hours."

Joss didn't know how long she just sat there, hands folded in her lap, silent except for the nervous flick of her fingernail.

"Just tell me what happened, darlin'."

She looked up at Patrick and sighed. "I didn't expect you."

"I know it's late, but I thought I'd just take a chance and—"

"No," she said with a chuckle. "I mean, I didn't expect to meet you."

"Ah."

"I came on this cruise as an escape, the same as every year. But there you were. And you're unexpected, and so . . . so . . . *in my face.*"

Patrick grinned and shook his head. "I know what you mean."

"I kind of don't know what to do with you now."

"I'm not really that complicated," he joked. "My care and feeding are pretty simple."

"I'm serious, Patrick." She reached out and stroked his hand. "You're wonderful. But you also just . . . tick me off!"

A surprised cough popped out of him, and he stared her down until she continued to explain.

"You're so pushy." Joss stood up and began to pace the cabin. "You just won't take no for an answer, and that drives me crazy because—"

"Because I'm so much like you," he finished for her.

She started to deny it, but she couldn't really—not with a straight face anyway.

"Maybe."

"So where do we go from here?" he asked. "We could call it a wonderful holiday surprise and just go back to our lives when we dock. Or we could take a chance on what's been growing between us and let it unfold to see if there's something solid to build upon. But either way, we owe it to one another to be honest, don't we?"

"Yes. We definitely do."

"I'll start," he said as she continued to pace. "I'm not ready to let you go. I want to see what happens to us on dry ground."

Joss stopped in her tracks and stared out the window as she considered his words. Her heart pounded harder, her palms felt clammy, and perspiration rose on her upper lip. How could so much relief and hope coexist with such a massive dose of anxious trepidation?

"I guess," she said when she finally broke the silence, "I just need a little time."

Patrick stood up and pushed the chair back over to the desk before he picked up her phone from the side table. "My cell number is in here, correct?"

"Yes," she said with a nod. "You put it in the day we docked in Mazatlan."

"Good. Then when you've thought this over—whether we're still on the ship or we've gone back home—you text me, and we'll meet and have this conversation again." He placed the cell phone in her hand and pressed it there. "If I don't hear from you before we disembark in L.A., I just want you to know I've really enjoyed getting to know you, and—"

"Patrick. I'm not going to leave the ship without saying goodbye. To you or your mother!"

"All right then. Take your time and think it over. If I'm not the kind of guy you can see yourself involved with, so be it."

"Thank you," she said, and it was heartfelt.

"But I believe I am, by the way," he added, holding her hand and phone in place. "I hope you'll give us a shot."

Joss could feel her heart pounding against her chest, far beyond simple palpitations, and she glanced down to see if her blouse revealed the rhythm. She broke the connection between their hands and dropped her phone to the table. Feeling suddenly faint, she sat down on the corner of the bed and sighed.

"I'm really tired," she told him.

"It's late. Get some rest." He leaned down and placed a firm kiss on the top of her head. "I'll wait to hear from you."

Joss felt as though she couldn't get a deep breath. Hand to heart, she managed to mutter her quiet appreciation before Patrick closed the door behind him. Within a few short minutes, she began to hyperventilate, and she hopped to her feet and began to pace again, sucking air sharply into her lungs as she wondered what on earth was wrong with her.

"Reese is right," she said, breathless as she dumped the contents of one of her shopping bags on the bed. "I'm a total head case."

Clamping the paper bag around her nose and mouth, she rapidly breathed into it.

Inhale. Exhale. Inhale. Exhale.

JOSS REALIZED IMMEDIATELY UPON opening her eyes that something was different. It took a few minutes to figure it out, but the clock on the nightstand verified it for her. She'd overslept, and the ship had docked.

She grabbed the remote to the television and flipped it on, switching to the onboard message channel. Sure enough, the third message that flashed onscreen announced the ship had docked. Breakfast was still being served, and passengers would not begin to disembark until 11 a.m. Joss flew out of bed, nearly crashing into her remaining carry-on bag she'd packed the night before and leaned against the wall.

Twenty minutes later, fully dressed, she grabbed her cell phone and purse and raced out the door and down the corridor. Why had she waited until morning to tell Patrick what she'd clearly figured out the night before? Despite all of her fears, she wanted to know what could happen between them. If Patrick was willing to overlook her neuroses and fears and craziness, she knew she'd be insane to let him go.

Joss made the dining hall her first stop, but their table sat completely empty except for Connie Rudolph as she sipped the last of her coffee while workers bused the dirty dishes from around her.

"Oh, sweetie! I'm so happy you showed up," she said, standing up and rounding the table to hug Joss. Connie's bracelet jingled in her ear as she did. "I'm so glad that we met. I really am."

"I am, too, Connie," she answered, grinning because she truly meant those words. Producing a business card from the pocket of her purse, Joss handed it to Connie. "My e-mail address is on here and both my numbers. I want you to keep in touch."

Connie looked genuinely surprised. "Really? Thank you, honey! I'll do that. I don't fly home for two days, but I'll write you as soon as I get back."

"Two days?"

"I couldn't get the supersaver price unless I booked a return flight for the third of January."

"What are your plans in the meantime then?"

"I booked a room at The Roosevelt Hotel right in the middle of Hollywood," she said. "They say it's haunted, you know."

Joss thought about the likes of Connie Rudolph wandering around Hollywood on her own, and concern closed a clamp on her good sense. "The only thing haunting about The Roosevelt is its location. You're not staying alone in Hollywood, Connie. You'll stay with me."

"What? No, honey. You don't hafta—"

"I know that, and yet you're going to stay with me."

"Oh, sweetie. I'm overcome."

"Listen," Joss said, and she grabbed Connie's wrist. "I have something I have to do right now. But I want you to meet me in the main lobby at noon. Okay? Over by that bench that goes around the big Christmas tree."

"Okay, sweetie."

"And if you don't find me, just raise your arm and shake that bracelet of yours. I'll follow the ringing bells."

Connie chuckled. "You're terrible."

"Just call my cell number. It's on the card I gave you."

"Okay, honey. I will."

And with that, Joss took off out of the dining hall at a full run, headed for the elevators. Just before she reached them, Marla called out her name and rushed toward her. "Joss, I'm so glad to find you."

Swallowing around the lump in her throat, Joss pushed a smile to her face. "Marla."

"Listen, Rod's been searching for you this morning."

"He has?" Her pulse thumped with hope.

"I think he'd really like to speak to you before we head out. Do you have a few minutes?"

Her reply got clogged somewhere deep in her throat. As much as she wanted to get to Patrick, could she really turn away from the possibility of clearing up the misunderstanding with Jenkins?

"Where is he?"

"He's back at the cabin getting the kids together. Just tell me where you're headed, and I'll have him meet you there."

"Oh. Well . . ."

"I'm sorry. If this is a bad time, I'm sure he can give you a call next week."

"No. No, of course, I want to talk to him. I'd been hoping for a chance to clear things up between us."

Marla leaned toward her and touched Joss on the arm. "I think it's a good idea."

"I was headed upstairs to say good-bye to some new friends," she explained. "I can—"

"You go ahead and do that, Joss. I'll go see how Rod's doing with getting things organized, and I'll tell him to meet you on the lido deck by the big swimming pool. Let's say in half an hour?"

"Perfect. I'll be there."

PATRICK CHECKED HIS PHONE again, the third or fourth time in the last twenty minutes. She'd said she wouldn't think of leaving the ship without saying good-bye to him and his mother, so he'd held true to his word and waited to hear from her. But there had been no contact at all. Checking his phone yet again, no message from Joss beckoned.

He should have gone to her room that morning when she didn't show up for breakfast. Or at least given her a quick call. But he couldn't really have done that after making those ridiculous declarations about waiting to hear from her, could he?

"Are you ready, dear? Should we return the wheelchair now?"

Patrick nodded at his mother. "I think you should remain right here in it until we're ready to leave the ship."

They'd packed up the night before, and Doug and Caroline had helped him navigate both his mother and their luggage down to the lobby since the cruise line's television message board had indicated that handicapped passengers would be allowed to leave the ship first.

"We still have an hour before the first passengers will be allowed to disembark," he told her. "Can I get you anything?"

"I'm fine, Patrick," his mother replied. "Go ahead, why don't you. Go and find her."

He looked into his mother's kind eyes and smiled. "She has my information, Mother. I don't need to go in search of her."

"Does she know, dear?"

"Know what?"

"How you feel. I think you need to tell her what's in your heart."

"We had a very nice discussion on the subject," he reassured her, and he knelt down in front of her and took her hand. "I'll hear from her again."

"If you're certain."

"I am."

Patrick hadn't often straight-out lied to his mother; at least, not as an adult. And this wasn't exactly a lie either. Just a partial . . . fib.

Ah, the truth is I may never hear from her again, he admitted to himself, and he checked his phone again in search of a text message that wasn't there . . . and might never come.

On the twelfth day of Christmas,
Murphy's Law gave to me . . .

twelve cell phones swimming,
eleven schemes a-forming,
ten sharks a-snapping,
nine Scrooges hiding,
eight careers crashing,
seven songs a-shrieking,
six teeth a-breaking,

five cold sardiiiines!

four dirty words,
three French friends,
two hearty shoves,
and a Partridge with the first name Keith.

12

Joss hadn't been able to find Patrick anywhere. Arriving on the lido deck with three minutes to spare, she scanned the area in search of Rodney Jenkins. When she didn't spot him, she moved over to the railing and began typing a text into her cell phone.

I need to see you. I—

"Miss Snow! There you are."

As Jenkins reached her, Joss reeled around toward him, and to her great devastation, she lost her grip on her cell phone and watched helplessly as it hurtled out of her hands and *down-down-down* toward the water below.

"Noooooo!!"

"Oh my. Was that your phone?"

For a long and frozen moment, Joss couldn't respond as she decided whether or not to dive overboard after it. Finally, she croaked, "My life is in that phone."

"I'm so sorry," Rodney told her. "I startled you."

"I can't believe that just happened," she cried, staring lovingly into its wake. "No joke. My life is in that phone."

"Perhaps this isn't a good time to talk then."

Joss's hand flew to her throat as she attempted to massage the words up and out. "No. No, I'm happy to . . ." She gave the departure path of her phone one last caring glance. "I really wanted to apologize to you about what you heard me say, Mr. Jenkins."

"I've given it a lot of thought, Miss Snow. And especially after my conversation with your Irish friend—"

"My . . . my what? You spoke with Patrick?"

"Yes, and he explained your unique situation and aversion to the Christmas holiday."

"Did he?"

"You have a very dedicated friend in him. I hope you know that."

Joss choked on the reality that, once Patrick stepped off that ship, she now had no way of finding him again.

"I want you to know, Mr. Jenkins, my business partner and I have worked very hard on preparing a proposal I think you're really going to love. In fact, now that I know you a little better and I've seen you with your beautiful family, I feel more confident than ever we can help set Vandermere on a really solid course."

She realized she'd been wringing her hands as she spoke, and she quickly dropped both arms to her sides.

"So will we see you next week at your office, sir?"

Rodney seemed to size her up before speaking. "Yes. I'll see you then."

Joss hopped to attention, and she snatched up his hand and began to shake it vigorously. "Thank you, sir. Thank you so much. You won't be sorry."

"We'll see, won't we?" he asked. "Now I have to get back to our cabin and help my wife before she decides to leave me."

Joss chuckled. "Thank you, sir. Please give her my best."

Once he'd shaken her hand one last time and headed off toward the doors, Joss rushed to the railing and peered over the side. She knew the odds against actually spotting her phone down there, but she looked anyway. She backed up her business contacts on a regular basis, so they could be restored.

But how would she ever find Patrick again without that phone?

She swallowed hard and glanced around cautiously before turning toward the railing.

"Okay, God," she whispered to the sky, "I know You haven't heard from me in a really long time, and I'm sorry about that. I don't even really know if You're listening or anything. But if You are, and You wouldn't mind helping me, I sure would like to see Patrick again. You know. If that's okay with You."

"I NORMALLY SPEND THIS night with my best friend, Reese," Joss told Connie as she carried fresh linens and an extra blanket into the guest room. "But she's engaged now, so I think our New Year's Eve traditions have pretty much gone up in smoke."

"So what are they?" Connie asked. "Your traditions."

Joss shooed Caleb off the unmade bed and dropped the linens there.

"Chinese food and mindless television. Last year, it was a *Keeping Up with the Kardashians* marathon."

"Oh, sweetie, you weren't kidding about mindless," Connie drawled.

Joss giggled. "Do you like Chinese food?"

"It's one of my faves."

"Then how about we order some and see what we can find on E!"

"Sounds like a plan. Can we watch the ball drop at midnight, though? I just love that Ryan Seacrest."

Joss arched an eyebrow at her new friend. "He is kind of cute. Maybe we could change the channel at five minutes before midnight and look in on Ryan."

Connie smiled victoriously. "Thank you."

"Tomorrow, you'll get to meet Reese and her fiancé, Damian. We have a big chow-fest at her house to watch football every year."

"A chow-fest?"

"All the food you can stand, in celebration of the end of the holidays."

"Oh." Connie thought it over. "I'm just the opposite from you. I don't usually want Christmas to end. But I'll try to get into the spirit of things."

Joss chuckled. "I'm glad you're here, Connie."

"Me, too, sweetie."

Connie followed her out to the living room where Joss grabbed the phone from its dock. "What kind of Chinese food do you like? Sweet and sour pork? Pepper steak? Ohh, crab rangoon? That's Caleb's favorite. He loves the crab rangoon."

"Any of that sounds luscious. Just order anything you like. As long as I get egg rolls. I love egg rolls."

Before she could dial the phone in her hand, it rang, and Joss grinned at Connie before picking it up.

"Hello?"

"Joss? Hi, it's Abby Metzger."

Joss covered the phone and mouthed, "My neighbor!" to Connie. "Hey, Abby. How are you guys?"

"We're good, but listen. I thought I should tell you that there's someone going house to house down here, and he's asking about you."

"Me? What do you mean? Who is it?"

"He's kind of cute, actually. With an accent."

"What kind of accent?"

"Scottish, maybe?"

Joss's breath caught in the back of her throat, and her mouth went completely dry. When she finally pushed the word upward, she nearly choked on it. "Irish?"

"Yeah, he could be Irish."

"Where is he now?"

"On my front porch. I told him to wait there while—"

Joss tossed the handset to the chair by the door without disconnecting the call.

"Where's the fire?" Connie exclaimed.

"I'll be back," she shouted, pausing to point a finger at Caleb as he tried to follow her out the door. "Caleb, stay!"

And with that, Joss took off running across the lawn, leaping over the shrubs that bordered the driveway. The Metzgers lived several houses away, and Joss barreled down the hill on pure adrenaline. When she reached the curve in the sidewalk that led to their driveway, she jumped through the line of enormous glowing candy canes, past the reindeer standing guard over the garden, and over the small—and somewhat eerie—elves in front of the house. Suddenly, Joss sputtered, clutching the stabbing pain in her side as she frantically scanned the front yard.

"Patrick!"

She could hardly believe her eyes as he turned around, that familiar grin spreading across his beautiful face like warm wax over a burning flame.

"What are you doing here?" she tried to ask while catching her breath.

Abby Metzger watched them from her doorway as Patrick moved down the driveway toward her. When Joss couldn't wait another two seconds, she shoved all thoughts of pain and the need for oxygen from her mind, and she took off toward him at an implausible full run again. When she'd nearly reached him, she leaped several feet toward him and landed in his arms.

Patrick twirled her around, laughing. "It's good to see you too."

"How did you find me?" she asked as he set her down.

"It wasn't easy. I just remembered what you said about the Spanish houses on the hill over the park, so I set out searching for you."

"I tried to text you before we left the ship, but I dropped my phone overboard, and I hadn't backed up your number, and—"

Patrick placed his finger over Joss's lips, shaking his head. "Breathe, darlin'."

As his words settled in on her, she began to sputter again. "I don't know . . . if I . . . can, actually."

"Joss?" Abby called from her front door. "Is everything all right?"

"Yeah," she frothed, waving her arm randomly. "Fine."

Patrick turned back toward the house and waved. "Thank you so much."

"Okay. Merry Christmas, you two."

Joss dropped to the ground beside one of the elves and draped her arm around its plastic shoulder, gasping for breath.

"Sorry. I just need a minute."

Patrick chuckled, and he stood over her until she recovered and returned to her feet.

"Where do you live?" he asked with a grin.

She pointed to the top of the street and grabbed his hand. "Come on. I'll show you. Oh, and you'll never guess who's in my living room! Connie Rudolph!"

"You're joking."

"No. I brought her home with me. Sort of a souvenir from my trip."

Patrick laughed. "Then I'd better do this here." Wrapping his arms around her waist, he pulled her toward him and pressed his lips to hers in a deep kiss.

"I wasn't sure I'd ever get to kiss you again," she said when they parted. "It's lucky you paid attention when I told you about where I lived."

"Not lucky, Joss," he told her. "Destiny."

And she almost believed him.

Merry Christmas

Humbug

It Came Upon a Midnight Deer

Merry ^Humbug Christmas

It Came Upon a Midnight Deer

SANDRA D. BRICKER

B&H
PUBLISHING GROUP

Nashville, Tennessee

Prologue

"Whoa, whoa, Mom. Hold on. Are you telling me I was named after *a peanut butter cup?*"

"Reese, please. Don't be silly at the Christmas dinner table."

"We don't even eat dairy, and Daddy's allergic to peanuts! How could you name your firstborn child after a chocolate-covered peanut butter cup?"

"It's not like we haven't ever tasted a dairy product," her mother replied. "Your father and I didn't embrace the vegan lifestyle until we moved to Berkeley in the sixties. Back then we still called ourselves vegetarians."

Her younger brother flashed a peace sign, and Reese giggled.

"I loved those peanut butter cups before I knew they were poison," her father lamented.

"The moment midwife Elaine put you into my arms, I thought you were the most delicious little thing I'd ever seen. Isn't that right, Alan?"

Her father's only comment came in the form of an arched eyebrow as he peered at them over the casserole bowl of vegetable stuffing.

"So your thought process went something like, 'Hmm. Delicious. Baby. . . . *Chocolate and peanut butter?*'"

"I think you had to be there, Sis."

Reese watched her father pour the Pendergrass family's version of gravy over the mound of smashed potatoes on his plate. The bald spot on the top of his head had widened in recent years, and he'd pulled what was left of his hair into a short ponytail at the back of his head.

"Hey, wait a minute," Reese said as realization dawned. "How did you come up with Herschel's name? Daddy! Was Herschel named after a *Hershey bar?*"

"What?" Hersch cried. "Is that true?"

"Reese Pendergrass," her mother warned. "Stop stirring the pot and eat your Tofurkey."

Tofurkey—a gelatin-like mound of tofu rolled around an herblike bread stuffing with the inexplicable and distant flavor of turkey—had graced the Pendergrass holiday table ever since Reese could remember.

"Will you think less of me if I run down to McDonald's for a Big Mac?" Reese asked.

Her mother flicked her long, straight hair over her shoulder, and her hand flew instantly to her heart. "Alan?"

Her father's eyes bulged. "What do you know about Big Macs? Is this what you do with your friends on the weekend now? You consume genetically mummified cattle in secret?"

Reese swallowed around the lump in her throat, averting her eyes to the slightly jiggling mound of tofu on her plate. "Only a couple of times."

Her mother's response came in the form of a moan muffled by the hand over her mouth.

"Herschel? You too?"

Hersch shook his head and closed his eyes. "And my friends wonder why I'm so messed up. Yes, Dad. I've eaten at McDonald's. I've also had tacos, and last weekend Brad's parents took us out for pepperoni pizza! With extra *cheese.*"

"Hersch," Reese muttered. "Really."

"Come on!" he exclaimed, and his pubescent preteen voice cracked. "Tell them, Reese. You've done it too. To all of the kids at school, we're nutritional freaks. But Mom, Dad, I think it's time you heard the truth. Reese and me, we like eggs and milk. *And meat.* I know it's hard to hear, but it's true. *We're carnivores.*"

"Perhaps you should invite all of your dairy-loving, meat-eating friends over at one time," their mother said. "I'll put on a roasted turkey and boil up some giblets." After a short dry-heave hiccup, she continued. "Then afterward, you can eat ice cream and put your father and me on display for everyone to see that it's not your fault. It's ours. We've abused our children." She stood up and raised one arm. "We are gastronomical child abusers! Call the FDA. Arrest us!"

As she crossed her hands at the wrists in anticipation of the cuffs, regret sizzled at the back of Reese's throat as she wondered why-oh-why she'd been grafted into such a strange, dysfuntional family tree. Was it some great cosmic joke that she—a girl with dreams of idyllic family Christmases around a twelve-foot tree packed with oodles of brightly wrapped packages tied with spools of curly ribbon and a holiday table boasting a golden roasted turkey and a cheesy broccoli casserole—had been plopped . . . *here?*

Reese glanced at her mother with a tinge of resentment, but the hurt swimming in her misty blue eyes strangled Reese with contrition instead. Touching her mother's arm, she said, "Oh, Mom. We didn't mean to hurt your feelings."

Pulling away, her mother replied, "And your father and I did not mean to single-handedly ruin your lives with a healthy diet. Now can we finish our meal?"

Reese nodded.

One day, Reese thought. *One day, I'll find the man of my dreams . . . and we'll have three children. . . . No, four! . . . and a twelve-foot Christmas tree with oodles of packages underneath . . . and a real turkey . . . and . . .*

"Good," her mother replied. "Now please pass the hummus *foie gras.*"

On the first day of Christmas,
Murphy's Law gave to me . . .

A big rockin' Harry Winston ring.

1

Reese held her left hand up to the window and subtly wiggled all of her fingers. It was something she'd taken to doing about thirty times every day since the one when Damian had proposed. She didn't suppose she'd ever tire of watching the light dance on more than two gorgeous carats of diamond set in a micropavé platinum Harry Winston setting.

"Look at the size of that thing," Joss had exclaimed when she first saw it. "I thought you didn't do flashy."

Reese winced as she recalled her reply. "I don't. But fortunately, Damian does!"

Way to waffle on your principles, she chastised herself. But only for a moment before a prism of light bounced off her ring and painted the wall with streaks of color that captured her focus.

"I'm sorry to keep you holding, Dr. Pendergrass."

Her thoughts snapped back to attention, and she pressed the phone harder to her ear as she shot a reassuring smile toward Caley, the sweet six-year-old patient looking up at her as a hovering nurse checked her vitals. "That's okay. So are you able to help me?"

"Absolutely! All of the plans are in place. One birthday cake delivered to the cabin of one Joss Snow on Christmas Day. It's all taken care of."

"Thank you so much."

Reese knew it wouldn't make up for the abandonment issues, but she couldn't very well allow her best friend to cruise off into the sunset without so much as a "Happy Birthday!" They'd always spent Christmas/Joss's birthday together, shooting at Santas with make-believe guns formed by their fingers, removing blinking reindeer noses, and knocking over elves with pointed jingle bell shoes. All in fun, at the beginning, but later their anti-Christmas activities had become a sort of diatribe shared by two best friends with their own private reasons for distaste of holiday cheer.

Joss—formerly (and unfortunately) known as *Merry Christmas Snow*—had been born on Christmas morning, and she'd changed her name as an adult in an effort to escape it. But she at least had memories of happy family Christmases with two parents who adored her and embraced every sappy holiday tradition from Christmas Eve caroling to visits from Santa and bulging stockings on Christmas morning. And Joss's descriptions of the traditional Snow family holiday feast! Reese had certainly never known anything like those.

Roasted turkey with chestnut stuffing . . . creamy mashed potatoes with thick turkey gravy . . . broccoli casserole swimming in melted cheese . . . pumpkin pie with . . . *oh!* . . . whipped cream. Reese imagined it all as a culinary and probably gastronomic delight.

Medical school had provided a pretty great excuse not to make it home for Tofurkey with the family over the years since she'd left home. Then her vagabond folks moved to Key West to pursue a laid-back lifestyle that included Hawaiian shirts, flip-flops, and a pontoon boat. By the grace of God, that's when she met up with Joss.

A chance meeting at a Pediatric AIDS fund-raiser had evolved into instantly recognized kindred spirits. After Joss's parents were killed in a car accident, her best friend revealed there had been no more Christmas/birthday celebration feasts. Joss had come to despise the holiday season as a monthlong reminder each and every year that she was utterly and completely alone. Except for Reese, of course.

And then Damian had proposed.

Reese had thought of Joss in those first seconds after he'd asked her. Staring down at the massive diamond ring, and then into the chocolate-brown eyes of one gorgeous neurosurgeon, she found it odd that Joss sprang immediately to mind . . . at least until she remembered their promise.

"From now on," Joss had said, "we'll avoid every Christmas together."

"We'll only celebrate it as your birthday," Reese had added. "We'll eat cake and Chinese food and watch movies and listen to music."

"But not Christmas songs. And absolutely no *It's a Wonderful Life*."

"Right!"

"It's a pact then," Joss had said, and she spit on her hand and extended it toward Reese.

"Really? Spit?"

"To seal the deal."

Reese had shrugged and only winced slightly as she placed her hand over the spit and they shook on it.

"There's no reason to be alone just because we're single," Reese added.

"So we'll avoid Christmas together."

"Until one of us gets married and starts a family," Reese had said.

It had seemed like an open-ended agreement that extended far, far down the road. There had been no sign of someone like Damian actually showing up in her life back then. But deep down, there had always been the hope.

Excitement surged inside her like a storm over the ocean. Now that the realization of those lifelong dreams peeked over the edge of her future, Reese felt torn between running toward them and shrinking back within the bracing fear of never fitting in to the world accompanied by an impending new last name.

"Okay, sweetie," nurse Karen said as she packed up her blood pressure cuff. "Your mommy should be back in about ten minutes."

Reese listened in from outside the door of the hospital room as anesthesiologist Jack Collins inched up on her before she noticed him.

"Are you spying on patients again, Dr. Pendergrass?"

She chuckled. "Waiting for Dr. Fielding. He's covering for me while I'm gone. What are your holiday plans?"

"Dinner with some friends on Christmas Eve," he replied. "Church on Christmas morning. Very low key."

Despite ten or more years difference in their ages, she and Jack had become fast friends when he'd joined the hospital staff a couple of years back. He'd joked with her about being a father figure, and she'd begun including him on special occasions like her birthday dinner in Newport Beach.

"But you're still planning to join us on New Year's Day, right?"

"I wouldn't miss it," he said, and he pulled her into a friendly embrace. "You and Damian have a great Christmas."

"We will, Jack. You too."

"Do you need anything? How about some of that banana pudding you like?" Karen asked her young patient as Jack walked away. Caley shook her head. "You know how to call me if you change your mind. The red button comes straight to me, all rightie?"

The little girl nodded, and the nurse tapped Reese's arm on her way out of the room. "Have a good Christmas, Dr. Pendergrass."

"You, too, Karen."

Karen passed Arthur Fielding as she hurried down the corridor, and Reese nodded him over toward the bed as she approached it.

"Caley, this is Dr. Fielding," Reese told her. "He'll be looking after you while I'm away over Christmas."

"Hi, Caley," Arthur said, squeezing her small arm. "I'm sorry you have to spend the holiday here, but I'm going to do everything I can to help you feel better as soon as possible. Okay?"

Caley shrugged. She'd been in and out of the hospital so many times throughout the year that Reese suspected she didn't really hold out much hope about feeling better.

"How long will you be gone?" Caley asked her, and Reese stroked her hair.

"I'll be back in just a few days. And Dr. Fielding will call me if there's anything out of the ordinary. I know he's not much to look at," she teased, and Caley giggled. The truth was Arthur gave George Clooney a real run for his money with those brooding blue eyes and dark floppy hair; unfortunately, he knew it too. "But he's a pretty smart man. And a very good doctor. I'm leaving you in excellent hands."

"You'll come see me as soon as you get back?" Caley asked.

"You'll be my first stop."

"Good to meet you, sweetheart," Arthur told her. "I'll see you again later."

Reese and Arthur strolled into the corridor, and Reese adjusted the stethoscope around her neck. "B12 and folate deficiencies," she explained. "The blood smear results should be back late today. She's still not holding much down, so you may want to order an IV if she has no luck with dinner."

"I've done this before, Reese," he joked. "I've got this."

Reese sighed. "Sorry. She's special."

"They're all special."

She grinned, supposing he was right.

"So," he said, slipping his arm around her shoulder as they headed down the hall, "when do you leave?"

"I'm headed home to meet Damian right now."

"Meeting the fam," Arthur said with a laugh. "Just be sure you don't blow it. You can never recover from a lousy first meeting."

"Oh, thank you for the support."

"You know me. Ever the encourager."

"Mm," she groaned.

"Hey, when are you going to set me up with that hot friend of yours, Reese?"

"Joss?"

"Joss," he repeated. "Right. Joss. She's a spitfire. So when are you going to hook us up?"

"Uh. Never?"

"C'mon!"

"Oh, yeah. I'm sorry. I'll set you up with my best girlfriend, Arthur . . . *said no woman on the planet, ever.*"

"Reese . . ."

"I find it quite alarming I have to remind you of this, but you're married."

"Semantics."

Reese pushed the elevator call button and stared him down. "Tell you what. Let's call your wife and discuss it with her and see if she agrees."

He chuckled.

"Yeah, I didn't think so."

"Can't blame a guy for trying."

"Actually, I can," she replied. The door slipped open and she boarded the elevator, tapping the button for the lobby. "Merry Christmas, Dr. Fielding."

"Same to you, Dr. Pendergrass."

DAMIAN RUBBED HIS EYES and yawned. Leaning back in his chair, he stared at the ceiling and wondered about traffic on Interstate 10.

"Dr. Palmer?" He looked up and smiled at his secretary as she stood just inside the door. "Do you need anything else before I head out?"

"No, Jackie, I'm headed out as well. Have a wonderful Christmas with your family."

"Thank you. I hope you and Dr. Pendergrass do the same."

"Here's hoping," he said with a grin. "My entire family is flying in, and we're joining them at our vacation home up in Sugarloaf. She's meeting them all for the first time."

"Be careful driving," she warned. "I heard on the news this morning that the ski lifts are fully operational at the resorts in Big Bear. Another foot of powder last night."

"A white Christmas," he mused. "We haven't had one of those for a couple of years."

On his way over to pick up Reese, Damian asked Siri—his best friend in the form of a cell phone—to check driving conditions on CA 38, the winding road that would take them up the mountain to Sugarloaf.

"State route 38 . . . to Sugarloaf Mountain," she confirmed in her friendly but robotic voice. "Currently thirty-one degrees. . . . Wind chill nineteen degrees. . . . Snowy conditions. . . . Expected snowfall . . . three additional inches . . . by ten p.m. . . . Road conditions . . . could be hazardous. . . . Driving speed slowed . . . from forty-five . . . to thirty-five . . . in some areas."

"Thanks, Siri."

"You are welcome. . . . Is there . . . anything else . . . I can do . . . for you?"

"Not right now. Have a good night."

"I am here . . . if you . . . need me."

Damian chuckled. He recalled the big deal of buying his first cell phone back in college, a boxy thing, too heavy to lug in his pocket, incessantly dropping calls. Now he carried less than four ounces of streamlined technology that conversed with him on a daily basis and performed more dependably than at least a couple members of his human office staff.

The garage door stood open, and two small-wheeled suitcases sat behind the rear bumper of Reese's car, a navy blue sweater looped through the handle of one of them. Reese stepped into view, smiling at him as he pulled up, stunning in lightly faded jeans and a pale blue blouse with glittering navy collar and cuffs. As she tossed her glossy blonde hair and began to gather her things, Damien popped the trunk and climbed out of his Mercedes.

"Your family's gifts are on the kitchen table," she told him, and he paused for a moment to take in the sight of her.

How did I ever land a girl like this? he wondered. From the bottom of her navy suede button-up boots to the wispy bangs of her honey-blonde hair, Reese Pendergrass could still take his breath away. She looked like a print ad for something decadent and fragrant. Perhaps a new cologne or shampoo.

She's even perfectly color coordinated, he realized. Right down to the metallic blue Lexus LS Hybrid parked behind her.

"You look great," he commented, and he gave her a sweet kiss before heading into the house to pick up the gifts.

He'd expected a cardboard box or a couple of shopping bags. Instead, two enormous red velvet stockings with white fur trim rested against the table, fat with presents wrapped with festive paper and curled ribbon bows.

"You do everything in style," he remarked as he carefully loaded the stockings into the trunk. She punched the code into the keypad next to the garage door to lower it.

"Too much?" she asked him once they'd settled into the soft leather seats.

"Not at all. I think they'll love it. Did you bring a coat? All I saw was a sweater."

"It's a heavy sweater. And it has a hood."

"Reese, honey. It's snowing up there. You're going to need a coat."

She looked as if she needed to consider the suggestion. "Oh. Okay."

"You own a coat, right?"

She frowned at him. "Of course I own a coat. I guess. . . . Well, you're right. I don't know what I was thinking. Hang on and I'll run inside and grab one."

On the second day of Christmas,
Murphy's Law gave to me . . .

two mismatched gloves
and a big rockin' Harry Winston ring.

2

Reese emerged from the house and walked through the garage, wearing a cute pink beanie and a long black coat with a pink fur collar. Walking the driveway like a runway, she paused at the front of his car and struck a model-esque pose, pursing her lips at him before spinning around and returning to the garage keypad to punch in the code once more.

At the front bumper she slipped out of the coat and tossed it into the backseat. Still wearing the hat, she plopped onto the passenger seat and tugged the door shut behind her.

"You're the cutest girl I've ever met," he told her, and they leaned together for a kiss.

"You better mean that," she warned, "because I intend to get the full scoop on your past from your sister Reggie. We've been conspiring by phone."

"You and Regg have been talking? When?"

"A few times now since we got engaged. I can't wait to meet her in person. She just seems like someone Joss and I would hang out with. And, of course, I'm counting on her to tell me some of the secrets of your past."

Damian chuckled. "Well, you've found the right inroad with Regg. She'll be more than happy to humiliate me. She was a real mother hen to the three of us boys when we were growing up. This is the longest I've ever gone without seeing her. Or any of my family."

"Three years!" she exclaimed. "As close as you all are, I can hardly believe you went this long without getting together for the holidays."

Damian turned the key in the ignition and backed down the driveway incline. "Matt and Courtney have been crazy busy with all of the holiday activities that come with four kids, so they opted to have Mom and Dad come to them. And Eli and his family moved to Puerto Rico three years ago and have only been home once since then. But this year we have the perfect storm where we can all get together. You're going to love the cabin. It's my favorite place on the planet. . . . Hey, I thought we'd drive for a while and then stop for dinner."

"Sounds good to me. How long until we get there?"

"If we stop at the base of the mountain, it will be another hour, hour and a half, depending on the weather. We may hit snow about halfway up."

They stopped for a pleasant, leisurely dinner at a little café about fifteen minutes from the base of the mountain.

"Okay," Reese exclaimed as they merged back onto Interstate 10. "I've been studying. Quiz me."

"Hang on," he replied with a grin. "First, I have a soundtrack."

Reese looked on as he cued up the first of the CDs he'd carefully and strategically chosen for the second leg of their trip. A tender pinch of guilt mixed with amusement pressed in as he recalled centering his search around music that did *not* contain any variation of Reese's favorite carol, "O Holy Night."

They'd only just met after Thanksgiving the previous year, so their first Christmas together peered around the corner of the still-getting-to-know-you phase of their relationship. Because she had traditionally spent Christmas with her friend Joss, Damian knew she wouldn't attend the Christmas Eve service with him, so he had invited her to church the Sunday beforehand. He would never forget that moment when Reese leaned toward him as the choir began to sing and declared in a whisper, "This is my favorite Christmas carol ever!"

As church members were encouraged to join the choir in song, Reese's passionate enthusiasm for that particular song came out in near screeches, and heads turned toward them from every direction, including the podium and the choir loft behind the pastor. At first he'd thought it to be a sort of tasteless and inappropriate joke on her part . . . until he really looked at her. With her eyes closed and her head turned upward, Reese wore an immaculate and reverent expression on her face.

He'd taken a lot of private ribbing from fellow church members in the months that followed. Despite the fact that he vowed to do all he could to avoid any repeat performances of that ear-splitting and somewhat horrifying enthusiasm for Reese's favorite carol, Damian also knew he couldn't bear the thought of ever spending another Christmas season without her.

He'd breathed a heavy sigh of relief when she agreed to spend the holiday with his family in Sugarloaf where he wouldn't need to worry about a church choir's song choices. On their way to dinner one night the week before, he'd quickly caught the first notes of Chris Tomlin's version of "O Holy Night" and changed the radio station before she recognized it. And now for their drive up the mountain, he'd orchestrated an "O Holy Night"-less soundtrack to accompany them.

"We're starting with *Christmas with the Rat Pack!*" he declared. And on the first notes of Dean Martin's "Let it Snow, Let it Snow," Reese giggled.

"You really do love your Christmas, don't you, Damie?"

"I told you. I'm not like Joss," he answered. "In fact, I'm the opposite of Joss. I put up my tree and hang the outside lights on Thanksgiving weekend, and none of it comes down again until after the New Year."

"Look who you're telling," she teased.

"And yet you agreed to marry me," he said.

"I know. It's a mystery, isn't it?"

Reese slipped her arm around his and kissed his cheek.

"You think I'm bad?" he asked. "Wait until you get a load of my family. All of them in one place too. I just hope it doesn't scare you straight off the mountain and back into Joss's Christmas-hating arms."

"I'll work hard to restrain myself."

He didn't really want her to sense how serious he actually was, but the sentiment slipped out with just one word. "Promise?"

"Yes, Damian. I promise."

The happy giggle that followed let him know she didn't have a clue of what awaited her in just a little over an hour. His growing-up years had been somewhat idyllic; at least, that's what he'd come to learn in the span of time since he left Vermont and his family home behind. In comparison to the vegan-hippie lifestyle with which Reese had been raised—and then the Christmas-hating years with her friend Joss—she might be in for a bit of a shock. He hoped it turned out to be a good one, of course, but it would certainly be a shock at first.

"Okay! Let's start with Reggie because she's easiest," Reese suggested, returning her attention to preparing for the big family meeting. "Forty-six years old, no kids, still lives in Burke where you all grew up, husband Kenneth died in '06, and she's never married again. That's so sad. I'll bet she misses him so much."

"Kenny and Reggie were the perfect couple," he said. "They started dating in high school and married right after graduation. She found out she had ovarian cancer when they were trying to figure out why she couldn't get pregnant. Kenny stood by her through surgeries and treatment, and she eventually had a hysterectomy. About the time they started adoption proceedings for this little baby boy from Kenya, Ken had a massive heart attack at forty-three years of age."

"That's horrible." Reese squeezed his arm and snuggled closer. "It's sort of amazing she's so upbeat and funny when she's had the most tragic things happen to her."

"Regg has always been that way. Nothing ever keeps her down for long. But her faith is really strong. I think that has a lot to do with it. Okay. Who's next?"

"Next comes Matthew," she piped up. "Thirty-nine years old, married for eighteen years to Courtney, lives in Colorado with four kids: P.J., fifteen—Paul Junior, named after your dad; Hannah, age thirteen; Sarah, ten; and Ezekiel, age seven."

"He likes to be called Zeke."

"Zeke," she repeated with a nod. "Got it."

"And then?"

"Elijah!" she exclaimed. "Eli is your younger brother by two years, thirty-one-years-old, married to Sofia for seven years. Two children: Abigail, age six, and Jeremy, five. Sofia is from Puerto Rico, where they moved when Eli took a job working for her father's real estate company three years ago. He's a marathon runner, and he recently broke his personal best to run a seven-minute mile. Are you dazzled?"

"Quite. Now what are my parents' names?"

"Oh. You have parents?" she joked, and Damian gave her a nudge with his elbow. "Dad Paul and Mom Jeane. Currently living out their retirement in sunny Sedona where it is very, very hot in the summer but—"

And they finished it in stereo: "It's a dry heat."

He kissed her head as she nuzzled into his shoulder for a moment.

"You really did study," he encouraged her. "You do me proud."

"That's the plan!"

"And the dog?"

"Paco," she said without missing a beat. "Belongs to Matthew's daughter Sarah."

Damian cleared his throat and raised an eyebrow.

She chuckled. "Chihuahua, six years old."

"Right," he replied. "And seriously, don't turn your back on him."

"No eye contact, no loud voices," she recited from memory, "and no quick movements."

"Ding, ding, ding," he rewarded her, and Reese returned the favor with laughter that sounded to Damian like a perfectly pitched choir singing on a distant hill. "You're amazing," he told her.

"And?" she prompted.

"And I am the most blessed man on the planet."

"Yes, you are."

Damian slipped his arm around Reese's shoulder, and she nestled against him as Frank Sinatra crooned "The Christmas Waltz."

"I'm a little nervous," she said softly.

"About?"

"What if your family doesn't like me?"

"Not possible."

"You said yourself, they're not usually all in one place like this. What if they get to talking, and they make a collective decision . . . like . . . I'm not good enough for you."

"That is not going to happen."

"You're so sure of your family that you know this for certain," she stated.

"I'm so sure of *you* that I know this for certain," he told her. "The only real worry we have is they might turn on *each other*."

"Why? Do they fight a lot? You never mentioned that."

"No. We don't fight, really. I mean, there are a few sarcastic jabs bantered about every now and then—especially when Matthew is in the room. It's important to just step back and get out of the way. Regg calls it our Family Power Surges. Like we're conductors for each other's electricity. Personally, from what I've deduced over the years, I'm pretty sure this is just called family."

Reese giggled and snuggled closer into him. After a minute or two, she sighed sleepily and told him, "I've never heard this song before."

"No?"

"Uh-uh. But I like it."

"Stick with me, kiddo. Okay, here's our turnoff to start up the mountain toward Sugarloaf."

"Alrightie!" she exclaimed, plucking two strange-looking gloves from her coat pocket. "Ah, Damie."

"What are those?" he said with a laugh.

"I can't believe I forgot to replace these stupid things. I can't meet your family, wearing these gloves!" she added as she tucked the bright orange, pink, and teal plaid mitten back into one pocket, and the purple and red one into the other.

WHEN REESE AWOKE, ROSEMARY Clooney softly crooned "It Came Upon a Midnight Clear," and the heavy snow outside looked as though it had been dumped by the barrelfuls over the roof of the car. They appeared to be the only travelers on the winding road, and Damian drove along at a conservative twenty-eight miles per hour as the high beams cut through the dance of thick, white confetti in front of them.

"Nice nap?" he asked as she squirmed upright in the passenger seat.

"Mm-hmm. Are we almost there?"

"About ten minutes."

"It looks like the roads are pretty clear, all things considered. Has it been scary?"

Damian chuckled. "I learned to drive in Vermont, remember? Snow on the roads doesn't scare me."

"Well, I grew up in northern California mostly. If a fog sets in, I'm your girl."

"I'll keep that in mind. We've actually passed a couple of snow-plows going both directions, so I think we should be fine all the way to the turnoff."

She glanced at the clock on the dash. The glowing blue light told her it was nearly eleven p.m.

"Did you call and tell them we were running late?"

"I guess I should have," he said with the lift of his shoulder. "They'll probably figure we decided to wait until morning."

"Do you have a key, or will we have to wake them?" Reese blinked as she spotted something up ahead, and she squinted for a better look. "Damian, what is that?"

"What's . . . what?"

"Up there on the side of the road. Do you see it?"

The beam of the headlights caught it in just that moment. An animal of some kind. A really big animal!

"I don't see—"

"No, look out!" she screamed just as the animal moved into the path of their car.

Damian jammed on the brakes, and the car spun sideways. It all seemed to evolve in slow motion as the grind of rubber sailing through snow and ice nearly drowned out her own screams and Rosemary Clooney's now-surreal soft, crisp undertones. The side and front airbags deployed and popped noisily at the exact moment the Mercedes crashed with a hard, sickening thump against the side of the large deer with the bad sense to cross in front of a car on a snowy mountain road at midnight.

Reese could barely breathe, and she frantically swatted at the bags pressing in on her while Clooney continued her serenade. It struck her strangely funny all of a sudden, as the white dust of the airbags cascaded over them inside the car and the thick white snow fell outside, that the soundtrack to the collision was soft and stunningly crisp, and—in her head, at least—became "It Came Upon a Midnight Deer." She tried not to laugh, but she couldn't help herself.

"Reese?" Damian sounded muffled and raspy. "Reese? Are you all right?"

Her heart began to race, and she reached over and felt for his arm. When she found it, she grabbed hold. "Damian? I'm okay. Are you?"

"I think so," he replied.

They pawed at the airbags, pushing them away until they finally looked one another directly in the face. Reese gasped when she spotted one lone trickle of blood winding its way down Damian's powder-white face.

"You're bleeding," she said. She blindly felt around for the package of tissues she recalled tossing to the console between them, and she quickly wrapped her fingers around it. Pulling one out of the package, she twisted a tissue around her index finger and patted his eyebrow while noisily puffing to remove the airbag powder from her lip gloss. "Pfft. Pffffftt."

The stereo, completely unaware that anything out of the ordinary had occurred, skipped to the next song. "White Christmas" by Bing Crosby elicited a chuckle from Reese. So much for dreaming of snow for Christmas.

Damian arched his clean eyebrow, and one corner of his mouth twitched slightly. "Was I delirious before, or did I hear you . . . *laughing?*" he asked as she tended to the gash.

"Pffft. . . . Pfft. . . . What do you mean?"

"When I came to, I thought I heard you laughing."

"Oh!" she exclaimed, and she spat out a few more puffs in an effort to blow her lips clean. "Yeah. It was that song that was on before, the Rosemary Clooney song."

"What song was it?"

"'It Came Upon a Midnight Clear.' But in my head, what I heard was . . . and you probably won't think it's very funny . . . but . . . well . . . in my head, she was singing 'It Came Upon a Midnight *Deer*.'"

Damian regarded her seriously for a long moment, and she prepared herself for the observation that was almost sure to follow—the one she always expected, but thankfully, never came from Damian:

Sometimes you can be so inappropriate. What is wrong with you?

I just don't understand what makes you tick! Laughing after a head-on collision?

But once again he astonished her to the very core when Damian snickered suddenly and then guffawed . . . snorted . . . gasped for air . . . and continued to laugh hysterically.

On the third day of Christmas,
Murphy's Law gave to me . . .

three wrenched necks,
two mismatched gloves,
and a big rockin' Harry Winston ring.

3

No doubt due to the combination of poor weather conditions and an elevation of more than seven thousand feet in the San Bernardino Mountains, Siri offered no assistance to them whatsoever. Reese's phone had only one bar, and she couldn't connect either, which made the fact that the rear wheels of the car spun in the snow without gaining traction even more troubling.

"What should we do?" she asked him, and Damian wished he had an answer for her.

"Well, we're only a couple of miles away from the road that leads toward the house, and not too far from there is a small general store that used to have a pay phone outside."

"Okay. Let's go then."

"I think you should stay here," he suggested. "Run the heater and stay warm. I'll hoof it and get back to you as soon as I can."

Reese's perfect little turned-up nose crinkled as she looked at him, her face bunched up like a fist. "You can't leave me out here, Damian. I want to go with you."

"You're going to trudge through a foot of snow in those suede boots of yours, Reese?" he admonished her, and he snapped the top of her button-up boot where it folded just over her knee. "They have three-inch heels on them."

"Four and a half."

He sighed. "Just stay here. Lock the doors. I won't be gone long."

"It's cold," she whimpered.

"News flash. It's much colder out there than it is in here." He tucked the flattened airbag behind the steering wheel and then reached over the seat and grabbed her coat. "Put this on and button it up. I'll be back soon."

She took the coat but then yanked her door open and stepped out into the falling snow to put it on.

"Reese, what are you—"

"Damian, he's hurt," she cried. "Look! The deer is just lying there . . . looking at me."

Damian popped the trunk and hurried out of the car to grab his own wool coat. After sliding into it, he grabbed the scarf and gloves he'd stashed in the back. He latched the trunk and tugged on the gloves and slipped the scarf around his neck as he rounded the back of the car. He found Reese crouched, peering down at the enormous deer lying on its side.

"Reese, back away from him."

She did, and the buck wriggled a bit and whined, but Damian thought it must be too injured to get back to its feet. He approached it, careful to maintain a safe distance from those sharp-looking antlers, and he squatted down to get a closer look. Its soulful brown eyes were as wide and round as saucers, and it made no move at all.

"I'm so sorry, buddy," he reassured the buck in a soft, steady voice. "I didn't see you. You needed to wear some reflective gear when you left the missus tonight."

The deer rocked his head, and Damian straightened with a lurch and backed away slightly. Reese stood behind him with a grip on the back of his coat.

"He's scared," she whispered. "Do you think there's anything we can do to help him? Without getting punctured, I mean."

Before Damian could reply, the buck heaved. Reese squealed and yanked Damian backward along with her until she pressed up against the hood of the car. They watched the animal cautiously as it struggled to roll over and regain its footing. After a moment it hopped up and stared at them with tentative suspicion. The thing was huge, and Damian scanned the area at the side of the car, wondering how quickly they could get back inside if it decided to charge them in retribution. But the buck took a step backward, still eyeing them closely, and then it bolted away with a significant limp.

"It's hurt." Reese winced, burying her face in the back of Damian's shoulder and clutching his coat with both hands. "It's really hurt, Damie."

"I know," he said, turning around and gathering her into his arms. "But you're not. And I'm grateful for that. Now get back into the car where you're safe so I can get going before I freeze to death."

Reese looked up at him and cringed. "It's going to get a lot colder out here, but if you want to keep standing here and arguing, I'm all in."

He groaned, knowing full well she could easily keep him engaged in debate for an incalculable amount of time. "Get that hat you had on earlier."

She shot him a triumphant grin and hurried back to the car and grabbed her hat. Placing it on her head as she walked ahead of him, she cried, "Come on, slowpoke! What's keeping you?"

Damian eyed those heels of hers as she trudged through the snow. Shaking his head, he set out after her. "At least you have some gloves to put on."

She reached into her coat pockets and pulled out the strange mismatched mittens and gave them a disdainful look.

"Put them on."

"I can just keep my hands in my pockets," she said, shoving them deep past the mittens. "See?"

"Reese," he said with a sigh. "Please put them on. Humor me, will you?"

She groaned, pulling them out again and tugging her hands into them. "Look at this," she said. "My suede boots are ruined from the snow, and now these stupid gloves. Your family will think you're marrying some hobo from the circus."

"I don't think hobos work at the circus."

"Oh, well, you know what I mean."

Damian turned his head away so she wouldn't see the smile on his face as they plodded along.

"You're afraid my family will look at you—a doctor with your own practice—and think you're . . . what? Too poor to afford some nice gloves?"

"I don't know," she snapped, rolling her arm at him. "I didn't really come from all that much, and your family has a vacation home near a ski resort. I guess I just feel . . ."

When her words trailed off, Damian smiled at her. "Less than?"

"Maybe. A little."

"You are not less than anything or anyone I've ever known."

She shushed him and tromped along. When she slipped and squealed, he caught her just in time to keep her from landing on her face in the snow.

"My neck hurts," she grumbled. "I think I have whiplash."

"It's a miracle we both walked away," he said, supporting her arm. "About those boots. If they're ruined anyway, will you let me break off the heels so you can walk like a normal person?"

"Break off . . . ! Are you joking?"

"I am not."

"Well, you should be. These boots cost over six hundred dollars, Damian. I got them at half off."

"Half. . . . They cost over a thousand bucks?"

"Honey, don't say *buck*. I just see those big brown eyes looking up at me. Do you think he's okay?"

"I don't know."

"Anyway, the boots are *Louboutin*." She said the name with such reverence that Damian almost expected to hear a choir of angels singing overhead.

"I don't care if they're Lou Ferrigno! A thousand bucks for a pair of boots?"

Glancing at him over her shoulder, she tossed him a sigh. "But . . . don't I look cute in them?"

"Not a thousand dollars cute."

He suspected the minute those words left his throat he shouldn't have said them, but when Reese slid to a stop, planted her hands on her hips, and glared at him, he knew for sure.

"Oh, really!"

Shaking his head in surrender, Damian snagged her arm and guided her forward. "I'm sorry. I shouldn't have spoken ill of your Lou Ferrigno boots."

Finally, she sniffed. "All right then."

"I'm just glad you have a successful practice of your own," he added. "No way I'm footing the bill for thousand-dollar boots."

"I told you. I got them for six hundred."

"Over six hundred," he reminded her, suppressing the laugh that wanted to pop out of his mouth.

"Have you always been like this?" she asked. "Or is this just what happens when you're freezing to death? It's good to know these things before the wedding, I think."

Damian chuckled and placed his arm around her shoulder. She wrapped her arm around his waist, and the two of them plodded along for several minutes without talking.

"Where did you get those horrible gloves, anyway?"

Reese giggled. "A couple of years ago, Joss and I went to Miami on our non-Christmas trip. Well, they had a ridiculous and unexpected cold snap that caught us completely off guard. So we had to go shopping for warmer clothes. That's where I bought this coat, as a matter of fact."

"Don't tell me. You got it for the bargain price of six grand."

"Hush. Anyway, you'd be surprised at how hard it is to find gloves in Miami, even at Christmas. Joss bought these for me as sort of a joke, and she tucked them into the pockets of my coat. When I grabbed it earlier today and saw the bulging pockets, I assumed they were my chenille gloves."

"Well, they're awful."

"Yes, they are. But I think I can pull them off, don't you?"

He laughed as she placed her hands over her bright red cheeks and smiled at him.

"All right, Fashion Plate. Let's pick up the pace, shall we? I can't feel three of my toes."

REESE DIDN'T REVEAL HER disappointment when they finally reached the closed general store to find the pay phone that used to hang on the wall had been removed. Damian's frazzled groan spoke volumes for both of them.

Thrusting his fist against the side of the small building provoked a shout, and Reese wrapped her brightly gloved hands around his and rubbed it, planting kisses on his leather glove.

"Ooooh, no. That's not going to help, Damie," she cooed. "We just need a different plan, that's all."

"You think?"

"Well, how far is it to the house from here?"

He removed his hand and shook it at his side. "Another mile."

"So we walk another mile. We can do that, right?"

She smiled with hope until his stormy glare melted.

"We're able-bodied, frozen people. We can walk one more mile."

Reese worked hard to keep from letting on what a lie that was. She didn't feel able bodied at all. And the thought of walking another *few yards* was almost more than her frozen, aching feet could bear.

She glanced down at her Louboutin boots. The wet snow had completely ruined the blue suede up past the ankle and darkened the calves in mortifying patches. She wished for a moment Damian had pushed through in their argument, plunked her down on the hood of the car, and broken off those detestable four-and-a-half-inch heels in spite of her best argument against it. Perhaps then she might have managed the grueling hike without losing the blood flow to both her feet.

Reese yanked off her hat and stuffed it under her arm, twisting her hair as she observed Damian and awaited word on their next move.

"Well," he said at last. "It looks like there's no alternative. Let's get moving."

Crushed, Reese nodded. She replaced her hat, stuffing her hair up underneath it, and she tugged it down around her stinging cold ears.

"Alrightie," she replied. It wasn't the enthusiastic battle cry she'd tried to muster, but it would have to do. "Onward then."

The late-night wind burned her face, and Reese's eyes began to water. She rubbed her nose with the back of her gloved hand, and a sharp pain elicited a wince.

"I think I have icicles hanging from my nose," she muttered. "No joke. My snot is frozen on my nose."

"Here," Damian said, removing the bright red cashmere scarf from around his neck. He gently covered her mouth and nose before wrapping it loosely around the back of her neck. He planted a kiss on the scarf where her mouth should have been. She couldn't be entirely sure if he'd hit his target because her numb lips only felt the distant impression of his. "Breathe into it for a few minutes. It will warm you up."

That familiar spicy scent of Damian soothed her as she pressed the soft cashmere to her face and they resumed their arctic hike. A mile might as well have been ten to Reese, and every step in those boots brought about a greater resolve—one she knew full well she would rescind at a later date—never to wear such high heels again.

Tennis shoes. That's the way to go. Athletic, comfortable, sensible.

There, she'd done it. She'd gone too far.

Sensible shoes? When Santa-bearded-Claus brought them down her chimney in person and placed them on her feet like Prince

Charming and Cinderella . . . then . . . then she would consider sensible shoes.

"You're doing it again," Damian commented.

She blinked and shook her head. "Doing what?"

"Laughing. What's so funny now?"

"Oh. Just . . . Santa Claus and sensible shoes."

He shot her a look and shook his head. She suspected Damian was about ready to stop trying to figure her out. Certain she would never know quite why, Reese paused and thanked God above that Damian loved her in spite of herself.

"When I met you, you despised him," he remarked. "Now you're thinking about what kind of shoes he wears."

Amusement bubbled up inside of her, and Reese pressed Damian's scarf tightly to her nose as she laughed.

"I'm pretty sure his boots are flats," he added. "You might think about that."

"Oh, I'm thinking about it," she assured him. "Now let's cut the chatter."

Damian playfully yanked the scarf away from her face and pecked the bridge of her frozen nose with a kiss before he replaced it.

"Sensible shoes," he mused as he took her hand. "That'll be the day."

On the fourth day of Christmas,
Murphy's Law gave to me . . .

four yapping dogs,
three wrenched necks,
two mismatched gloves,
and a big rockin' Harry Winston ring.

4

"Welcome to the Palmer Family Flophouse."

"Are you kidding me?" Reese exclaimed as the magnificent home came into sight. "I thought we were walking down another road! This is *the driveway?*"

Damian chuckled as he took her hand and tried to lead her toward the house, but Reese stayed rooted to the spot and squirmed out of his grasp.

"It's . . ." Dropping the scarf from her face, she gawked at the sight at the end of the driveway. ". . . spectacular."

The sophisticated—*and massive!*—home looked like something out of a Thomas Kincaid painting or a movie set. Three stories, the first of them fronted almost entirely by glass . . . perfect, clean lines of twinkling, white lights framing every inch . . . a snow-covered walkway outlined with immaculate red-and-white lanterns . . . a twenty-foot evergreen standing at one side like a muscular sentry, ignited with thousands of colored bulbs and sporting a blazing white-gold cross at the top.

"Exactly how much money am I marrying into?"

"You're betrothed to a neurosurgeon," he replied with a snicker. "Unless you marry my father instead, the keys to all of this would only be on loan for a weekend getaway or a few days at Christmas."

Reese's heart palpitated, and she tapped her chest with her ugly gloved hand. "I . . . can't really . . . *breathe*."

"Reese?"

She loosened the scarf and yanked it from her neck, stuffing it into his hands. Flapping the collar of her coat, she gasped for air. "I don't know . . . what's . . ."

Damian stood before her, straight and serious, and he placed his hands on her shoulders and looked her squarely in the eye. "Take in a deep breath and just hold it for a minute."

She did as he instructed, her eyes bulging and her cheeks puffed with air.

"Now just let it out very slowly."

Instead, the air pushed through her puckered lips with the sound of a sputtering raspberry. Before she'd expelled all of what she'd taken in, she prattled, "I've never even seen anything like this, Damian. I mean, it's probably the biggest house I've ever seen in person . . . well . . . outside of a hotel we stayed in once in Seattle. My mom got some sort of special deal on it, and we were only there one night before my dad insisted on checking us out so we could stay somewhere more realistic. Not that your family home isn't realistic. I mean, in all seriousness, it's not really, but I just mean—"

"Reese," he interrupted with a sweet smile. "Calm down, baby. It's going to be fine. It's just a house."

Waving her arm over his shoulder with a dramatic flourish, she exclaimed, "This is not just a house, Damian. This! This is an *event* in logs, stone, and glass."

"No, it's—"

"I won't know how to act, Damie." She felt the caving-in process as it set in, and she tried to pull herself together to no avail. "You haven't met my parents yet, so you have no way of knowing. They grow their own vegetables, Damian. They make side dishes like sweet and sour pickles marinated in Kool-Aid. And I'm not entirely certain, and I could be wrong I guess because I don't have any real proof, but I'm pretty sure they sometimes smoke weed in the basement!" The rambling had begun, and she couldn't stop the snowball from plummeting down the hill. "Our big Christmas tradition was watching my brother do a dance from *The Nutcracker* in the living room, which was alarmingly entertaining when compared to the fact that, from the day they retired to Key West, my father hasn't worn anything besides a Hawaiian shirt and Bermuda shorts even one day. The last Christmas I spent with them, he played a ukulele and sang "Jingle Bell Rock" until Hersch and I couldn't stand it anymore! I don't . . ." She glared at the house again for a long moment and rubbed her forehead. "I don't fit here."

Damian held both of her hands to his heart and smiled at her. "Look at me."

You poor, sweet, deluded man, she thought as she gazed into his chocolate-brown eyes and melted a little. *You really think you can shove this square peg into that giant round hole up there, don't you?*

Damian kissed her wacky mittens and smiled. "You fit with me," he stated. "There's not one single doubt that you fit with me. This is just a remote and distant part of who I am . . . like your family isn't the sum total of who you are. You'll do fine here because you fit *with me.*"

Reese sighed. "You need an intervention."

He arched an eyebrow as he asked, "Out of the two of us, you think *I'm the one* who needs an intervention?"

"All right. I need one too."

"So we're perfect for one another," he deduced. "Now can we go inside and warm up before we freeze to this spot? My mother despises those little statues people put on their lawns. I don't want us to become the life-sized ones she finds on hers in the morning."

"Gnomes," she croaked, shaking her head and nodding at the same time. "My parents have three of them in the vegetable garden." She slapped her hips with both hands and moaned. "My parents have gnomes in their yard."

"I won't tell if you don't."

Reese followed him up the sidewalk to the massive front door. Damian cranked the knob and sighed.

"Wait here."

She watched him jog down the sidewalk again, stopping at the end of it and peering up at the top floors.

"What are you doing?" she asked him from the porch.

He raised his index finger at her without reply and hurried around the side of the house.

"You are not going to climb that Christmas tree, right? Damian?"

It seemed like a really long time since he'd disappeared, and Reese had begun to shiver, wishing she'd held on to that scarf of his. She yanked the hat down onto her head and folded her arms, shifting from one foot to the other in the vain hope that it might help her get warm. Just about the time she'd decided to sit down on the rustic pine bench angled off to one side, the ornate wrought-iron lamp over her head flooded the whole porch with bright yellow light.

The front door flew open, and she expected Damian's victorious greeting. Instead, a large and sleepy young man in a tight thermal shirt and jeans glared at her.

"Who are you, and why are you standing at our door?"

"Oh. I . . . I'm . . ."

"Who *iss* it, Eli?" a young woman asked in a thick Spanish accent as she approached the open door.

"Dunno yet."

"Oh, you're Eli!" Reese exclaimed. She started to reach out to shake his hand, but she caught sight of her horrible mismatched mittens. She discreetly yanked them off and slipped both hands behind her back, tossing them off the porch and into the snow before she took his hand and shook it awkwardly. "And you must be Sofia?" she asked the stunning, dark-haired woman standing next to him. "I'm Reese." Not even the remotest spark of familiarity. "Damian's fiancée?"

"Oh," Eli said as he slapped her hand and then excitedly twisted his own out of her grip. "Where is he?"

She glanced toward the side of the house and shrugged. "I'm not exactly sure. I think he went looking for a key or a way into the house so we wouldn't wake everyone."

A mischievous smile began to form, and Reese recognized it instantly.

The Palmer family grin.

"Come on inside," Sofia invited her with the whisper of her Puerto Rican accent. "You look like you're *frosen* solid."

"We hit a deer a couple of miles back, and the wheels got jammed. . . . Anyway, we had to walk the rest of the way . . ."

She hadn't even noticed Eli's departure until a wild growl drew her attention to the ground in front of the evergreen. Eli had already tackled Damian, and the two of them wrestled around in the snow like ornery schoolboys.

"Is that Damian?" another one cried as he appeared in the doorway, presumably Matthew, and he flew off the porch, his bathrobe flapping behind him like a superhero's cape as he dove into the mix.

Sofia rolled her eyes and grabbed Reese's hand. "Come on. They'll need coffee and blankets."

Reese chuckled and began to follow her inside when Damian shouted, "Hey! Where are you taking my bride?"

"Away from the three of you before she finds out the truth about you *imbéciles* and runs for her life." Muttering, she added, *"Idiotas."*

"Good to see you too, Sof," he called after her. "Merry Christmas!"

He'd barely gotten the words out before Sofia slammed the front door behind them and led Reese through the towering foyer toward the cavernous kitchen and great room. A twenty-foot spruce tree captured most of her attention, even with its six million or so lights extinguished, stretching toward the rafters next to an open loft.

Reese's hand rested on her heart, and she gasped when she saw it. "That's . . . so . . ."

"Enorme?" Sofia finished for her. "I know."

"I was going to say exquisite!"

"Really?" she asked as she stood next to her and inspected the tree with fresh eyes. "It's just a *leetle* . . . too much for my tastes. But then what else are you going to get with ceilings this tall, heh?" She shrugged one shoulder and tucked a wisp of wavy dark hair behind her ear as she smiled. "Let's put on the coffee, shall we?"

The impressive kitchen nearly stole Reese's breath away. Hickory cabinets with leaded glass fronts bordered the space around a large center island with a sage green and beige granite counter and a low-hanging row of amber pendulum lights. The appliances appeared to be built right into the cabinetry, and a huge stainless steel hood hovered over a six-burner gas range with a griddle on one side.

"Ah, *hermosa*. I'll bet those were cute boots before you introduced them to the snow, heh?" Sofia commented as she produced five ceramic coffee mugs with a white-on-white swirled design, and she set them on the island.

Reese's lip curled slightly as she looked down at them. "Yeah," she said with a groan. "They were."

Three noisy men rumbled into the house, drawing the women's attention.

"I'm warning you, *chicos*!" Sofia exclaimed just above a whisper, and she pointed an erect finger at them and wiggled it toward the railing beyond the Christmas tree. "There are six sleeping children in that loft. If you wake even one of them, you're all *dormir en el bosque*."

Damian looked to Eli who translated. "Sleeping in the woods."

Damian and Matthew both nodded.

"Ah!"

"Gotcha."

The family resemblance sang true and clear as Eli, Matthew, and Damian—with their arms around one another's shoulders—stifled their harmonious laughter.

"You think I'm joking?" she asked them.

"We would never think that about you, Sofia," Matthew said with a snort. "You don't have a humorous bone in your body."

She glared, and Eli smacked his brother hard in the ribs. "Don't be a blockhead, Blockhead."

Matthew rounded the island and pulled his sister-in-law into an embrace, kissing her cheek. "We're sorry, Sof. We'll be good boys."

"Like you would know how."

Damian stood behind Reese and wrapped his arms loosely around her waist. "Can you all pretend to behave, at least long enough to say hello to my best girl?"

The three of them turned toward her, and Reese suddenly felt like a suspect at the front of a lineup.

"Hey. She looks like a normal human being," Matthew remarked, and Sofia smacked his arm.

"Estúpido!"

"Reese Pendergrass," Damian said. "Meet the first segment of the Palmer clan. My older brother Matthew, my younger brother Elijah, and Eli's forgiving wife Sofia."

"You're here?"

They all reeled before the introductions came to full fruition as a woman slid into the kitchen in a green terry bathrobe and matty pink slippers.

"Reese?" she cried, and Reese unlocked the mystery immediately at the sound of her voice.

"Reggie?"

The two women collided in an embrace, and Reggie rocked her from side to side as she told her, "I'm so happy to finally meet you!"

"You too."

Damian chuckled. "What about me? You're not happy to see me?"

"Only because you brought Reese with you," she teased, and then she set Reese free long enough to hug her brother.

When they settled down onto barstools around the island, Sofia had already added another cup and filled each of them with steaming coffee.

"What happened?" Reggie asked Damian as she doctored hers with cream. "I thought you were arriving early in the evening."

"Dr. Perfect hit a moose," Matthew cracked.

"You what!"

"A deer," Damian corrected. "We hit a deer, and the car veered off the road and got stuck in the snow."

"How did you get here then?"

"We hiked."

Reggie looked at her for confirmation, and Reese shook her head.

"Nice indoctrination to Sugarloaf Mountain, huh?"

Reese shrugged.

"Oooh!" Reggie cried. "Let's see the ring."

Reese grinned. Those had been her four favorite words ever since Damian had proposed. She lifted her hand and extended it out into the middle of the island, wiggling her fingers.

"Where is it?" Damian asked dryly.

She didn't *actually hear* the piercing music from Janet Leigh's shower scene in *Psycho*, but it sure did seem like it in the first instant her eyes lurched against her completely ring-free hand.

Turning to Damian, she cried, "Where is it?"

"JUST CALL ME HOLMES," Damian said as he looked up at Reese on the porch. "Sherlock Holmes."

He produced the mittens from the mound of snow where she said she'd thrown them, and with one little shake, Reese's engagement ring tumbled out into the palm of his hand.

"Elementary, my dear Pendergrass."

She shook her head as he joined her on the porch. "I can't believe I did that."

"And all because you were embarrassed by these fine-looking winter mittens," he teased. "You really think my family is shallow enough that they'd think less of you for these gloves . . . when they have those *boots to judge you on?*"

She nudged him and reached for the ring, but Damian yanked it back.

"Not so fast," he said, moving in close until they stood face-to-face with no more than a couple of inches between them. "Let's do this right."

Damian took her left hand and kissed it before placing the ring back in its rightful place on her finger.

"Will you still marry me?" he asked.

"Hey, if you still want to, that's your problem," she joked. "You're not getting out of this, mister. I know a good thing when I'm offered it, so yeah. I'll marry you."

"It's a good thing," he told her. "I've already ordered the monogrammed towels."

"We have the same last initial," she reminded him, and Damian lifted one shoulder into a shrug.

"See, I told you. Match made in heaven."

He pulled her closer into a warm kiss. They parted quickly as the frenzied scamper of little claws on the floor accompanied a familiar bouncing growl. When the tiny brown-and-white Chihuahua reached the door, he skidded to a stop just a few feet away from them and kicked into a chorus of high-pitched barks.

"Shhhh," Damian said, raising an index finger. "Paco, hush. You know me."

Paco paused for a moment before he wagged his tail so hard it nearly knocked him off his stubby little legs. He stretched up the length of Damian's calf, wagging as he gave the dog a scratch behind the ear.

"There, that's better," he said.

But when the dog noticed someone standing next to him, it turned toward Reese and growled.

"No eye contact," Damian reminded her, and Reese lifted her gaze to the top of the doorway.

"Okay," she said. "Tell it I'm friendly. Tell it, Damian!"

"Come here," he said, but Paco flattened both ears and sneered, showing a full mouth of sharp, white teeth.

After a long, disenchanted growl, the dog's attention jerked to somewhere beyond the porch. When Damian heard the distant crunch of snow, he turned, expecting to find someone approaching on foot. Instead, a large deer stood at the edge of the driveway, about fifty yards out.

"Damian, is that—?"

"I don't know."

Paco flew off the porch and bounded across the yard toward the animal, barking and snarling. With every leap came a landing down into snow taller than the dog, but the Chihuahua pressed on in his pursuit. The buck bolted away, a severe limp evident as he did, Paco hot on his tail.

"Paco! Be nice!"

Damian recognized the familiar sound of his mother's voice as she padded quickly across the foyer rug toward the open front door.

"You're here!" she cried and nearly leaped into his arms. "I'm so happy you're both here! Come here, Reese." When she grabbed Reese and hugged her, Paco reappeared and exploded into another wave of spitting barks.

"Paco!" she reprimanded before she looked Reese in the eye. "They should have named him A-Paco-lypse."

Reese chuckled, and Damian lifted Paco into his arms and began to coo softly in the dog's ear. Not because he wanted to but because he knew a soft lilt to the voice was often the only thing that kept the peace in The World According to Paco.

"Mrs. Palmer, I'm so happy to meet you."

"Mrs. Palmer was Paul Senior's cranky old mother," she said with a twinkle in her pretty brown eyes. "I'm Jeane to you."

"Jeane. I'm really thrilled to be here."

"Mom," Damian interjected. "Let's get in the house. We've been out in the elements for hours."

"Why? What happened?" she asked as he closed the door and they all went inside.

"I'll tell you all about it in the morning. Just tell us where you want us to bunk, go back to sleep, and we'll see you at breakfast."

"Oh, no, you don't!" she exclaimed. "You think I could go back to bed now? Let's have some tea, shall we, Reese?"

Paco continued to growl all the way down the length of the hall. When Reese turned around to look at Damian, the dog nearly leaped out of his arms to nip at her, and she jumped back at least two feet.

He nudged the dog with two fingers. "Hey! Be nice."

As they walked toward the kitchen to find his eldest nephew standing next to his Aunt Sofia, Damian exclaimed, "P.J.! Is that you?"

Paul Jr. had sprouted a full foot since the last time he'd seen him. Lanky and tall and sporting a shaggy head of dark unruly hair, P.J. looked every bit the fifteen-year-old rebel his father Matthew had been.

The boy looked Reese up and down before offering, "'Sup."

"What kind of greeting is that?" Damian teased. "This is my fiancée, Reese Pendergrass. Reese, this is Mattie and Courtney's oldest, Paul Jr."

"P.J.," she said with a smile, and Damian beamed with pride that she remembered. "It's good to meet you."

"You too."

"Did we wake the other kids?" Matthew asked.

"Nah, they're all out," P.J. told his dad. "And Zeke is snoring like a bear. I hadda get outta there."

"Which rooms are we in, Mom?" Damian asked.

"Are we . . . *doing separate rooms*, bro?" Matthew teased.

It felt as though every eye turned expectantly toward him. "Yeah, we are."

"You don't have to on our account," Eli chimed in. "You're engaged."

"This is Damian and Reese's choice," his mother defended, "and I support it. There won't be another word about it."

"I'm gonna sleep on the couch in Grandpop's den." P.J. shook his head as he headed out of the room. "Dude," he chuckled as he passed Damian.

"Hey, if you're going in there, take this guy with you, huh?" Damian suggested, plopping Paco into his nephew's arms. "Close the door too."

"I thought you could take the small bedroom next to ours," his mom told him. "And Reggie has offered to share her room with Reese." Turning to Reese as if she needed to justify the decision, she added, "It's a nice big king-sized bed in there. You won't even know she's on the other side of it. Is that all right with you? We've kind of got a full house this year."

"It's fine," she exclaimed, and Reese grabbed Reggie's wrist and shook it gently. "I'm looking forward to the girl talk. As long as you don't mind me barging in on you."

"Are you joking? It was my idea."

Damian's heart puffed up a little as he watched them. In defiance of all her worst fears, Reese seemed to fit right in with this clan. Not that he'd doubted it in the least, but it felt nice to see it for himself. And more importantly, he knew Reese needed the validation.

"We don't have our bags," Damian announced. "So Reese will need something to sleep in, Sis."

"You just worry about finding your room. I've got this."

On the fifth day of Christmas,
Murphy's Law gave to me ...

five frozen thiiiings!

four yapping dogs,
three wrenched necks,
two mismatched gloves,
and a big rockin' Harry Winston ring.

5

A platter of scrambled eggs, fried potatoes overflowing a large bowl, a tray of bacon, three baskets of warm croissants, a variety of cubed fruits, and two dozen pastries. Breakfast at the Palmer table looked like a restaurant buffet line to Reese.

Mismatched chairs, stools, and benches flanked three six-foot folding tables on both sides. Set up in front of the glass windows overlooking the rolling hill in the backyard, nine adults and six children indulged in the meal while the chatter of more than a dozen people at once gave Reese a bit of a headache.

A soft snowfall took on the look of silver glitter sprinkling out of the morning sky, and the tree skeletons doing their shimmy in the wind all around the property foreshadowed the hint of a breathtaking view come spring.

"Okay, okay," Damian's father called out above the din, "simmer down. Let's talk about the plan for today. What are all of you doing to get out of this house at the same time so I can take a conference call at ten o'clock?"

"Eli, Matt, and I are heading down to the main road to dig out the car," Damian told them. "If we can't get it out, we'll call Jacob in town and see if he can bring his winch and help us."

"Reese and I will follow the boys in my rental car," Reggie chimed in. "We'll unload the bags and the gifts and bring them back to the house after we take a ride down the hill so I can show her around."

"Sofia, Mom, and I are going into the village with the kids," Courtney said. "Why don't you two meet up with us at The Teddy Bear for hot chocolate, and we can all go to the square afterward to hear the carolers."

"When are we going tubing?" seven-year-old Zeke cried. "Can't we just stay here and go tubing?"

"Tubing this afternoon," Jeane mandated. "After your Grandpop's important phone call. Or else in the morning."

"The morning?" he objected. "I don't want to wait until the morning. Daddy said we could go tubing."

"Let's see how things unfold with Uncle Damian's car, buddy," Matthew said. "Maybe we'll get back in plenty of time to do some tubing today."

"Who are you calling, Grandpop?" little Abigail inquired. "Who's the important person?"

"I'm just helping a friend back in Sedona with a decision he has to make about his company."

"Pop, you're still consulting?" Damian said as he plucked another roll out of the basket across from him. "If you want to, we can have a talk later about the full meaning of the concept of retirement."

"It's just a favor for a friend, son." Paul sipped his coffee and winked at Reese. "Now everyone has a plan, and every plan is in place. Are we clear?"

"We're clear, Grandpop," ten-year-old Sarah piped up, and Reese noticed for the first time that she held her little sleeping Chihuahua to her chest in a baby sling.

"Mom," P.J. said as he leaned toward Courtney. "Do I have to go? Grandpop won't even know I'm here if I stay in my room and listen to music."

"This is a family vacation," she replied. "We're going into town together."

He blew out a puff of exasperated impatience, and he and his sister Hannah both rolled their eyes.

"Can I at least go with Aunt Reggie then?" Hannah whined. "I don't want to spend the whole morning with the little kids."

"What did I just say?"

"Family vacation, blah, blah, blah," she replied. "But Aunt Reggie is family. And Reese *will be*."

"Pass me the eggs?" Reggie asked her softly.

But when Reese reached out to pick up the platter, a strange rumble drew her attention to Sarah. Paco had shifted in the little girl's arms and stared at Reese, growling under his breath.

"Paco!" Jeane scolded to no avail, and the little dog snapped at Reese's outstretched hand. She jerked it back with a squeal.

"Really, Matthew," Jeane said, and she stood up and grabbed the platter of eggs, walking it around the table to Reggie. "That dog is a menace."

"You just have to let him get used to you," Courtney told Reese. "He'll warm up to you."

She nodded and tried to smile, but Reese felt pretty certain Paco's warmer days had been left back in Colorado. Clearly the dog hated her.

"He's really a sweetheart," Matthew added. "Come on, the dog wears a yellow slicker when it rains and a fur coat in the snow."

"Daddy, he's little," Sarah pointed out. "He gets cold."

"I know, honey. I was just making the point that, after a few years of wearing high fashion, he just needs to remind people he's still a bad dude."

"I think he just doesn't like Reese," Abigail, Sarah's young cousin, said.

"Oh, don't be silly," Jeane said, smoothing Reese's hair. "There's nothing about Reese not to like."

"Well, Paco sure found something," Abigail said with a snicker.

"That's enough, Abs," Damian said. "Who wants more coffee?"

Reggie leaned over from the chair beside her and grinned. "Don't let us scare you. Despite appearances we really don't tear apart our prey."

"Nah, I'm good," Reese said with a chuckle. "I find it's best to approach the pack by first hanging back and observing. It's easier to assess potential danger that way."

"Well, if Hannah gets to go with Aunt Reggie," Abigail told them in her high-pitched six-year-old voice, "then Sarah and me want to go too."

"You're going with *mamá, mi hija*," Sofia told her. "Drink your juice and finish your huevos, heh?"

"But I can go with you, right, Aunt Reggie?" Hannah exclaimed in hope.

"It's up to your mom."

"Notice they never say it's up to Dad. Only that it's up to Mom," Matthew pointed out.

"Oh, please," Courtney countered with a good-natured grin. "Feel free to take this one, if it will make you feel better. Hannah, if you want to go with Aunt Reggie and Reese, ask your father."

Hannah leaped upon Matthew and tugged his arm. "Please, Daddy. Can I?"

The corner of Matthew's mouth quirked as Courtney groaned. "Yes, darling daughter. As your father, I declare that you may go with your Aunt Reggie and Reese and meet up with your mother for hot chocolate in the village afterward. So it is written; so it is done!"

"What's the word, Sofia?" Courtney asked her sister-in-law.

"*Idiota.*"

"Right," she said. Turning to her husband, she repeated the word. "*Idiota.*"

"Nice," Matthew retaliated. "Very nice."

"Play nice, children." Jeane chuckled as she returned to her chair, and Matthew shared a smile with Courtney before reaching around their daughter and touching her hand.

Reggie sighed as she leaned back against her chair and smiled at Reese. "Sometimes when we're all in one location together, it's kind of like this weird familial magnetic pull, and we all have power surges at the same time. Do you know what I mean?"

Reese chuckled. "I believe I do."

"THERE THEY ARE!" HANNAH exclaimed, and Reggie tapped the brake to slow the car before easing onto the shoulder of the road behind her brother's minivan.

"It doesn't look like they've had much luck yet," Reese said, pushing open the front passenger door.

She strolled up to the car where Damian and Eli pushed hard against the rear bumper while Matthew sat behind the wheel in hopes of steering it out. The grind of the spinning tires accentuated the problem as a shower of snow and ice sprayed them.

"Whoa, whoa!" Damian called out to Matthew who lifted his foot off the gas pedal. "We need more muscle. Why don't you let Reese slide behind the wheel, and you come back here and help us push."

Matthew cranked open the door and complied. "I'll bet it pains you to admit you need this impressive physique to accomplish anything, doesn't it, bro?"

"Just stand right here at the edge of the bumper. That's where the spray of snow will pelt you the hardest."

Reese chuckled as she slid into the car.

"Hannah and Regg, you stand back," Damian called as they took their positions behind the car. "Reese, put it into neutral and just keep control of the wheel."

She did as he'd instructed, but the car barely budged.

"Okay, okay, ease up!" Turning to his brothers, Damian suggested, "Let's spread out to the sides and see if we can rock this thing out of the rut around the back tire." As soon as they moved into place, he tapped the trunk three times. "Reese, we're going to try again."

She gripped the steering wheel tightly as the guys groaned in unison, working together to create a rocking motion that seemed to make some meager headway. Suddenly Reggie and Hannah rushed to the back of the car and pushed with all their might. Reese watched the crown of Hannah's dark, shiny hair bob in the rearview mirror. Finally Damian's Mercedes inched forward, and Reese cheered as the car moved all the way onto the shoulder.

"Honey, shift into park," Damian called out to her, and she waved her hand out the driver's-side window.

The next couple of moments turned into a blur. She meant to shift up into park, but instead she pulled down into drive, and the car lurched forward, bumped, and skidded slightly as she jammed on the brake. In the middle of the action, she heard a scream, and Eli threw himself to the mound of snow at the side of the road, writhing and howling.

"She ran over my foot!" he wailed. "She broke my foot!"

Reese threw the gearshift into park and dove from the car to find Matthew, Damian, and Reggie bent over him.

"I start training for the Puerto Rico Marathon in San Juan in a few weeks!"

"Eli, I'm so sorry!" she cried as he yelped in pain. Both hands clamped over her mouth, she continued to squeal. "I'm sorry, I'm sorry, I'm so sorry!"

Once the initial panic had settled, she rushed toward him and reached for his ankle.

"What are you doing!?" Eli cried.

"Let me get a look at your foot and see if anything is broken."

"Of course something is broken!" he screeched. "You just ran over my foot with four thousand pounds of car!"

Reese swallowed around the lump stuck at the center of her throat. "I'm so sorry, Eli. But I'm a doctor. Let me take a look."

"You just go over there," he answered. "I don't want you anywhere near me right now."

"Elijah!" Damian exclaimed.

"Dude," Matthew chastised him. "It was an accident, man."

"Well, I don't want to be the recipient of any more of her accidents just now," Eli insisted. "Just make her back away from me!"

She felt the sting of pure emotion behind her eyes and down her throat as she stood up and backed away. Reggie moved in and loosened the lace on Eli's boot.

"Don't feel bad, Reese," Hannah offered immediately from beside her. "It was definitely an accident. Uncle Eli didn't mean what he said."

Damian looked up at her, and Reese burst into tears the moment their eyes met. "I'm sorry," she mouthed.

He rose from the ground and marched straight to her. In that fraction of an instant, even though she knew the thought to be ridiculous, she wondered if he approached in anger. But the moment he reached her, he pulled Reese into an embrace and rocked her from side to side, smoothing her hair.

"I didn't mean to . . ."

"Of course you didn't," he reassured her. "It was an accident. We'll get him down to the hospital in Big Bear Lake and get an X-ray. He'll be fine."

After a moment, he let her go and kissed her head before returning to Eli's side.

"Mattie, let's help him into the back of the van and drive down the hill into town," Damian said. "Regg, you drive Reese and Hannah and follow us to the hospital. We can come back for my car later."

"No, I . . ." Reese began, pausing to wipe her dripping nose. "I can drive your car."

"You are in no shape to drive, Reese. We'll pick it up later."

She didn't have the energy to argue, so she simply turned and stalked toward the passenger side of the car.

As usual, Damian's cool head prevailed in a crisis. He took charge, told everyone what to do, and they all instinctively followed. Reese loved that about him, and she also knew it to be one of those qualities that made a brilliant neurosurgeon.

Once she'd climbed into the passenger seat, Damian jogged over and tapped on the window. She lowered it, and he leaned in and touched her arm.

"You okay?" he asked.

"Me?" she said on a bitter chuckle. "I'm just great. After lunch I'll look into which member of your family I can do in next."

Hannah laughed from the back seat, and Reggie let out a soft snicker while Damian kissed his finger and touched it to her lips.

"I'll see you in a few." He leaned in deeper and smiled at Reggie. "I'll call Mom. She can tell Sofia."

Sofia hadn't even entered Reese's frame of reference until that moment, and she groaned out loud. "Oh . . . no . . ."

"Take a few deep breaths. See you in town."

On the sixth day of Christmas,
Murphy's Law gave to me . . .

six ER visits,

five frozen thiiiings!

four yapping dogs,
three wrenched necks,
two mismatched gloves,
and a big rockin' Harry Winston ring.

6

"They took him down to X-ray," Damian told his mom over the phone. "It's pretty black and blue, and he's in a lot of pain, but it doesn't look like anything's broken . . . against all odds. He'll walk with a limp for a couple of days but no cast or crutches."

"I think your father's cane is still in the bedroom closet. Should we come to the hospital then?" she asked him.

"Not unless Sofia insists. But tread lightly when you tell her, huh, Mom? Reese is pretty shaken up, and a Puerto Rican tornado in her face isn't going to help."

"Well, sweetheart, it was an accident. Did you tell her you know it wasn't her fault?"

"I did," he replied with a smile. "But she still ran over your son's foot with a car."

His mom chuckled. "No one's going to blame her. You're sure your brother is going to be all right?"

"I'm pretty sure. I'll call you with an update, but I think we can get him back to the house and onto the sofa without further incident."

Reggie sat down in the chair next to him and smiled. "We live in hope."

Damian heard Sofia in the background, chattering in her version of fast-forward Spanglish. She must have heard Jeane ask if "his brother" would be all right.

"Okay, Mom. I'll call you later and let you know what's going on."

As soon as he disconnected the call, Reggie touched his arm and nodded in Reese's direction.

Reese stood at the window, gazing out, a long and serious expression on her face. As he got up from his chair, Hannah rounded the corner carrying a foam cup with a teabag string hanging over the edge. She offered it to Reese as Damian joined them.

"It's herbal," she said. "The nurse said it's good for calming your nerves."

Reese chuckled as she accepted the cup. "Thank you, Hannah. How old are you again?"

"Thirteen."

"Going on thirty," Reese told her with a grateful smile. "You're very sweet, especially considering the fact that I just ran over your uncle."

Without missing a beat, Hannah pointed out the obvious. "Not my whole uncle. Only one foot of him."

Damian laughed out loud.

"What's that? Like, 10 percent of my whole uncle?"

Reese giggled as she slipped her arm around the girl's shoulder and pulled her in close, taking a sip of tea. "Thank you, Hannah."

Matthew had just joined them in the waiting room to announce that Eli had been released when Sofia pushed through the glass doors like a mother bear in search of her missing cub.

"Where is he, *Domion*?"

It always tickled him the way she pronounced his name.

He headed straight toward her. "Everything is fine, Sof. He's just been released, and we're taking him back to the house."

"I want to see him. Where *iss* he?"

"Come on," Matthew told her. "I'm headed back there now."

As she passed Reese, Sofia narrowed her eyes and glared at her. Damian slipped his arm around Reese's shoulder and tucked her in close. "Let's go back to the house."

"The car," she muttered. "If it snows again today, we might never get it out."

"Right." He looked to Reggie and asked, "Can you drop us at my car?"

"Sure thing. Are you going with us, Hannah?"

She nodded happily and jogged after them.

"Why don't you ride shotgun with Regg," Damian told Hannah. "Reese and I will get in back."

Once they settled into the car, Damian opened his arms to Reese, and she fell into them. A few minutes passed before he felt her body shake and realized she'd been crying. Reggie must have noticed it in the rearview mirror, because she commented to Hannah, "Well, that was an eventful morning, wasn't it?"

Hannah chuckled. "Word!"

"Elijah has always had two left feet," she said. Then, glancing into the mirror, she said, "Reese, one time he walked right up behind one of the wild burros that roam around up here in the spring. That thing must have kicked him ten yards! Remember that, Damian?"

Damian laughed, more for Reese's benefit than at the recollection. Eli's ribs had been bruised for a month.

"There are wild burros up here?" Hannah exclaimed. "Like . . . donkeys?"

"Oh yeah," Reggie told her. "The rumor is that they escaped or were left behind by miners. But they walk around in small herds, and they'll mosey right up to your front door."

"Remember when they demolished Mrs. Hillsborough's strawberry patch?" Damian piped up.

"Oh, she was so mad," Reggie cried. "She chased the whole herd of them down the road with a shovel."

Reese giggled, and Damian felt the rumble of it against his chest. Relief surged through him, and he kissed the top of her head, breathing in the citrus scent of her shampoo.

"Can we see them?" Hannah asked.

"They're harder to find in the winter months," Reggie told her.

"A few years back they rounded up about ninety of them," Damian said, "relocating them to an adoption program in Ridgecrest. There are a couple of herds still roaming around, but they tend to move to the lower elevations when the snow falls."

Hannah groaned in disappointment. "I want to see them."

"Then you'll have to come back again in the spring," Reggie suggested with a smile.

Hannah seized the opportunity. "Maybe I could come and visit Reese and Uncle Damian for a while over summer break. After they get married and everything. Could I, Uncle Damian?"

"We'll have to talk to your mom and dad about that," he replied.

Hannah's obvious connection to Reese came as no real surprise to Damian. He'd seen her with a few of her patients in the time that he'd known her, and kids just seemed to respond to her in profound and immediate ways. When he'd initially realized the depth of his feelings for her, he'd imagined what a wonderful mother she would make one day, knowing he only had the most remote chance of witnessing that first hand. When Reese had confessed she'd fallen in love with him as well, Damian had been astonished, wondering how such a perfect and amazing woman could have settled for the likes of him.

"Are you joking?" she said when he revealed his fears. "I can't believe you would want to be with *me*! I'm a total mess, and you're . . . perfect."

Time had exposed those imperfections in both of them, but even their shortcomings fit together well.

"Like pieces of a puzzle," Reese had once observed, and the conclusion had stayed with him. Since she'd come into his life, Damian did feel a bit like a finished jigsaw puzzle.

Reese squirmed a little closer, and he smiled and wrapped his arms tightly around her.

"I love you," he whispered into her ear, and she sighed.

BY EARLY AFTERNOON, THINGS seemed almost right in the world again, although Reese didn't want to take anything for granted. Paul Sr. moved the plump loveseat close to the massive window looking out over the backyard, and Jeane helped Eli get settled into it with a cup of hot chocolate, a bowl of her traditional trail mix, and a crocheted red blanket he said smelled of Christmas. Damian queued up a few holiday CDs on the stereo, and Eli seemed unexpectedly content to watch the action through the window. To the soundtrack of Judy Garland's "Have Yourself a Merry Little Christmas," Matthew and several of the kids flew down the hill on inner tubes and sleds.

Reese slipped into her coat and tugged on a pair of slightly too small gloves she'd found in the mudroom, and she stepped out the front door and closed it behind her. The snow had let up for the time being, and the sky had turned dark gray as the temperature plummeted. She closed her eyes and lifted her face, sharply breathing in the brisk air.

In with the good air, out with the bad.

After half a dozen of those, she felt invigorated again. She opened her eyes and sighed before she processed the bizarre sight before her. When clarity came to rest on her, she gasped.

Just twenty feet away from her—right in the middle of the snow-drifted yard—stood a huge buck, his massive antlers held high and his black-brown eyes perfectly round and fixed squarely on her smaller blue ones.

He had a meaningful sort of expression on his deer face, and he held her gaze so tightly she couldn't possibly squirm out of it. She wasn't entirely sure she wanted to.

"Hi," she uttered, and it took all of the breath she had.

The deer didn't even blink. He just stood there, staring at her, conveying some important secret message she couldn't quite understand.

"Are you okay?" she asked him. Strangely, Reese waited, as if she expected him to speak up and tell her the reason for his return visit. When he didn't respond, or move a muscle, she willed herself to breathe again before telling him, "I'm really sorry about the car hitting you." With a chuckle she added, "You wouldn't believe how many times I've said those words since we first met. It seems like I have something to apologize for every couple of hours."

The buck's chest twitched, and he jerked his tall antlers, but he remained planted in his spot, his saucer eyes alert and fixed on her.

"Well, you look strong now," she said softly. "Much better than when we first met. And I'm so glad. I wish you could tell me if you need something because I'd be happy to get it for you."

And with that he bobbed his massive head at her, breaking the connection between them. Then he turned and dashed way.

It took Reese several minutes to pull herself together after the encounter. Finally she took a couple more cleansing breaths and pushed the front door open.

Reggie and Sofia sat on barstools at the island chopping and dicing while Jeane tended to an enormous pot on the stove, and Damian and Paul unpacked the final box of ornaments and hung them on the massive Christmas tree.

"Hey, Mom," Eli called out over Bing Crosby's rendition of "Let it Snow, Let it Snow." "Are there any more sugar cookies?"

Jeane flashed a smile. "Yes, honey. Give me one minute and I'll get them."

"I'll do it," Reese said as she removed her coat and gloves.

Jeane handed her a sealed canister, followed by a paper plate covered in poinsettias and a matching napkin. "Just give him a couple," she said softly. "If he gets his hand on the container, they'll disappear."

Reese carefully chose a Christmas tree covered in green sprinkles and a red glittery bell, and she placed them on the small plate. She took a deep cleansing breath before heading across the great room toward Eli.

He looked up at her strangely before reaching for the cookies. Once he'd taken them, she just stood there for a moment, weighing out the best way to speak her mind. Eli gave her a "What do you want?" look, and she smiled.

"Eli . . ." She sat down on the edge of the nearby table and tried again. "Eli, I just wanted to say how sorry I am."

"Yeah. I know."

"I keep replaying that moment in my mind, and I just . . . can't . . ."

"I know the feeling."

"It was just . . . horrible," she said, and she gingerly reached out and touched his hand. "I'm so sorry."

"I get it, Reese," he replied. "I shouldn't have yelled at you like that, but the pain . . ."

"I know. I know."

". . . I was just out of my mind with it, you know?"

"Yes! I know. And I'm so sorry."

"Will you do me one favor?" he asked her.

"Anything. Do you want more hot chocolate?"

Eli snickered and shook his head. "No."

"What then?"

"It was an accident."

"Yes! It was."

"And you're sorry, we've established that."

"So sorry," she reiterated.

"So it's done, and you're forgiven."

"Really?"

"Yes. So please stop apologizing."

Reese gazed at him as relief surged through her. "Really?"

"Yes. Stop now."

She grinned and zipped her lip with a quick motion. After a moment she touched his hand again. "Thank you." Eli nodded, and she stood up. "Okay. I'm going to find out my chopping duties for the soup."

Just as she began to walk away, he added, "Oh. About that hot chocolate . . ."

Reese giggled. "Marshmallows?"

"The little ones."

It was the most wonderful cup of hot chocolate Reese had ever prepared in her life—not that she'd made very many of them.

As she placed the marshmallows, Damian caught her eye from across the room. She wondered if she detected relief from him as well. It couldn't have been easy for him, being so deeply entrenched in his Palmer family ties, to think of future Christmases and Thanksgivings where his younger brother and his wife could hardly look at one another.

She quickly looked at Sofia and thought, *Now she might prove to be a completely different mountain to climb.*

But when Sofia looked up at her, instead of disdain, she saw acceptance in her striking dark eyes. When she smiled at Reese, a flood of deliverance crashed over her heart in a tall wave.

After she handed the cup to Eli, Reese moved to the window and stood next to Damian as they surveyed the festivities on the other side. Flurries of snow had begun to fall again, and the distant squeals of the children playing soothed her heart somehow.

"Yeahhhh!" P.J. exclaimed as his inner tube took up speed over the slope of the hill.

Sarah and Ezekiel followed him, sharing one large sled. Matthew tailed them, shouting like a child as the inner tube he rode pitched to one side. At the top of the hill, Abigail and Jeremy encased in puffy little coats, gloves, and ear muffs looked like festive sausages building a short, stout snowman. Reese and Damian chuckled in perfect harmony when Frosty's misshapen head rolled off his round body.

"I think they need some help," Damian commented. "Are you game?"

"You get the coats."

But just as they turned to head outside, Hannah appeared behind them.

"We're headed out to help the little ones with their snowman," Reese told her. "Want to come too?"

Something in Hannah's greenish eyes stopped Reese in her tracks.

"Could I talk to you a minute?" the girl asked her. "Just us?"

Reese raked her fingers through Hannah's chestnut hair. "Of course."

She looked to Damian, and he nodded. "I'll meet you out there."

Following Hannah's lead, the two of them filed past the Christmas tree and down the hall in silence. When she reached the closed door to the bedroom Reese had shared with Reggie, Hannah asked her, "Is this your room?"

"Yeah," she said with a nod. "Let's go in."

Once they'd stepped inside, Hannah shut the door behind them, double-checking to make sure it had latched. Reese sat on the corner of the bed and waited, trying to imagine what might come next.

Hannah turned around, but she made no move from the door. Her eyes misted over almost immediately, her nose reddening as she angled her head down until her copper-brown hair nearly covered her face.

"Hannah. What's going on?"

When she finally raised her head again, tears streamed down both cheeks.

"Come on," she said, patting the mattress beside her. "Sit down and tell me what's going on."

Hannah took only two steps forward and she froze to the spot, digging the toe of what looked like combat boots into the thick sage carpet.

"I can't help if you don't talk to me."

After another moment of heated silence, Hannah tugged on her oversized chambray shirt and slid one arm out of it. Reese's eyebrow twitched as she tossed the shirt to the floor and lifted the black knit tank underneath.

"You're a doctor, right?"

Reese nodded, and without another word, Hannah turned around so Reese had full view of her bare back where a large and vivid tattoo peered back at her from just below Hannah's small waist. Angel's wings with a heart in the middle and a halo over the top glowed in vivid color.

On the seventh day of Christmas,
Murphy's Law gave to me . . .

seven backs a-blazing,
six ER visits,

five frozen thiiiings!

four yapping dogs,
three wrenched necks,
two mismatched gloves,
and a big rockin' Harry Winston ring.

7

"Oh, Hannah, . . . Sweetie, what did you do?"

The base of the left wing radiated with red, and Hannah reached back and touched it. "I think something's wrong," she said, sniffling.

"Yes," Reese replied. "Come here."

Hannah clutched the front of her tank shirt to cover her as she approached. "We have to be really quiet because my mom is taking a nap just across the hall, okay?"

"Stand right here," Reese told her, and she placed her hand on her arm and guided her. "Turn around so I can get a closer look."

Her heart pounded hard as she realized what a terrible infection had begun to take hold, and Hannah's muffled sobs punctuated the seriousness of it.

"Honey," she said, nudging her around to face her. "Do your parents know you got this tattoo?"

"N-no."

"How long ago did you get it?"

"Last week."

"And when did it start bothering you?"

"It's been . . . you know . . . sore. But it didn't start really hurting until a couple of hours ago. Then I went in the bathroom and looked in the mirror, and I could see my skin is really red, and when I touched it, I could hardly stand it."

"Okay. Well, the first thing we need to do is tell your mom and da—"

"No!" she cried, hopping backward. "No, Reese, please. They'll kill me. I can't tell them. Can't you just put something on it or something? You're a doctor."

"Yes, I am, sweetie. And I'll help you, but if you don't tell your parents, I'm going to."

"No, you *caaan't*," she insisted.

"Talk to them, Hannah."

"Can't you just fix me up, and then I'll tell them after Christmas? It's going to ruin the whole thing."

"What whole thing?"

She jerked her head down again, letting her wavy hair fall across her face.

"Hannah."

"My parents haven't been getting along very well," she muttered, and Reese's heart jumped over the next few beats. "But they've been nicer to each other since we came on this trip. I don't want to do anything to mess that up."

Reese sighed, and she rubbed Hannah's arm warmly.

"I heard them fighting. Daddy's mad at Mom for taking a job and being away from us kids, and my mom says she wouldn't have had to take a job if Daddy made enough money to support us kids."

Sadness turned sour at the back of her throat, and Reese tugged Hannah into a hug. "I'm so sorry, honey. Your mom and dad never meant for you to hear that."

"Yeah, but I did."

"Yes. But it has nothing to do with their love for you," she explained, and Hannah sat down next to her on the bed, holding her knit shirt close over her chest. "Sometimes grown-ups just have to argue a little to make their way toward working something out."

"I bet you and Uncle Damian don't argue."

Reese clucked out a chuckle. "Oh, we argue, honey."

Hannah shifted gears. "Couldn't I just wait until after Christmas to tell my mom and dad?"

"I'm afraid not." The girl's disappointment rang through her silence. "Here's what we're going to do. I'm going to go and ask Grandma Jeane for a first-aid kit. We'll start by treating the infection and getting this cleaned up. Then you're going to go in there, take your mom and dad aside, and show them your back. All right?"

She nodded unconvincingly.

"Hannah, I'm very serious about this. You're thirteen years old. This is way too important to keep from your parents."

The young teenager kicked the carpet with the toe of her boot and lifted one shoulder in a hopeless little shrug.

"And how does a thirteen-year-old get inked anyway? Who did this, Hannah?"

"My friend Brittany's brother, Buddy. He's a tattoo artist." As an afterthought, she added, "I'm fourteen next month."

Reese swallowed the angry sentiment toward some random villain named *Buddy*. "I'll go and see about some first-aid supplies. You wait right here."

Relief washed over her when she returned to the kitchen to find Jeane at the stove alone, her helpers scattered. Reese approached and stood close to her.

"Jeane," she said softly. "Do you have a first-aid kit?"

"Are you hurt?" she asked.

"No. I'm fine. I'm just looking for some antiseptic like there might be in a first-aid kit."

"Under the sink in the master bathroom, dear. Help yourself."

Reese found the bright red metal box tucked to the side of the cabinet, consoled with the sheer size of it. The substantial box surely held what she needed.

She carried it to the bedroom where Hannah waited on the bed just where she'd left her.

"Did you tell?" she asked.

"No. Telling is your job. One thing at a time." Reese unclamped the box and lifted it open. The first thing she noticed was an array of bandages and a large tube of Neosporin. "Oh, this looks really good. It has everything we need for the time being." After tearing a corner of the plastic bag that held a supply of cotton gauze, she placed her hand on the reddened skin to the side of the ink. As expected, it radiated an unnatural amount of body heat.

"It's hot, right?" Hannah said.

"Yes, it is. You know, what you did was very dangerous," Reese told her as she cleaned the infected area. "And your friend's brother was extremely irresponsible to help you do it."

"He does it all the time."

"To adults," she pointed out, and Hannah jerked from her touch. "Oooh, sorry. I know that's tender. Anyway, I want you to promise me you're never going to do anything like this again until you're old enough to *legally* decide for yourself. And even then, I want you to give it some serious thought, Hannah. This is no small thing."

"Okay," she agreed, albeit with a grudge.

"You promise."

"I promise."

"After you talk to your mom and dad, I want to drive you back into town to the hospital."

"What? No!"

"Yes. I don't have my prescription pad with me, so we'll need them to check you out and write you a script for an antibiotic."

"Reese, nooo. Please."

"There's no please or thank-you about it, honey. We need to do this right."

"But I don't want to!"

So much for being quiet, Reese thought just as a knock sounded at the door.

"Hannah?"

Before they could even react, the bedroom door slipped open, and Hannah's mother poked her head inside.

"Hannah?" Courtney exclaimed, but her eyes were fixed on Reese. "What's going on here? What's that on my daughter's back?!"

"Mom, calm down, I—"

"Don't tell me to calm down, young lady," she said as she stalked into the room. "What's going on here? Where's your father? *Matthew!*"

"DR. PLUNDERERS."

Reese popped up from her chair and hurried toward Rick Dalton, the emergency room attending physician who had examined Hannah.

"Dr. Dalton. How's she doing?"

"Her mother's with her, and the nurse is reviewing the care procedures. You were right to hold off on the Neosporin. I've written a script for an oral antibiotic, and she's going to keep the tatt clean and dry for a couple of days before applying antiseptics."

"Thank you so much, Dr. Dalton."

He grinned at her and pushed the glasses up the bridge of his long nose. "Didn't I see you here earlier today, Doctor?"

Reese chuckled. "Yeah. That was for my fiance's brother. Hannah is his niece."

Arching one of his bushy eyebrows, he asked, "Are you sure you want to marry into this family? Two emergency room visits in one day. Are they safe?"

"I think they're wondering that very thing about me." Rather than explain, she simply thanked him and hurried down the hall.

Damian stood outside the curtained cubicle when she reached it, and Reese heard Courtney and Matthew grilling Hannah about her tattoo. She slid her arm around Damian's waist as they waited.

"This is so not cool, Hannah," Matthew said. "You're way too young for a tattoo. What made you pull a stunt like this?"

"Well, I think that's obvious, don't you?" Courtney snapped.

"If it was obvious, I wouldn't have asked."

Reese pinched the sleeve of Damian's coat and nodded toward the nurse's desk. He followed her out of earshot, and they found a couple of chairs nearby.

"Mattie and Court have always been like the perfect couple," he said, shaking his head. "I've never heard them bickering like this."

"Hannah said they've been arguing a lot at home."

"She did?" The concern showed on Damian's face, and a storm brewed in his eyes. "That really comes as a surprise."

"I know."

"I don't know what to do for them."

"It's not up to you, Damie," she told him with a stroke to his hand. "It's something they have to work out as a family on their own."

"I'm really sorry, Reese."

She smiled. "For what?"

"I thought I was bringing you up here for this idyllic Palmer family Christmas," he said. "It's turned into a bad episode of *Meet the Parents* times ten."

"Well, it would have been much more joyful if I hadn't run over your brother."

Damian snickered. "Or somehow made my sister-in-law think you'd taken some ink and a needle to her thirteen-year-old's pink skin!"

Reese leaned into Damian's shoulder and chuckled. "I guess Joss doesn't seem so strange to you now, does she?"

"Oh, I wouldn't go that far."

She playfully smacked his arm just before glancing down the hall as Hannah and her parents approached.

Standing up, Reese asked Hannah, "How are you doing, honey?"

"I'm okay, but I'm grounded for life."

"Life," Damian repeated. "I remember your father serving out that sentence a time or two. There was this one time, Hannah, when your dad—"

"All right, that's enough," Matthew interrupted, and he threw a chokehold around Damian's neck and dragged him along down the hall toward the door.

"Wait!" Hannah cried as she ran behind them. "Tell me what Daddy did."

Reese and Courtney followed, silent until they reached the glass doors.

"I need to thank you," Courtney said with her hand on Reese's arm. "I don't know what would have happened to her if she hadn't come to you. There's no telling how long she might have hidden it from us."

"When I saw it, I wanted to find that tattoo artist and give him a tonsillectomy on the house," she joked, and Courtney laughed.

"If you get a postcard from my prison cell after we get home, you'll know my effort to control myself was an epic fail."

"Seriously, I hope you plan to file charges."

"Matthew and I will talk about it and decide how to go about it, but he's certainly not going to escape consequences. I just thank the Lord that Hannah's been seen by two doctors now, and she's going to be fine."

Reese buttoned her coat as they passed through the breezeway and stepped outside. The occasional flurries had progressed into a full-fledged snowfall, and she surmised that more than an inch of new powder had fallen in the couple of hours since they'd rushed through those hospital doors.

"Don't you have a hat and gloves with you?" Courtney asked as they hurried toward the car.

"I left my hat back at the house in the rush to leave," she replied. "But I threw away those horrible gloves I brought along."

"Jeane has a chest full of scarves, gloves, and hats out in the mudroom. We might even find some snow boots that aren't complete eyesores. We can hit that for you when we get back. It will be like a condensed shopping trip."

Reese laughed. "Sounds like a plan."

By the time the five of them returned to the house, the sun had descended for the day. Despite the falling snow, the midnight blue night sky twinkled with countless silver stars, and the Christmas lights framing the Palmer house completed the picture.

"It looks like the front of a Christmas card," Reese said as they pulled down the long driveway.

Hannah reached the front door first, and the savory scent of vegetable beef soup wafted on the winter breeze to greet them as they filed up the sidewalk behind her. Inside, a fire roared in the huge stone fireplace, and the lights on the massive Christmas tree reflected off the windows behind the line of tables set with burning candles, mismatched stone bowls, and baskets of fragrant warm rolls wrapped in festive red-and-green linen napkins.

"Perfect timing!" Jeane exclaimed. "Hang up your coats and have a seat. Dinner's on the table."

Paul Sr. stood at one end of the table and Jeane sat down at the other end, both of them using large stainless steel ladles to fill each bowl with chunky vegetable beef soup that looked more like stew than soup.

"Wait," Jeane called to Ezekiel at the middle of the table as he dipped his spoon into the bowl set before him. "Let Grandpop say the blessing first."

He pushed the spoon into the bowl and waited obediently.

With the last of the bowls filled, Paul sat down. "Father God," he said, and everyone around the table, from the youngest to the eldest, bowed their heads. "The Palmers are one grateful family, but never more so than when we sit together, all of us around one table. We ask that You bestow your blessings upon each of us here with safety, good health, and peace, and we ask that You bless the food we eat as well as the hands of its preparers. In Jesus' holy name we pray. Amen."

As the amens resounded all around, Reese couldn't help tacking on a silent thanks of her own. She'd always wondered what it must be like to be part of what her brother Hersch called "a *Normal Rockwell*" type of family with actual meat and dairy products on the dinner table, Christian prayers exchanged before the meal, and packages under the tree wrapped in shiny foil and crinkled ribbons rather than plain brown paper and undyed twine.

Please don't let me mess this up, she prayed.

"Grandmom, when are we making the birthday cake?" young Abigail asked, and Reese wondered whose birthday they planned to celebrate.

"You know what, Abigail," Jeane replied. "I heard about this wonderful bakery in the village, and I got one from them there."

"Then they made it for us? Where is it?"

A sudden low growl punctuated Paco's arrival at Reese's feet, and she glanced down to find the dog standing next to her chair. The moment their eyes met, he began to bark and spit at her.

"Paco, can it!" Matthew exclaimed, and the dog backed away.

"It's in the refrigerator out in the laundry room," Jeane continued. "Why don't you kids have a look after dinner, and if you don't like it, then we'll have to make a different one."

"Can I go now?" her younger brother asked. "I want to see Jesus' birthday cake."

Reese's heart squeezed.

"It's a family tradition from when we were all little kids," Damian said as he leaned close to her. "Our dessert on Christmas Eve is always a birthday cake for Jesus."

Reese chewed the corner of her lip in an effort to hold back the tears that threatened to crest over the top of her emotions.

A birthday cake for Jesus.

She'd never even heard of such a thing, but what a beautiful tradition.

"What kind is it?" Sarah asked.

"It's Grandpop's favorite this year," Jeane told them.

"Red velvet!" Zeke piped up.

His grandfather nodded and raised his hand, allowing Zeke to smack it in a high-five.

"With cream-cheese icing," Jeane said. "And chocolate sprinkles all around the sides."

"We gotta see!" Jeremy cried, and he flew from his chair.

Once Jeane gave her blessing, Sarah, Zeke, and Abigail followed on his heels.

The children thundered into the laundry room, banging the door against the wall behind it. As the adults and teens left behind reacted to the children's squeals of joy, Reese felt a sudden warmth hit her ankle.

Glancing down at the floor, she discovered Paco had seized the opportunity to return, and while poised at her feet, the dog lifted his leg in an expression of how he truly felt about her.

On the eighth day of Christmas,
Murphy's Law gave to me . . .

eight geese a-roasting,
seven backs a-blazing,
six ER visits,

five frozen thiiiings!

four yapping dogs,
three wrenched necks,
two mismatched gloves,
and a big rockin' Harry Winston ring.

8

"Just grab the bean firmly between your thumb and index finger. Now twist the tip downward toward its seam in a quick, even motion."

Reese followed Jeane's instructions to the letter, and the tip of the bean gave a firm, crisp *snap!*

"Perfect!" Jeane said. "Now do the other end of the bean." She rubbed Reese's shoulder before moving on to stand behind Reggie. "Regina, don't go so quickly that you toss the tips without looking. You've got more of them on the floor than in the bag."

"I'm doing just what you told me," she objected. "Snap-toss-snap-toss."

"Do I need to update it for you?" Jeane countered. "Snap-toss *in the bag*."

Reese tried to keep up with the rhythm of the snap-toss-snap-toss song, but she hadn't spent much time around string beans. Her mother rarely prepared them, and when she did, Reese hadn't been asked to *snap* anything, and aside from *tossing* a prepared bag of them into the microwave in the break room at the hospital, there hadn't been much of that either.

Hannah smiled at her from across the island. "It takes a lot of food to feed our family. We're like a small country or something."

"I don't want to hear you complaining over there," Sofia teased her. "It's the wives . . ." She paused and glanced at Reese. ". . . and the girlfriends who are responsible for the *side deeshes*. You could be outside in the snow with the other children and your *grandpapi*."

"How many thousands of string beans do we need?" Courtney asked. "Haven't we been at this long enough to feed a village?"

"You know the drill," Jeane retorted. "Each boy gets to choose one side dish, and all of the women work together to make them." Reese grinned as she imagined her own mother's reaction to such an antifeminist statement. "And it's your husband who chose string beans with almonds and thyme, missy, so get to snapping. You're nearly finished."

Courtney chuckled as she stepped up the pace.

"What did Damian choose?" Reese asked.

"The same as always," Sofia chimed in, and the other women surrounding Reese sang along in four-part harmony. *"Chest-nut stuf-fing."*

She didn't even know Damian liked chestnuts.

"Jeane's chestnut stuffing is to die for," Courtney told her.

"She doesn't put it inside the goose. She makes it in this giant glass dish," Hannah said, "and she bakes the goose with all this fruit and stuff instead."

"Goose?"

"That's our traditional Christmas Eve meal," Jeane explained as she lifted the massive colander filled with cleaned string beans, set it into the deep stainless steel sink, and turned on the cold water.

"What's the matter?" Hannah asked when she noticed Reese's expression. "You don't like goose?"

"I have no idea," she admitted with a grin. "I've never met one."

"Just wait until you find out what you've been missing!" the young girl exclaimed. "Grandmom's goose is the best in the world."

"One son down," Jeane announced as she shut off the water. "Next son is up. Elijah has chosen candied sweet potatoes. Let's get started skinning those sweet potatoes."

Sofia and Courtney groaned, but Hannah hopped up from her chair and rounded the island, hugging Jeane around the neck. "Little marshmallows, right Grandmom?"

"Of course."

"You're going to love her candied sweet potatoes, Reese."

"Shall we stop and have some hot tea and cookies before we start them?" Jeane asked, and everyone, including Reese, chimed in their agreement.

They scattered for a short break, and Reese took her cup of Darjeeling and a sugar cookie with her to the large picture window beyond the Christmas tree in hopes of getting a look at Damian and the boys out in the snow. When she spotted movement off to the side of the house, she squinted to get a closer look.

Reese drew in a sharp breath when her line of sight landed on a large deer standing just beyond the woods at the edge of the Palmers' property. She wondered if she'd imagined the eye contact between them just as the buck reared its head and lifted its tall antlers, staring straight at her with wide, bright eyes.

"What does a deer eat?" she asked as she flew past the women and into the kitchen. "Do they like carrots, like a horse?"

"I believe they do," Jeane said, reeling around to watch Reese speed past her. "I believe they like sweet potatoes too. There's a sack of them in the pantry on the—"

Reese remembered seeing them. She grabbed several carrots from the counter, and then found two misshapen sweet potatoes in the netted bag on the pantry shelf. Snagging her coat on the way, she dashed out the side door and hurried around the back of the house.

Panting for breath, she skidded to a stop when she saw it. She couldn't be sure, but something told her she'd looked into those very same eyes—black and glassy, outlined in unique white fur circles— at least once before.

"Hi," she said, and her voice sounded gravelly as she spoke. "I'm Reese. You might remember me, right?"

The deer didn't even blink. He just kept his sight fixed on her. She noticed his back leg trembling, no doubt in preparation for quick flight.

"Reese, what are—"

"Shh!" She stopped Damian in his tracks. "Do you see him?"

He moved cautiously toward her and came to a silent stop at her side. Finally, "I see him," he whispered. "What are you doing?"

"I think he's hungry."

Damian snickered. "Baby, the chances of this deer being the one from the other night—"

"It's him, Damie. I know it. Do you think he'll let me get any closer?"

"I doubt it."

Reese thought it over for a moment before giving the buck a timid smile. "I feel really bad about what happened," she told him, and she took one step forward. "It's not that I think food will make up for everything, mind you. But I'm pretty sure it couldn't hurt."

"Uncle Damian, is that one of Santa's reindeer?" Jeremy cried as he rounded the corner of the house. Reese shushed him sweetly.

"Don't scare him, okay, sweetie?"

"Okay," he said, and Damian picked him up. "It's not Rudolph," the little boy whispered, "because he's got a regular nose. Maybe it's Blitzen!"

"I don't know, buddy."

Reese took another step forward. The buck quaked slightly, but he didn't bolt.

"I thought maybe you'd like some carrots," she said and took one more step. "I'm hoping you like sweet potatoes too. I've got a couple of those here."

Before her foot touched the ground again, the deer backed up and blinked at her.

"Okay, okay," she said with her hands raised. "I won't come any closer. I'll just toss you a carrot. Okay?"

She pitched one of the carrots toward the animal, and it landed a foot or so from its front hooves. Instead of sniffing the offering the way she expected, the buck simply turned and bounded away into the woods, its fluffy white tail standing erect, an unmistakable limp as he ran.

"That's him!" Reese cried, and she grabbed Damian's free arm and shook it. "Did you see him limp as he ran away? That's him, Damie." After a moment she tossed the rest of the vegetables, and they landed near the carrot she'd offered the deer. "Maybe he'll come back if we all go inside."

"I gotta go tell the other kids!" Jeremy cried, and he nearly leaped out of Damian's arms.

Reese and Damian clasped their hands together and meandered around the house behind him.

"My brothers and P.J. went sledding up the road. I came back for the little ones. Do you mind if I join them up there?"

"Not at all," she replied. "The womenfolk are busy preparing the Christmas Eve dinner anyway."

Damian chuckled. "I can't come to grips with my pediatrician fiancée as one of the womenfolk. It's just too *Doctor Quinn, Medicine Woman*."

"You like Jane Seymour," she reminded him with a giggle.

"Yes. Yes, I do."

"So why don't you go off and chop some wood and ride some sleds while we stay behind and rustle up some grub."

Damian laughed and planted a kiss on her. "See you later, Jane."

Once inside, Reese found the next segment of the food preparation triathlon already in gear. Hannah, Sofia, Reggie, and Courtney had resumed their places around the island while Jeane stood over the sink rinsing the beans they'd prepared.

"How can I help?" Reese asked.

"You can put away the lemon and creamer while I baste the bird."

Reese happily picked up the condiments and headed for the refrigerator. Jeane opened the oven door and pulled out the rack, removing a tent of aluminum foil. Reese's eyes bulged open at the disconcerting sight before her: *A fat, headless goose sitting naked in a large, shallow pot.*

Its partially raw flesh looked strangely acne ridden. An epiphany crested on the fringe of her suddenly numb, vacant thoughts; and, in that instant, Reese knew where the term "goose flesh" had originated.

"Meet Gerard," Hannah said as she stepped up beside her. "Our Christmas Eve dinner."

A decade or more of Tofurkey-laden holiday tables flashed across her mind, and an operatic reminder of parental monologues extoling the humanitarian virtues of veganism chimed in echoes throughout her brain . . . all while Blitzen limped around outside and Gerard sat there in that pot, still and lifeless, his head chopped off and his little webbed feet glaringly absent from his light golden brown torso.

A wave of nausea crashed over Reese, and cold perspiration erupted all over her body.

"Reese?" Hannah asked her. "Are you . . . all right?"

The room began to spin, and it felt as though she'd been socked in the stomach really, really hard.

By the time she realized what might occur, she had to gag back the acidic liquid on the rise in her throat, and she covered her mouth with both hands. In a frantic effort not to hurl everything she'd consumed for the last two days over naked, half-baked Gerard, she spun around and threw herself over the edge of the sink and spewed into it.

Unfortunately, her short-lived relief capsized and fell, the gasps of everyone around her echoing in her thrumming ears.

"*Ay caramba!* Did she just *vahmeet* on the string beans?"

REESE HADN'T SAID A word in the entire fifteen minutes that had passed since Damian found her on the front porch. Every time he tried to inquire about her obvious distress, she simply held up her hand, shook her head, and lowered her face over the side of the icy railing.

"Come on," he prodded, wrapping his arms around her. "What's going on?"

"Puke," she finally muttered. At least he thought that's what she said.

"You feel sick? You're going to throw up?"

She shook her head, then nodded on second thought, then shook her head again.

"Reese. Help me out here. Are you feeling sick?"

"Hey, bro," Eli called from the side yard. "We're making another run down the hill. You in or what?"

"So much for his sore foot, right?" Damian commented. "I'm out," he shouted, waving one arm at his brother. "Are you sick?" he repeated softly to Reese.

"Yes," she managed before leaning over the railing again, her glossy blonde hair falling down around her face.

"Can I get you something?"

She shook her head in frantic swipes before suddenly gasping and popping upright in front of him. "Unless . . . Can we go into town and buy a whole lot of string beans?"

"You . . . want string beans?"

"Well, no," she said with a soft shrug. "I mean, they're not for me. I don't really care for string beans, if you want to know the truth. But your brother Matthew really does, and that's what he picked for his side dish and . . . Why don't I know how much you love chestnuts?"

That one left him reeling a little. "Pardon?"

"Oh. Sorry. Your mom told me you choose chestnut stuffing every year as your side dish, and I didn't even know you liked chestnuts. My mom has a recipe for roasted chestnuts. I could try and make it for you."

"Reese."

"Oh. And Eli picked candied sweet potatoes with little miniature marshmallows on them, and then Matthew chose string beans, and we spent two hours snapping and tossing and snapping and tossing—"

"Baby."

"And then I saw the goose," she cried, her blue eyes glistening, round and shiny as freshly packed snowballs. "You know?"

He leaned forward and put his hands on both of her shoulders. "Not really," he told her. "No."

"The goose, Damian! The goose!"

"The one we're having for—" And it dawned like a floodlight ignited over the yard. "Ohhh. You saw the goose in the oven?"

She nodded slowly.

"And it made you feel kind of sick."

Faster nodding . . . wider eyes . . .

"And . . . the . . . string beans?"

"Yes!" she replied with insistence that lost him, and Damian just couldn't translate.

"Yes," he repeated.

"I threw up."

"Because of the goose."

"Yes."

"Oh. Are you—"

"On the string beans."

Okay. It's coming together now.

"Oh!" he exclaimed. "You . . . threw up *on the string beans?*"

Reese simply nodded frantically as tears popped into her eyes and streamed down both cheeks. He tugged her into an embrace and held her there, and she finally cried out into the lapel of his coat. "I puked all over Matthew's string beans!"

Damian tried to hold it back; he really did. But the laughter sputtered out of him until Reese hauled off and socked him in the arm.

"Stop it."

"Sorry."

She pulled back and gazed into his eyes with raw emotion brimming in hers. "That's why we have to get our hands on a whole bushelful of string beans, cleaned and ready to be boiled. Or grilled. Or whatever your mom does to them when she adds the . . . something. Thyme and almonds?"

"Steamed. She steams them. Okay. I see."

"Can we? Can we go and get some string beans, Damie?"

"What, now?" he asked.

"C'mon," she replied, yanking on his arm. "Let's go."

"Where are you going?" They both turned to find Damian's mom standing in the open doorway. "Are you feeling better, dear?"

Reese blinked a new stream of tears down her face and shook her head. "Not really, Jeane. I feel just awful about the string beans. But we're going into town to see if we can find replacement beans. Maybe Matthew won't have to know."

"Oh," Jeane said sweetly, and she cocked her head to the side. "I'm afraid he already knows."

"They told him?"

Reese groaned and spun around on her heel, shielding her face with both hands.

"Things like this happen," his mom reassured her as she pulled on Reese's arm gently. "Hannah said it was Gerard that made you so sick?"

She groaned again and looked to Damian. "He had a . . . *name*, Damian!"

"Baby, the goose gets a name every year. It's just a silly thing we do. It doesn't mean—"

"That it was once alive?" she interrupted, almost whispering through clenched teeth. "That it didn't have a face before his head was *chopped off*?"

"I'm surprised you're this squeamish," Jeane said. "You being a doctor and all . . ."

Damian shared a smile with his mother. "Reese's parents are vegans," he explained. "She and her brother were raised on no meat or dairy."

"Ohhh. You're vegetarian?" she asked, concerned.

"No."

"She didn't follow the lifestyle," he continued. "She eats meat."

"I've just never . . . you know . . . seen anything like that close up . . . in the oven . . . *baking*."

Jeane chuckled. "I can imagine what a shock that was then. I'm so sorry, dear. Had I known, I could have kept him . . . *it!* . . . I could have kept it covered."

Reese wiped the tears from her face with the back of her hand. "No. You shouldn't have to hide your goose from me." Realizing how strange it sounded, she shared a reluctant laugh with mother and son. "I mean, I just feel awful about the way things have gone since we arrived. I ran over one son with the car, and I threw up on the other one's string beans, . . . and the dog absolutely hates me!"

"Paco doesn't hate you. He just——"

"Mom," Damian interrupted. "He peed on her."

"Oh. Well. I guess he did."

Reese giggled softly, and Jeane and Damian bubbled with laughter.

"Poor child," Jeane said, and she placed an arm around Reese's shoulder. "Come inside."

"No, we might be able to find some string beans for the dinner."

"We'll be fine without green beans, Reese. You just come inside and help the children string popcorn and cranberries for the tree while Damian's father hangs the stockings on the mantle and I get dinner on the table. When it's time to eat, I'm going to make you a nice green salad."

"Mom," Damian interjected, "she's fine with meat. She eats meat all the time."

"Oh."

"Maybe we could just carve the bird in the kitchen so she doesn't have to look at it."

"I'll speak to your father."

On the ninth day of Christmas,
Murphy's Law gave to me . . .

nine cornball sleigh rides,
eight geese a-roasting,
seven backs a-blazing,
six ER visits,

five frozen thiiiings!

four yapping dogs,
three wrenched necks,
two mismatched gloves,
and a big rockin' Harry Winston ring.

9

"There she is!" Matthew called out the instant Reese and Damian appeared, and Reese's heart sank. "Hey, Reese. Wanna hear a joke about barfing?"

"Matthew!" Jeane exclaimed.

"Really, Mattie?" Courtney scolded.

"Ah, come on. It's a really *sick joke!*" he teased.

"Enough," Damian warned as he helped Reese out of her coat. "I'm not kidding. Not another word."

"Maybe just one?"

"Estúpido!" Sofia snapped, and she hurried toward Reese and grabbed her by the hand. "Nobody else likes those beans anyways, *chica*. I'm replacing that *deesh* with a Puerto Rican specialty. *Verde del arroz.* You'll love it, and it's already started."

"What's that mean, Aunt Sofia?" Hannah asked.

"It means 'green rice,'" five-year-old Jeremy stated as he handed Sarah another cranberry for the string. "It's yummy."

"Papi says Mama's green rice is spicy just like she is," Abigail piped up, and Sofia chuckled.

"Yah, but I'm going to go easy on you *Americanos*."

Reese pulsed with gratitude. The banter about green rice took the focus off the single most humiliating moment of her entire life, even for just a few minutes. She had no delusions about the jokes that would no doubt ensue at her expense over every Christmas celebration for the rest of their married lives, but for this one instant she felt overwhelming thankfulness for the diversion of spicy Puerto Rican rice. She squeezed Sofia's wrist as she passed her—just a quick, private gesture to let her know how much she appreciated the support.

"How about some eggnog, you two?" Jeane said as she approached with two lovely glass mugs. Leaning in and whispering, she added, "It's store bought. No raw eggs involved. Just in case that's relevant."

Reese giggled and accepted the mug. "Thank you."

Damian nudged her arm. "You okay?"

She nodded as Reggie strolled toward her and grabbed her arm. "Why don't we give you a chance to freshen up," she suggested. "Come on with me, huh?"

The two of them made their way back to their shared bedroom, and Reggie fetched a washcloth doused in warm water. Taking the eggnog from her hand, Reggie pressed the cloth to Reese's forehead.

"Are you rethinking the wedding?" she asked with a lopsided smile.

"No. But I hope Damian isn't."

"Are you kidding? The way that boy looks at you tells me he's just praying he can get you to the altar before you run screaming into the snowy night."

Reese sighed and closed her eyes, pushing the warmth of the cloth against her skin.

"Honestly, I've never seen my brother so completely happy," Reggie said softly. "He loves you very much."

Without opening her eyes, Reese smiled. "Thank God . . . because I can't imagine a life without him."

After a few minutes, she felt surprisingly refreshed. They chatted about Reggie's life back in Vermont while Reese repaired her makeup and ran a brush through her hair.

"Are you ready to face the lions' den again?"

"Not quite," she replied with a smile. "I'd like to give my family a call before we sit down for dinner."

"I'll give you some privacy," Reggie said. "See you out there."

When she grinned at Reese from the doorway, Reggie's pretty brown eyes seemed to sparkle, and she looked so much like Damian that Reese's chest clenched with emotion.

"Thank you so much, Reggie."

"Any time," she replied. "We're sisters now."

Sisters.

Joss fluttered across Reese's mind, and she wondered how the cruise had shaped up for her best friend. She imagined Joss on her *Bah! Humbug* Christmasless journey, surrounded by clear-blue waters and white sugar sand, sipping something fruity with a colorful little paper umbrella, probably wishing she'd done more abdominal crunches before putting on that swimsuit.

One particular escape fluttered across Reese's thoughts. Snickering at the recollection of an adult Joss evaporating into *Merry Christmas Snow*—her former teenaged self—at the sight of a grown-up Keith Partridge after one of David Cassidy's holiday shows in Las Vegas, Reese unplugged her cell phone from the charger. She had snapped several pictures of Joss talking (or trying, at least!) to David Cassidy as they told him about their holiday tradition of avoiding Christmas together.

"There really is just something about the bond between women, isn't there?" he'd observed. "I hope you two have a beautiful time!"

As Joss floated off on a tropical bubble of thought, Reggie bobbed back into view. Reese had always been close to Hersch, and she often supposed that having a sister wouldn't have been much different from Hersch. But remembering Joss, and getting to know Reggie, had ignited something—kindredship she hadn't expected.

What a total genius Keith Partridge grew into! she thought. *There really is something to the whole girl power thing.*

Reese tried dialing Joss, but her friend's voice mail picked up on the first ring.

"I miss you," she said after the beep. "That's all. I just miss you."

Fortunately, Hersch beat his voice mail to the punch. "Is this my sister calling on Christmas Eve?"

"It is," she replied, and a mist of emotion rose in her eyes and tingled over the bridge of her nose. "What's up in Key West tonight? What are you all doing?"

"I'm not eating Tofurkey, that's for sure!" he exclaimed. "Mom made a vegetable lasagna with tofu cheese that wasn't half bad. How about you? How's life with the Rockwells?"

"Ha!" she popped. "Well, not so *Rockwellesque*, I'm afraid."

"No? McDreamy's not all he's cracked up to be?"

"Oh, Damian is dreamy, Hersch. But I don't really fit in the way I'd hoped."

"Come on!" he blurted. "You? Name one person who doesn't love you on sight! You're freakishly lovable, considering where you came from."

"His family is wonderful, actually. There's a lot of them!" she pointed out with a chuckle. "They're great."

"So what's the problem?"

"Promise you won't tell mom and dad?"

"Of course."

"One look at the giant goose in the oven, and I hurled all over the string beans."

"No!"

"Oh, yeah."

"Mom would be so . . . *proud* . . ."

Reese had to pull the phone away from her ear and adjust the volume as Hersch's cackling laughter spilled over her in booming waves.

"WELL, YOU SOMEHOW MADE it through Christmas Eve dinner," Damian said as he swatted Reese's hip. "Nice work!"

"Oh, hush."

His heart surged when her grimace transformed into a smile that seemed to melt the new snow around his boots.

"Admit it," he said, shifting the heavy bag of sand from one arm to the other. "You liked it."

"Yes," she replied with reluctance. "Fine. The goose was delicious. Once it wasn't bird-shaped any more, I actually enjoyed it."

"You know what would have made the dinner perfect?" he asked her with a serious expression.

"A hollow leg so you could consume even more than you already did?"

"That," he acknowledged, "and some string beans. Man, that meal would have been perfect if we only had some of my mom's string beans!"

"You're a dark and tortured man, Damian Palmer."

Out of the corner of her eye, Reese thought she saw something race past them, and she whirled around. "Did you see that?"

"See what?" he asked as he walked on down the driveway.

"I . . . don't know."

Stopping, she held her breath and surveyed the area around them. Beyond the house several of the shrubs shimmied, and she squinted and watched to see if it was nothing more than a December wind.

"Did you guys see it?" Hannah called out to them from the front porch.

"See what?" Damian asked her.

Zeke peered at them from behind Hannah's jeans-clad legs. "It was Blitzen, Uncle Damian. He came back and ate the sweet *patatahs*!"

"He just snatched them and ran in this direction," Hannah exclaimed. "He's huge!"

Reese looked toward the woods, wishing she'd caught a glimpse of him. "Was he limping?" she asked Hannah.

"A little. His back leg looked like it might be hurt."

"I told you," she said to Damian, shaking her head. "He's the one."

Damian slipped his hand into the pocket of his coat and produced the long-necked lighter he'd stashed there.

"Okay, let's get back down to business," he said, and Reese took a long look toward the woods before trailing him.

"How does all this luminaria stuff work, exactly?" she asked.

"You open up one of the white paper lunch bags," he said, and she followed his instruction. "I pour in a few cups of sand."

Reese held the mouth of the bag open as Damian emptied some sand into it.

"Now you place the candle in the sand, like this, careful not to get too close to the sides. I fold down a cuff at the top of the bag. Then we do that about six hundred more times down the driveway and along the road."

"Wait, shouldn't we light it?"

"No, we wait for everyone to get their sections set up, and then we go along and light them all at once."

Damian used his teeth to pull off one of his gloves, and he left it hanging there while he adjusted the opening on the bag of sand. He glanced back at Reese just in time to see her twist her gold hair around one hand and tuck it underneath her pink beanie. Although a nearly full moon reflected off the snow-covered ground, and new flakes gave the landscape a light dusting of glitter, all of it paled in comparison to the quiet beauty of Reese standing there in her long black coat with the pink fur collar that matched not only her cute little hat but also the stain of frigid pink on her cheeks from the plummeting temperature. Damian knew the woman had no clue how exquisite she really was.

"What are you grinning at?" she asked when she caught him watching her.

"Just dreaming about those string beans," he said with a shrug. "Sure wish I had some of those tonight."

He felt the heat of her glare bearing down on the back of his neck, and Damian couldn't help but chuckle as the boots Reese had borrowed from the mudroom crunched along through the snow behind him.

"Hey," she said when they stopped to prepare the next bag with sand. "Where does this tradition come from, anyway? And why do they call it a *luminaria?*"

"It came from a Spanish tradition, actually." When he noticed Sofia, Eli, and their two kids ahead of them at the end of the drive-way, Damian called out to Sofia. "Hey, Sof. It started out as a celebration of the birth of Christ, right?"

"Chez, Domion," she said as she broke away and headed toward them with little Jeremy holding her hand. *"Las Posados.* It's a celebration of when Mary went into labor, and they had to search for *lotching."*

"Search for lodging," Damian translated for Reese in a whisper.

"Ohhh."

"Elijah, he says the Palmers have been lighting the *farolitos*—the little lanterns—for years back in Vermont, so I tell him he had a Spanish influence even before he met me."

"A foreshadowing of what was to come," Reese said with a grin.

"Si. Foreshadow."

"When my folks bought this place in Sugarloaf," Damian told Reese, "we carried on the family tradition every Christmas Eve. Pretty soon, Mr. and Mrs. Hillsborough down the road liked it so much they organized all of the other neighbors, and it became a regular thing up here. In an hour or so, we'll go for a sleigh ride, and you'll see lanterns like these placed every few yards for nearly three miles."

"A sleigh ride!" Reese cried. "You have *a sleigh?"*

"Well, we don't, no," he said, laughing. "Pop rents one every Christmas Eve. It's more of a huge wagon, really, pulled by a couple of horses owned by the Ferncliff family down in Erwin Lake." When he saw the astonished expression on her face, he smiled and lifted one shoulder into a shrug. "The kids really love it."

"Don't let him fool you, Reese," Eli said as he joined them. "The adults like it just as much as the kids do."

"The Palmer boys are just big *niños*, anyhow," Sofia added. "*Cheeldren*, right?"

"Oh?" Reese teased. "I'd hardly noticed."

On the tenth day of Christmas,
Murphy's Law gave to me . . .

ten carols screeching,
nine cornball sleigh rides,
eight geese a-roasting,
seven backs a-blazing,
six ER visits,

five frozen thiiiings!

four yapping dogs,
three wrenched necks,
two mismatched gloves,
and a big rockin' Harry Winston ring.

10

Two large brown horses—one of them with streaks of white running through its mane and long, bushy tail—trotted down the road, the clomp of their hooves muffled by another inch of fallen snow. Three generations of Palmers huddled together on two long bench seats on either side of the open wagon.

Reese leaned close to Damian, and he tightened his arm around her shoulder, drawing the soft woolen blanket up to her chin. The temperature had dropped below thirty degrees, but the wind had gone still, and snowfall had thinned to a scant flurry, making the ride up the road and over the hill somewhat pleasant when well prepared with thick blankets and thermos cups of hot chocolate and warm mint tea.

Jeane and Paul, seated at the reins with Zeke and Abigail between them, seemed to know every neighbor they passed along the way. In the distance Reese heard a choir of voices singing "Joy to the World," and Paul brought the wagon to a stop as they crested the ridge at the top of the hill. A family of six had just gotten around to lighting the candles inside the paper lanterns at the end of their driveway, and the eldest of them shouted out a greeting as the others continued to sing.

"Palmer clan!" he beamed. "Merry Christmas!"

"Same to you, Jake," Jeane returned. "How about some hot chocolate?"

"Thank you, thank you," the white-haired man answered. "But we have Margaret's apple cider a-flowing already. Join us in song?"

"Come on, Palmers," Paul called out. "Let's show the good Lord what you've got!"

And with that Damian and his family began to sing along.

"He rules the world with truth and grace, and makes the nations prove . . ."

A teen from the group stepped forward and rubbed one of the horses on the nose. When the animal whinnied, her laughter cut her song into pieces.

Reese felt as if she'd stumbled into some cheesy Hallmark movie with the townsfolk singing carols, drinking apple cider, and taking sleigh rides in the snow. Even though she secretly adored those Christmas movies each year, she recognized a good fantasy when she watched one! Looking around her now, it was almost a little too much for her to believe. She didn't know whether to call Hersch later and describe the scene in mocking disbelief or just to dive in and enjoy the cornball beauty of it all.

"How about one more?" Jeane suggested when they'd completed the carol.

Jake basked in the glow of the suggestion, and he rallied his troops.

"O holy night, the stars are brightly shining . . ."

Reese's favorite Christmas song! She grinned so hard at Damian that her cheeks throbbed.

"I love this song!" she exclaimed.

A strange expression shadowed his face as he replied, "Right. I know."

And with that Reese sang out with all her might.

"Faaaaall on your knees. O hear the angel voooices. O ni-ight diviiiiine . . ."

Was it her imagination, or was everyone staring at her?

She felt exhilarated as the beautiful carol came to a close. Squeezing Damian's arm as tightly as she could, she whispered in his ear. "I can't believe this is for real . . . that people actually live like this. Let's bring our children here every year, okay? I want them to grow up with this view of Christmas, Damie."

He touched her cheek with his leather-gloved fingers and gazed into her eyes for a long and frozen moment. She could almost see the wheels of thought turning in him, and she wished she had a computer screen handy where she could read the transcript. The steam of his warm breath meeting the cold air between them fogged her eyes, and she closed them as he kissed her.

"I love you so much," she told him when they parted. "I never even knew there was a man like you out there somewhere."

"Just wandering around looking for you," he replied.

A cacophony of good wishes exchanged, Paul steered the horses into a soft u-turn, and they headed back down the hill toward the Palmers' house. From above it all, the winding border of shimmering candle lanterns seemed to light the way home, and the magnificent sight filled Reese's heart with a seasonal thrill that she hadn't felt in . . .

Maybe, ever!

But certainly not in many, many years. The sensation almost struck Reese as a form of betrayal, and she wondered how Joss might feel if she shared the experience with her Christmas-avoiding best friend.

"Traitor!" she would surely exclaim. "You are such a traitor!"

For a moment Reese supposed Joss might be right. But as the flickering lanterns guided them down the hill and around the curve of the road, she snuggled against Damian and sighed. She didn't really mind the label of *traitor* so much.

"NO, YOU CAN'T GET dressed," Reggie said, still lounging in bed, pausing to stretch her entire body and give a hearty yawn. "It's Palmer tradition. Christmas morning is for my mom's eggs benedict and opening up our stockings, and all of that takes place while still wearing your pajamas."

Reese glanced down at the ensemble she'd worn to bed on Christmas Eve: red flannel pajama pants and top with holly wreaths stamped all over them, and a pair of thick, nubby green socks. When she looked up again, Reggie laughed out loud.

"I have a red flannel robe that would finish off that look for you," she suggested. "Do you want to borrow?"

Reese folded her hands and placed them dramatically on the side of her cheek. "Oh, could I?"

Reggie nodded toward the attached bathroom. "Hanging on the door."

What she really wanted was a shower; but instead Reese headed in to brush her teeth and wash her face, and she quickly ran a brush through her disheveled hair. Using the red scrunchie normally relegated to the bathroom counter or the front pocket of her workout bag, she gathered up her hair into a bun at the top of her head, a hairstyle Joss always called her "controlled mess 'do." After applying a coat of moisturizer to her freshly washed skin and dabbing her lips with shiny cherry lip balm, she found Reggie waiting in the bedroom wearing green, one-piece pajamas with large reindeer heads printed all over them.

"I always buy the silliest pajamas I can find, just for Christmas morning," she said with a broad grin. "How do I look?"

Reese giggled as Reggie did a little twirl, one hand on her hip and the other behind her head.

"You win the prize. Those really are the silliest pajamas I've ever seen."

"Score!" Reggie exclaimed. "Next stop, eggs benedict!"

As the two of them strolled down the hall, it struck Reese again how sad it was that Reggie had remained alone for so many years after the death of her husband. It just seemed wrong somehow for such a unique and personable woman to spend her life alone in the shadow of one great love that disintegrated far too soon. Reese never thought of herself as much of a sentimental, romantic sort, although that had changed a lot since meeting Damian, but something about Reggie living such a solitary life seemed like such a waste.

The sight that greeted her in the great room inspired Reese to pop with laughter. All of those Palmers—each one wearing pajamas more outrageous than the next—scattered around the great room and gathered around the island in the kitchen reminded Reese of the digital camera she'd tucked into her bag at the last minute. But it was the sight of Damian that made her turn and run back to the bedroom to retrieve it.

He looked like a decorated gingerbread man from head to toe, the feet in the one-piece pajamas rounded and the puffy painted tie around his neck blinking with red and green lights. Beside him, the normally reserved P.J. wore large antlers on his head and a red T-shirt with white blocked letters on the front: Ho3.

Jeane greeted her with a kiss to the cheek and a large cup of steaming coffee. Her long flannel nightgown had a six-inch lace ruffle at the hem and a three-dimensional manger scene protruding from her chest.

"It's pumpkin spice," she said as she handed over the coffee, but the fragrance gave it away before she identified it.

"Wait," Reese said, and she raised her camera before Jeane turned.

Damian's mom posed with her hand behind her head, much the same way Reggie had earlier, and Reese composed a full-length photo in the viewfinder of her camera. Taking her coffee with her, she snapped away.

Hannah wore a short, plain red tee over boxers screened with the large green face of the Grinch, and little Abigail's long, sun-kissed braids framed a blinking red Rudolph nose on the front of her footed pajamas. Sarah shuffled across the floor with a small glass of chocolate milk in her red-and-white pajamas and a strange little curved hat that made her look like a walking candy cane. Stranger still, Paco scampered along behind her wearing the very same thing. When Reese raised her camera, the dog shot her a menacing, low-pitched growl, and she lowered it again without taking the shot.

Not one member of three generations of Palmers, however, looked as silly—or adorable—as gingerbread man, Damian.

"Really?" she said when she caught his eye and raised her camera. Instead of a reply, she got bulging eyes and a goofy smile.

"I don't know, Damian," Matthew said, shaking his head and looking Reese up and down. "She's a little pajama-challenged, isn't she?"

"I forgot to warn her," he replied.

"You mean she just had those pajamas in her suitcase? And you're looking at all of us like we're out of the ordinary?"

"Hush, Matthew," Jeane said. "You look charming, Reese."

"Remember Courtney's first Christmas with us?" Paul chimed in, and Reese snapped a quick picture of him dressed like Scrooge with his full-length night dress and cap. "And remember the way Sofia looked at us all? They both thought the Palmers had lost their minds."

Sofia waddled across the room in a knee-length romper, wearing awkward padded knee socks made to look like reindeer hooves. She plopped down on Eli's lap and kissed her husband on the cheek. "We haven't changed our minds either, Paul. The whole *familia es loco!*"

"Give me your camera, Reese," Hannah offered. "I'll take one of you and Uncle Damian."

Reese complied and then stepped behind Damian, wrapped her arms around his neck, and smiled for the camera. The thought fluttered across her mind that it would be one of those photos that would keep their children—and grandchildren—laughing for decades to come.

"BRO, I THOUGHT SHE was joking!" Eli whispered.

"You mean she wasn't?" Matthew asked, mock serious.

Damian shook his head and tried to ignore them, concentrating instead on refilling his coffee cup.

"And nobody's told her? Ever?" Eli went on. "*You* haven't told her?"

"What am I gonna say?" Damian flared, trying to keep it to a whisper through clenched teeth. "How do you tell the woman you love that her singing cuts through steel?"

"How do you *not* tell her?" Matthew countered. "You've got fifty years with her ahead of you with any luck. *Not even you* can face that down, can you?"

Damian snickered. "When I weigh it against all of the qualities in her that I absolutely cannot live without, yeah, I can face it down. Gladly."

"Talk to me in three years," Matthew replied, and he walked away shaking his head.

The memory of the looks on everyone's faces when Reese had broken out into song the night before kindled a chuckle in Damian, one that quickly galvanized into full-on laughter, and Eli caught the fire.

"What are you two laughing about over there?" Jeane called out to them. "Bring it over here to the tree. It's time to open our stockings."

Damian grabbed his coffee and headed across the room, and he sat down on the floor in front of Reese's chair.

"What's so funny?" she whispered in his ear.

Fortunately, his mother unwittingly saved him from answering.

"Reese, Damian," she said, taking her husband's hand. "We've been talking, and we'd like to make you an offer. You can certainly refuse it, but we're hoping . . . well . . ."

"What is it, Mom?"

With a quick glance to Damian's father, she smiled. "We were wondering . . . what you might think . . . of getting married here at the cabin."

Before he could even take a breath, Reese hopped out of her chair and rushed across the room, hugging both of his parents at the same time.

"What a wonderful idea!" she cried. "Damie, isn't it a wonderful idea?"

They hadn't talked much about the actual ceremony since becoming engaged, but he'd sort of imagined it taking place at their church down the mountain. The joyous fire in Reese's sky-blue eyes, however, put a different slant on those plans.

"If it makes you happy, it's a wonderful idea," he told her. "I don't care where we get married, as long as we do." And while they were on the subject of marriage, Damian got up and plucked a stocking with Reese's name embroidered on the fuzzy white cuff from the long line hanging from the mantle. "This is a good transition. Here. Why don't you open your stocking first."

He watched the curiosity bubble up in her, and she returned to her chair and accepted the overstuffed green velvet stocking. First, she removed several of the Palmer stocking traditions—a couple of cinnamon candy canes; a rolled pair of fluffy, colorful socks; a tree ornament hand-made by his mother—and then she reached it. Damian's heart began to race.

Reese pulled out the small blue velvet box and perched it on the open palm of her hand. Glancing up at him, she smiled before looking back at it again.

"What is this?" she asked him. "I thought we agreed not to exchange gifts and to save our money for a really extravagant honeymoon."

"This didn't cost me a thing," he replied, and his mother's beaming smile burned the corner of his eye. "Open it."

She lifted the platinum-hinged lid with slow anticipation, and in the exact moment his eyes landed on the contents, hers did, too, and she gasped.

"What . . . ?"

Damian straightened and knelt in front of her. "They were my grandparents' wedding rings. I think Gram's will work perfectly with your engagement ring, and Mom let me have it sized for you, but if you don't think—"

"Damian, let the girl think for a minute," his dad cut in. "She's hardly had a chance to open the box."

Reese gazed down over the thin silver bands, hers with a row of small round diamonds across the top. "They're . . . beautiful."

Damian couldn't contain himself another moment. He pulled the diamond band out of the box. "Try it on. Let's see how it looks with your ring."

With an eager grin, she held up her hand and wiggled her fingers. When Damian slipped on the band and it rested against her engagement ring, it looked to him as if the two had been made as a perfect set. He glanced up at Reese and waited, holding his breath.

Instead of a reply, she simply slid her arms around his neck and squeezed. "It's just exactly right," she cried at last.

"Really?"

Over his shoulder she thanked his parents and waved her hand at Reggie and the girls, all of whom moved in for a closer look before she'd even released her hold on his neck.

"Each of the boys' wives got something that belonged to Paul's mother for their wedding," Jeane explained. "Courtney wore a lovely pearl and diamond necklace on her wedding day, and Sofia had the florist work a beautiful diamond brooch into her bouquet."

"*Maravilloso!*" Sofia exclaimed. "It's just beautiful. *Mi hermana es* an artist, and she built a very pretty shadow box for us with all the things from our wedding. Grandmother Palmer's *peen* is at the center of it."

As Reese let go of Damian, he smiled at her. "Did you get all that?"

"Sister is an artist. Shadow box. Diamond brooch."

Eli guffawed. "Do you know how long it took me to get that fluent at speaking Sofia?"

Sofia brushed her husband's arm and grinned.

"*Mi madre habla un lenguaje muy personal,*" young Jeremy stated, and they all turned toward him, surprised.

"He say his mama . . . speaks a language all her own," Sofia translated, and she drew her son into a playful embrace. "That's my boy."

On the eleventh day of Christmas,
Murphy's Law gave to me . . .

eleven houses burning,
ten carols screeching,
nine cornball sleigh rides,
eight geese a-roasting,
seven backs a-blazing,
six ER visits,

five frozen thiiiings!

four yapping dogs,
three wrenched necks,
two mismatched gloves,
and a big rockin' Harry Winston ring.

11

"The thing is, Damie, I've never even held a football before, much less played the game."

"You'll do fine. Just stick close to me. It's our Christmas Day tradition."

"Yeah. So you said," she replied. Pressing her lips together, she gave him an odd little smile. "But you know, I don't really enjoy getting knocked down, even if . . . or maybe especially when . . . there's a lot of snow to cushion the fall."

"It's just touch football, Reese. No one's going to knock you down."

Just as he completed the thought, a crunch of bodies caught their attention, and a pile-up of brothers and children thumped to the ground a few feet away. Reggie stood next to Damian and Reese, and she let out a peel of laughter.

"Hey! *Touch* football, morons!" he shouted, but Matthew just snorted at him as he grabbed the ball and took off running.

"Mom, Daddy's cheating," Sarah called out. "Tell him he can't just pick up the ball and keep on running."

"Matthew, you can't just pick up the ball and run," Courtney said from the sidelines in a lackluster tone of disinterest.

"Ha!" Matthew cried from the tree-lined end zone. "Touchdown!"

Damian tried to frown as he watched his brother dance around, waving the ball over his head, but he just couldn't manage it. Despite his ridiculous behavior, Damian found Matthew entertaining. He always had.

"All right, enough with the warm-up," Eli exclaimed. "Everyone under the age of forty out on the field."

"The field," Sofia muttered as she and Courtney headed into the snow. "*Eet's* a lawn covered in snow, Elijah."

"Keen observation," Eli announced. "That's why she's on my team."

Damian could almost see the anxiety simmering in Reese. Just as he began to formulate some sort of excuse for her to bow out, resolve crested in her crystal blue eyes, and she grinned at him.

"I can do this!" she assured him, and she straightened her sweater and stalked out toward Eli. "Which team am I on? Just tell me what to do."

Eli's eyebrow quirked as he stared at her for a moment. "Well," he finally said, "you line up with your team. And you protect your quarterback at all costs."

"Okay!" she said, nodding. Her expression melted a bit as she added, "Who is my quarterback? And how . . . exactly . . . do I protect them?"

Damian snorted and placed his arm around her waist. "When Eli runs with the ball, you just block anyone from Matthew's team so they can't get near him."

She nodded vehemently. "Got it. Block . . . protect."

Damian's chest tightened as he looked at her, so eager to find her place in his world and so obviously out of her element. As she lined up next to Abigail, she mimicked the young girl's stance by hunching over and pressing both hands to her legs, mid-thigh.

Damian chuckled. "Okay! Let's play ball. It's two-handed touch, and there is no tackling, Matthew. This is touch football. Women and children are present."

"Yeah, yeah," Matthew returned, and he took his place at the center of the opposing team. "Just try not to get in my way, *Nancy*. That way, you won't get hurt."

"Hush yourself, Matthew," Sofia snapped. "*Tochito* already."

Matthew laughed as P.J. hiked the ball to him, and he fell back and surveyed he field. His eyes met Damian's for only a split second before he sent a perfect spiral sailing toward Sarah. When it became clear the throw had no chance of connecting, Damian rushed toward the other side of their makeshift playing field.

"Oooh, I got it! I . . . I think . . . I got it!" Reese squealed, and she scrambled toward the hurtling ball over her head.

It might have been a brilliant interception, too, if not for the thud of her body slamming into Abigail's, sending Damian's small niece crashing to the ground beneath Reese.

Abigail wailed as P.J. recovered the ball and lifted it over his head with a victorious shout.

"Oh, Abigail, I'm so sorry!" Reese cried.

"Come here, *mi bebé*," Sofia cooed, placing her arms around her crying child and lifting her from the ground. "*Que está bien, bebé.*"

"Really," Reese said, almost frantically. When her eyes met Damian's, she shrank. "It was an accident. I would never—"

"I know," he said, offering both hands to her.

She took them, and he pulled her to her feet.

"I didn't see her," she continued as he led her to the sidelines. As they passed Sofia, rocking Abigail in her arms, she added, "I'm so sorry."

Damian's mother stood up and touched Reese's arm. "Reese, sweetheart . . ."

"It was an accident," Reese exclaimed. "I didn't see her."

"I know, dear. Would you mind going inside for me?"

"Yes!" she exclaimed, and she tossed Damian a sweet and grateful smile. "Of course!"

"I think I forgot to turn down the heat on the tomato sauce for tonight's lasagna. Would you give it a quick stir and turn down the burner?"

"Absolutely!"

His mother had saved the day yet again. Reese eagerly disappeared before Damian could even swat her with his scarf. A clamor of angry barking accompanied her entrance to the house, and Reese cried out.

"Hey! Cut it out!" A moment later a doggie tirade of barks and snarls ensued that Damian felt certain, if translated, included some very offensive language. He hardly heard Reese underneath it as she exclaimed, "Seriously, Paco? Tell it to someone who cares."

REESE GLARED AT PACO as he unleashed an ear-splitting rant, apparently over the simple fact that she dared enter the house. When he lunged at her for the third time and sunk his sharp little Chihuahua teeth into the pant leg of her jeans, she grabbed the dish towel hanging on the oven door and swatted at him.

"I'm not kidding, dog," she exclaimed, dancing out of his way. "Kids and animals love me! What is your—" And one more jump away from him. "—problem!?"

Standing on one foot while maneuvering her other one like a jousting lance against Paco's advances, she stirred the chunky tomato sauce in the large simmering pot. She checked the setting on the burner and smiled. Set on the lowest temperature possible, she realized Jeane had concocted the mission with the idea of relieving Reese of her position on the field of touch football.

She tapped the wooden spoon against the side of the pot before cradling it in the wreath-shaped spoon rest and replacing the lid. When she spotted the plastic baggie of miniscule dog treats on the counter, an idea sparked, and she snagged a handful of them. Using the dish towel as a defensive weapon, she planned to cast herself as the bait that would lead the barking dog around the center island, but he bit down on the end of the thing, and she was able to drag him around it by the teeth instead. When he relaxed his clenched jaw enough for Reese to snap the towel away from him, she scattered the smelly treats on the floor; and as Paco scurried after them, she tossed the towel back into the kitchen, bustled out the back door, and slammed it behind her.

An ingenius plan, she congratulated herself, hoping no one would notice her return and force her into the Palmer reindeer games. With her head down, she stalked across the snow to where Jeane sat, holding Abigail. Reese descended into the empty folding chair next to Jeane and smiled.

"How did the sauce look?" Jeane asked her.

"Good enough to eat," Reese replied with a grin. "The fire was already set on low, so I just gave it a stir."

"Thank you, dear." She looked down at Abigail and rocked her slightly. "Do you have something to say to Reese, sweetheart?"

Reese's stomach lurched. She couldn't even imagine.

Abigail peered up at her while still shielding part of her face with the collar of her grandmother's coat.

"I know you didn't mow me over on purpose, Reese," she offered.

"No, I really didn't," she replied. "And I am so sorry."

"I know. Grandmom says we always have to forgive somebody if they mean it when they say they're sorry."

Reese grinned at Jeane. "That's a really good rule. I think I'm going to keep that one for myself."

"So you shouldn't feel bad about it, even if I get a bruise on my arm."

"Well, I won't be able to help that," Reese told her sincerely. "I mean, I hate to think of you with a bruise. But you know what helps bruises?"

"No," the young girl said, perking. "What helps them?"

"Cookies," she answered. "Like the ones in the tin on the kitchen counter. When this game is over, what do you say you and I go and get ourselves a couple?"

"Did you get a bruise too?"

"I don't think so," she admitted. "But I have a different sort of boo-boo."

Reese glanced down at her leg and swirled her finger around in the small tear in her jeans.

"What happened?"

"Paco," she stated. "Man, oh man, but that dog really doesn't like me."

"He *bit you?*" Jeane exclaimed.

"Well, it was more of a good strong gnawing, I suppose. I tried to reason with him and explain that kids and animals usually like me, but he was having none of it . . . or me."

"I'm so sorry."

"Do you need a Band-Aid, Reese?" Abigail asked her.

"No," she assured her with a shake of her head. "He didn't even break skin. Just denim."

Jeane chuckled. "Still. I'm very sorry."

"So who's winning?" Reese asked as she surveyed the field of snow.

"Team Damian by one," Paul answered from Jeane's far side.

Reese grinned. "Any injuries?"

"Not in the last few minutes. Unless you count yours in going up against Paco," Jeane teased.

Sofia heaved the ball in a sort of underhanded, two-fisted pitch, and Matthew intercepted it. Paul hopped up from his chair so hard it fell over behind him, and the audience of three at the sideline shouted as he passed it to P. J.

"Get him, Damie!" Reese yelled.

But P. J. ran ahead of him, Matthew and Reggie backing him up, all the way to the far side of the yard for the touchdown.

As Reggie, P. J., and his father danced around like roosters, Jeremy consoled Sofia for the incomplete pass to Eli.

"Uncle Mattie's just taller than you, Mama."

Damian shot Reese a quick little wink and headed toward the equivalent of the fifty-yard line. Just then, however, Paco's incessant barking from the house drew Sarah's full attention.

"Grandpop," she called out. "I think something's not right."

Everyone turned toward the house, and Jeane popped up from her chair with a gasp. Reese's heart nearly stopped when she spotted the black smoke billowing from the house.

"Something's on fire!" Hannah shouted.

Matthew spiked the ball to the ground, and the whole lot of them took off running toward the back door. Through the expanse of windows, Reese could see the flames reaching from the stovetop to the hood over it, curving around the edge and straining toward the ceiling.

"Stand back," Paul bellowed. "Nobody open that door until I see what's going on inside. Just stand back, all of you. Jeane, get the kids away from the door."

"Does anyone have their cell phone out here?" Reggie called out to no reply.

Reese cupped her eyes against the window with both hands and peered inside. On the marble kitchen floor, she spotted the towel she'd tossed back on her departure, one end of it charred by flames. Surely, she hadn't started the fire with the thoughtless toss of a dish towel!

"No!" she cried. "Nooo."

Her helpless archenemy circled the island and ran into the great room, barking relentlessly.

"Paco's in there!" Sarah cried and headed straight for the door, but Damian grabbed her at the waist and yanked her back again.

"Not a chance!"

Reese couldn't help herself. She weaved around them and pushed past Paul before cranking the knob and shoving open the door.

"Reese, what are you—"

With her arm folded over her mouth to block the smoke, she raced into the great room and searched the tables until she caught sight of a cell phone and grabbed it.

"Mom, where's the fire extinguisher?" she heard Damian call out.

"Damian, get outta there, son!"

"It's under the shelf in the pantry!"

Reese searched the room for Damian, but a substantial wall of ashy fog blocked her view. She took a deep breath and began choking on the thick smoke.

Paco—*You ignorant little thing!*—made her chase him around the sofa before she got close enough to catch him by the collar. He chomped down on her hand as she did, and she screamed, but she didn't lose her grip.

"Mattie!" Damian called out. "Do you know how to work it?"

"I got this," Matthew returned. "Get Reese!"

Disembodied arms wrapped around her waist and hoisted her straight off the ground. By the time she recognized Damian's muscular biceps, he'd heaved her right over his shoulder and carried her toward the back door, Paco dangling by his teeth from her bleeding hand.

"PAUL, JEANE, I AM so sorry. I'm just so, so sorry!"

Reese could hardly breathe. She didn't know if the smoke had smothered her, or if the guilt had done it, but she couldn't seem to get a deep breath. Damian wrapped a blanket around her shoulders and sat down on the bench next to her.

"En qué estabas pensando? Has perdido el juicio?" Sofia rattled. "You threw a towel on a burning flame on the stove?"

"Is that what happened?" one of the firefighters asked from the doorway.

"Yes!" Reese confessed, and she jumped to her feet. "It's all my fault. I just went inside to stir the sauce, and the dog bit me—"

"Paco bit you?" Damian interjected.

"He didn't mean it," Sarah piped up.

"Oh, I know, honey. He just doesn't know me."

The fireman cleared his throat. "The towel?"

"Oh. Right. I was using it to swat the dog away from my leg, and I tossed some dog treats to distract him—"

"What dog treats?"

"Don't interrupt, Sarah," her mother told her.

"But I ran out of dog treats yesterday."

Reese looked up at Damian, her heart racing. "What was in the plastic bag on the counter?"

"Those were Grandpop's vitamins!" Hannah exclaimed, and Sarah began to cry.

"What will happen? Will he die? Did you try to kill Paco just because he doesn't like you?"

Reese collapsed into Damian's arms.

"Let's just settle down. Everyone," he said. "Mom, go with Regg and call the emergency animal clinic in town. They'll want to know Pop's pills and dosage."

"I'm going with you!" Sarah blurted.

"So you tossed the towel toward the kitchen," the fireman led Reese. "And you didn't know it landed on the stove."

"Of course, she didn't," Damian answered him.

"No," Reese confirmed. "I didn't know." Looking frantically at Paul and Jeane, she descended into a full-on ugly cry. "I'm so sor-ry . . ."

"We know, dear," Jeane said with an exasperated sigh. "We know."

"No one was hurt. That's the important thing right now," Paul added, and he turned to the firefighter. "What's our next step?"

"You'll want to contact your insurance company, and they'll send out an inspector to make sure there's no structural damage."

"Is that a possibility?" Jeane asked.

"It could be, but I really don't think so. It looks like you're just facing some cosmetic repairs. Still, you'll want to take care of that right away. We don't see any residual hot spots, and no water damage. There is, however, some concentrated smoke damage. If you'll come into the kitchen with me, I'll show you."

The entire Palmer clan filed in behind the fireman, except for Damian and Reese who stayed outside the door. Tightening the blanket around her shoulders, Damian looked into Reese's eyes and gave her a tired smile. For the first time she noticed the smudges of soot on his face and neck, and she instinctively bunched the blanket with her hand and used the corner to gently rub it away.

"Reese," he said with a gravelly tone to his voice.

"Please don't."

"Don't . . . what?"

"Don't anything," she replied as he brushed the tear stains from her dirty face with his thumb. "Don't tell me it's going to be okay, that it was just an accident, because I'll break down completely. And please don't tell me how badly I've messed up and that you're finished with me because I would like to be your fiancee as long as I possibly can. You can break up with me after we get back to the city, all right?"

"Is that everything?"

She thought it over then nodded. "I think that covers it."

Glancing down at her blackened hands, Reese noticed her beautiful and brilliant diamond ring had lost every bit of its luster beneath the soot. As she realized it was likely a living metaphor for all that had happened, she dropped to the bench, tossed her face into both hands, and began to sob.

On the twelfth day of Christmas,
Murphy's Law gave to me . . .

twelve reindeer hauntings,
eleven houses burning,
ten carols screeching,
nine cornball sleigh rides,
eight geese a-roasting,
seven backs a-blazing,
six ER visits,

five frozen thiiiings!

four yapping dogs,
three wrenched necks,
two mismatched gloves,
and a big rockin' Harry Winston ring.

12

"Are you sure you don't want to go back and get something to eat with the rest of your family?" Reese asked Reggie as they meandered down the sidewalk. "It's not like we're going to find anywhere else open on Christmas night."

"I'll be fine," she replied, and she looped her arm through Reese's. "Mom's going to take out a platter of sandwiches we can all have later. Right now, it's just about getting the kids fed. There's nothing more trying than a pack of hungry Palmer children."

"And since Christmas dinner was pretty much sidelined by me . . ."

"Well, when you said you wanted to go for a walk while the others got something to eat, I pretty much knew that translated to being too uncomfortable to sit there and—"

"And look into the faces of the family whose home I had just burned down?"

Reggie chuckled. "You didn't burn down the whole house. Just a little corner of it."

"The kitchen, Reggie. That's a pretty important corner."

"Besides," Reggie cut in. "I wasn't going to leave you wandering the streets of Big Bear Village all alone with your thoughts."

"You mean the ones where I flail around in them until I finally drown?"

"Those would be the ones."

Reese shook her head and groaned softly. "You're a very kind person, Reggie. I appreciate the company."

The normally bustling village streets stood rather empty beneath the border of candy cane lamps and scalloped tinsel. Most of the stores were closed for the holiday already, and only a few bundled families wandered past them as she and Reggie made their way down Pine Knot Avenue.

"Let's recap," Reese suddenly exclaimed. "Bailed on my best friend for Christmas . . . hit a reindeer . . . ran over Eli . . . barfed on dinner . . . burned down the house . . . poisoned the dog. Did I miss anything?"

Reggie couldn't hold back her laughter. "If you did, I'm not going to name it. I try never to kick a friend when she's down."

"Thank you." Reese tilted her head and rested it on Reggie's shoulder for a moment. "I think it's always important to make a good impression on the in-laws, don't you?"

After a few beats of silence, Reggie sniggered in the effort to keep from displaying her amusement, and the mere sound of it ignited something in Reese. The two of them began to laugh—almost hysterically—as they ambled on.

When the soft strains of a choir of voices beckoned, they both straightened.

"Do you hear that?" Reese asked.

"Angels we have heard on high, sweetly singing o'er the plains. And the mountains in reply echoing their joyous strains . . ."

As they turned the corner, Reese spotted a group of people gathered around a tall lit Christmas tree with a living nativity staged in front of it. About fifty people held small candles as they gathered around a man, woman, and baby in a constructed manger lined with hay. Next to them, Reese noticed a shy little lamb, two goats nibbling on straw, a brown-eyed calf, and a small donkey. The scene, enhanced by the beauty of the combined harmonies, touched Reese in a raw place deep within her.

As they reached the group, a smiling woman in a red-velvet coat handed them both candles. "Welcome," she said as she lit them. "God bless you both."

Reese and Reggie exchanged curious smiles, but neither one questioned whether to join in. Just as they became part of the circle, her emotion weighed on Reese until she couldn't help from bowing her head.

"Glo-o-o-o-ria! In excelsis deo!"

She'd had such high hopes about spending time with Damian's family and getting to know them. Would they ever be able to forget her horrendous first impressions? Could they eagerly accept her into the fold after such an awful first Christmas together? After the childhood she and Hersch had experienced, a family like the Palmers seemed like a dream come true. But once again Reese felt as if she stood on the outside, looking through a frosted window at the joy and celebration inside.

Suddenly she thought of her parents and smiled. The last Christmas she'd spent with them had been the year they'd moved to Key West. They'd strung gaudy colored lights on the palm tree in the front yard, and her father had danced around in a Hawaiian shirt and flip-flops singing "Jingle Bell Rock." A far cry from a Palmer family Christmas, that was for sure. Still . . . she missed them.

A sudden yearning for her mother's embrace put a chokehold on Reese, and tears stung her eyes. What she wouldn't give for a chunk of her father's peppermint soy bark and a big glass of eggless nog, shared out on their screened lanai under balmy seventy-degree breezes, listening to Hersch's latest tale of chorus lines in Peoria winter stock.

As one song ended and the singers embarked on a new one, Reese dried her tears and resolved to call her family before the night concluded. She wished she'd been able to reach Joss earlier that day, and she wondered if she'd received the birthday cake Reese had sent to her cabin.

"O holy night, the stars are brightly shining . . ."

She smiled. "I love this song," she told Reggie.

But just as she opened her mouth to sing along, her future sister-in-law touched her arm and gazed at her with a curious arch to her brow. Before she had the chance to inquire, Reggie shook her head of short brown curls.

"Uh-uh, honey. No."

No? Why not?

"Let's just quietly listen, okay?"

The sentiment stung a little, but Reese swallowed it just the same. Despite her best efforts, she couldn't help softly humming along, but she purposefully restrained the urge to sing out in her normal way.

She just wished she knew why.

At the close of the carol, a young reverend addressed the gathered crowd. "We're so happy you all could join us tonight on this holiest of nights and that you've chosen to leave your warm homes and shiny new gifts to bring honor and glory to the true meaning of the Christmas season. I urge you—every one of you—to put the thoughts and stress of the holidays behind you here, to leave them outside the door of the manger, and give a moment of reflection to the Child born so that you might be set free."

Reese's cell phone jangled out a notification that she'd received a text, and she handed Reggie her candle and pulled the phone out of her coat pocket as she stepped away from the group.

Vet says Paco will live. Come back to clinic? —Damian

"Let's go down to the restaurant and gather the troops," she muttered to Reggie. "Paco's ready."

"Is he okay?"

"Damian says the vet thinks he'll live."

"Sarah must be so relieved. Let's go."

Reese glanced at the manger one more time as they blew out their candles and headed back. The little baby swaddled in a light blue blanket blinked at his mother before his eyes fluttered shut.

"Hey," she said to Reggie as they marched up the walk again. "Why did you tell me not to sing along back there?"

Reggie sighed and gave Reese an odd, crooked attempt at a smile. Damian's smile. The one that said he didn't want to reply.

"I say this in love," Reggie prefaced. "But even Mariah Carey is challenged by a song like 'O Holy Night.'" After a short pause, she added, "And I'm sorry to be the one to tell you, Reese, but you are no Mariah Carey."

"DID DADDY MAKE HIS peppermint bark?"

"Of course!" her mother replied, and Reese pressed the phone to her face and closed her eyes. "Would you like me to box some up and send it to you?"

"Would you? I'd love that."

"Really! I didn't think you'd want any. I'll have to stop your brother from eating every last crumb. You know how that boy can be when anything sweet is in the house."

Reese chuckled. "Can I speak to Daddy?"

"Of course. In a minute."

Her mother paused for a long moment. While Reese waited, trying to figure out what might come next, she glanced out the window and gasped as her eyes met those of the large buck standing beneath the trees.

"Are things not going well with the future in-laws, Reese?"

She pinned back the curtain for a closer look at the deer as she asked, "Mom. Why do you say that?"

"Just a feeling. You seem strange."

"Do I?" Reese sighed as the deer tossed her a quick nod of his antlers and bounded off into the woods without a trace of a limp. "This is the first Christmas I've spent without you all or Joss. I guess I'm just feeling a little *tofu out of water*."

"You and Damian will make your own memories now," she reminded her. "And Herschel tells me Damian's family is very Norman Rockwell." Reese laughed, and her mother put her amusement into words as she added, "But then, compared to us, they would almost have to be, wouldn't they?"

Still chuckling, she said, "Mom, I really want you and Daddy to come and visit us in California. What do you think?"

"I think that would be lovely," she replied. "Hang on, honey. Your father wants to wish you *Mele Kalikimaka*."

After she had a few minutes of conversation with her dad, Damian poked his head through the open bedroom door and smiled at her.

"Eli and Sofia are taking off for the airport."

She nodded. "Dad, I hate to interrupt, but Damian's brother and his family are about to leave."

"Go ahead, kiddo. You and Damian have a happy New Year, okay?"

"You guys too. I love you."

As Reese and Damian reached the great room, Sofia knelt in front of her two young children and helped them zip their jackets while Eli embraced his mom and dad.

"It was the most eventful Christmas we've ever had," Eli told them. "Thanks, Reese. I never liked the paint color in the kitchen anyway."

She shook her head and walked over to him. "Yeah, I wasn't wild about your foot either. I do what I can."

Eli let out a hearty laugh as he embraced her. "Welcome to the family. I'll see you at the wedding."

"I wish we could have got another flight," Sofia said. "Christmas night with the children. *Ai yi yi!*"

"Have a good trip," Reese said, and she hugged Sofia.

When they parted, Jeremy walked right up to her and stretched out his arms for a hug of his own. "*Feliz Navidad*, Jeremy," she said.

He giggled, and she kissed him on the head as he and Abigail moved into her arms.

"Happy to meet you, Reese," Abigail said. "Even with everything."

Damian chuckled, and he grabbed Reese's hand. "Safe travels, guys!"

Reese hadn't noticed until the rest of them settled into the living room, but the layers of black soot the flames had left behind in the kitchen were all but gone except for a light gray glaze over the sage-green wall.

"The smoke damage," she commented, and Damian sat down next to her on the loveseat.

"Pop knows a guy. He came over while we were at the animal clinic."

"That's wonderful," she said.

It didn't look nearly as horrible as it had before. A couple coats of paint, and they might actually have some shot at forgetting.

"While you were on the line with your folks," Damian said, hijacking her thoughts, "Regg got a call from her neighbor in Vermont. They got more than a foot of snow last night, and they're expecting another two. Flights are going to be backed up for days."

"Oh, that's terrible. How will she get home?"

"Well, I've talked her into coming back to L.A. until after the New Year."

Reese gasped, and she and Reggie exchanged grins. "You can stay with me," Reese exclaimed. "And we're having our tailgater . . . well, it's held in my living room, but we treat it like a tailgater . . . on New Year's Day. Oh! And you can meet my friend Joss!"

"Can I go with them, Daddy?" Hannah cried. "It would be so much fun."

"Afraid not," Matthew answered. "We're all going back to Colorado together."

Hannah's face bunched up like an angry fist, and she stomped her foot and fell back into the sofa cushions. When another idea dawned, she sprang forward with a gasp. "Well, maybe I could come and see you over Easter break?" she asked Reese.

"Sure, if your parents say it's okay. You're always welcome, Hannah. And you know what? I can take you into Hollywood, and we can get matching tatts!"

Courtney looked as if she'd been shot. "Somebody please tell me she's joking."

"Hey," Reese teased. "Paul isn't the only one who knows a guy. I know a guy too."

Damian and Matthew howled, and Hannah followed up with laughter of her own. "I'm so happy you're joining the family, Reese."

"I'm just glad you all still want me," she said.

And in the very next moment, a true Christmas miracle occurred to seal the deal on all of that joy and good tidings.

Paco tiptoed across the floor and looked up at her for an instant before hopping up to the loveseat and curling into a ball in her lap.

"Well, now I've seen it all," Jeane chimed in.

EPILOGUE

 "You're back!"

Reese flew down her driveway and collided with Joss before she even closed the car door behind her.

"You missed me, huh?" Joss teased. "Sorry you blew me off for that fiancé of yours?"

"Hush and hug me again. I can't believe we've only talked one time all week!"

When she noticed two complete strangers rounding the car, her grasp on Joss loosened. The only thing more surprising than the platinum blonde with Christmas wreath earrings and bright coral lip gloss was the really handsome guy who followed her. He raked his hand through his shaggy hair and smiled. His deep hazel eyes and rugged face lined with stubble seemed to revolve around one deep dimple at the center of his chin.

"Uh, hi," Reese greeted them.

"This," Joss told them with the wave of her arm, "is my best friend Reese Pendergrass. Reese, this is Connie Rudolph. We met on the cruise, and she's spending a couple of days with me."

"Hi, sugar!" Connie said with a painfully white smile. "Pleased to meetcha."

"And this is Patrick Brenneman," Joss told her. No matter how hard she tried to disguise it, the excitement over the introduction simmered over into a full boil.

Patrick reached for Reese's hand and shook it. "Happy to meet you. Joss has told me a good bit about you."

His Irish brogue took the Score-O-Meter well over the top, and Reese locked eyes with Joss in unspoken and heartfelt congratulations, easily translated between two such close friends.

"Damian's sister is with us too. Come on in so you can meet her and say hello to Damian. We have a ton of food, and lots of great people." Slipping her arm through Joss's, she grinned. "I want to hear everything. Don't leave one thing out."

Damian greeted them at the front door and hugged Joss. "Happy New Year. How was your cruise?"

"Surprisingly great!"

"And she brought souvenirs home with her," Reese said with a chuckle. "Meet Connie and Patrick. This is my fiancé, Damian Palmer."

While Damian took drink orders and went off to fill them, Reese borrowed Joss from her new friends and tugged her into the bedroom and closed the door.

"That's the guy you said is *me on steroids*?" Reese asked her. "Because I haven't looked that good even in my dreams!"

"I know," Joss said on a bumpy giggle. "He's gorge, right?"

"Beyond gorgeous. Status report?"

"Delirious."

"Joss. Really?"

"Reese, it's crazy. We've known each other for a week. But I am deliriously crazy in love! At least it feels like love. It might be too soon to get a true reading."

"It's not a fever, Joss. It's your heart."

Joss grinned at her, and Reese realized she'd never seen her friend with that look in her eyes. She reached over and grabbed Joss's wrist and jiggled it.

"I hope it's love," she confided. "I really hope it's love. You deserve to find love, Joss."

"Hush," she blurted. "Tell me how it went with the in-laws?"

"Couldn't have been better. We started out getting into an accident with a deer, and the next day I ran over Damian's brother Eli with the car."

"You did not."

"Then I poisoned a little girl's dog—"

"Stop it!"

"—and I topped it all off by knocking down a little girl and setting fire to the Palmer family mountain home."

Silence gripped them as they sat there staring at one another.

"Please tell me you're making this up."

"It would be so great if I could, wouldn't it?"

A soft rap at the door preceded Damian as he poked his head around the corner and smiled. "Game starts in twenty, and I put the chili on the buffet table," he declared. Then, walking in a step farther, he whispered, "And I think we've got a love connection out here between Regg and Jack Collins."

Reese gasped. What a perfect example of god-like kismet! Working with Jack had been a high point in her time at the hospital, and she couldn't imagine a nicer man for Reggie to spend some time with.

"That's a happy accident!" she said, grinning. "And guess who else might have found love over Christmas."

Damian smiled. "Really?"

Joss shrugged.

"I like Patrick," he told her. "He seems cool." Glancing at Reese, he nodded. "Now, come out here and get a load of them together."

"Give us five minutes."

"Who's Regg?" Joss asked after he'd gone.

"Damian's sister. Reggie. You have to meet her. You'll love her!"

"Okay, but we have so much more to talk about. Let's have lunch tomorrow over near my office."

"Done," Reese said with a nod. "But there are some things that can't wait until then, so let's shorthand it."

"Okay. Go!"

"Patrick. Does he feel like you do?"

"He thinks we're destiny," Joss beamed. "The mother-in-law. Is she tolerable?"

"More than. She's heaven."

"The dog you poisoned?"

"Freakish little Chihuahua that belongs to Damian's niece, Sarah."

"Accident, right?"

Reese tilted her head and glared at Joss. "Of course! I wouldn't poison a dog on purpose."

"Right. Was it Norman Rockwell up there like we imagined?"

"Times twelve. There was—*get this!*—a sleigh ride on Christmas Eve!"

"Stop it!"

"There was!" Reese vowed. "Now come on. I'm hungry. That'll have to do for now."

They both stood up, and Joss turned to Reese at the door and looked at her seriously. "Don't laugh, but it's not really so bad, is it?"

"What's that?"

"Christmas," she mumbled. "I mean, under the right circumstances."

Reese heard her own heartbeat *rat-a-tatting* in her eardrums. "Joss."

"I know. Don't tell Damian. He'll just get all self-righteous on me."

"I won't. And how does Patrick feel about Christmas?"

"He thinks it's overcommercialized. He's all about the true meaning and all that."

"Really."

Joss grinned. "Check us out."

"I know. Want to know what I did on Christmas?"

"Spill."

"Invited my parents for a visit."

Joss popped with laughter. "Stop it!"

"I did."

Placing her arm around Reese's neck, she squeezed. "Just one last one for the road, okay?" she said.

"What did you have in mind?"

"Did you see those wreath earrings Connie has on, with the little Santas swinging on them?"

"Like I could miss them?" Reese teased.

"If I can get them away from her, let's bury them in the potted plant out back."

"Bring it! And if I get them first," Reese added, "you buy lunch tomorrow."

"You're on!"

"For a child will be born for us,
a son will be given to us,
and the government will be on His shoulders.
He will be named
Wonderful Counselor, Mighty God,
Eternal Father, Prince of Peace."

—Isaiah 9:6